Jenny Roberts is a 55-year-old Yorkshirewoman – born in Bridlington and now living in York, where she runs the Libertas! Women's Bookshop, which she founded in 1998. She has a grown-up son and daughter. This is her first novel.

NEEDLE POINT

JENNY ROBERTS

First published 2000 by Diva Books
an imprint of Millivres Limited
part of the Millivres Prowler Group
116-134 Bayham Street, London NW1 0BA

A catalogue record for this book is available from the British Library

ISBN 1 873741 42 1

Printed and bound in Finland by WS Bookwell

Acknowledgements

Writing a book is a major project and I'm grateful for the support, encouragement and critical help that I have received from my friends.

Particular thanks to Rachael, who was there in Amsterdam with me right at the start, and encouraged me to begin; to Eve for never mincing her words when she read the work in progress; to Jane for her creative support; to Annie, Jenny and Kati for reading and commenting on the finished draft, and to Nick, Chrissy and Eve (again) who took the strain in the bookshop whilst I completed the final version. Finally, thanks to Ann for all her patience, encouragement and help on the final draft.

Special thanks to Peter Kalu, who taught me the rudiments of thriller writing and convinced me that I could do it.

Despite any inferences to the contrary, I must stress that I admire the Amsterdam police enormously and regard them as one of the most professional and least prejudiced forces in the world. I am indebted to their press office for help on background information. Thanks also to Gert van Ingen MD from the Netherlands Laboratory of Forensic Pathology and Richard Vos of the Free University Hospital for their kind and helpful advice on various pathological and procedural details.

Marriette's Guest House is loosely based on Liliane's Home, a women-only guest house in Sarphatistraat but, I hasten to add, Liliane is not Marriette. Thanks to Angèle of the Vrouwencafé Saarein for checking much of my detail; sadly her bar is no longer women-only and the Vrouwencafé Juno is but a figment of my imagination. Thanks too to Trees for help with some of the Dutch phrases. I also acknowledge the assistance of *The Women's Travel Guide to Amsterdam*, by Catherine Stebbings, published by Virago, in providing some background information.

Thank you Amsterdam for just being there. You are a beautiful city.

Major thanks to my editor, Helen Sandler, who with her incisive criticism and her unerring support and friendship has enabled me to make this into the book I always wanted it to be.

Since I have not stopped talking about *Needle Point* for the last eighteen months, thanks also to dykes everywhere who have patiently listened to – even encouraged – my obsession. Bless!

To Dorothy Mabel Walkington
(1900-1983)
who would have understood

Prologue

The demons retreat, still pointing at me as they go. Sneering. Accusing. Laughing at my discomfort. I stir uneasily from a deep, dark sleep.The fog in my head is smothering my senses and it is some time before I am able to focus my eyes. Only then does my waking memory begin to take shape again – like a computer booting up, opening its programmes, checking its systems. The light falls into the room through a gap in the curtains, but my body feels like lead and my spirits seem to have lost their way again during the night. Another morning, another daily battle to keep going: to make some kind of sense out of it all. Carrie's face floats into my mind as it has done for the last two months: a beautiful, smiling, happy face, the face of a big sister who I thought would always be there for me. Except now she won't be ... ever.

Now she is dead.

Crawling out from between the sheets, I shiver in the iciness of the morning and peer out from behind the curtains on to a gloomy deserted street. A light mist swirls around the nearby rooftops, almost hiding my view of York Minster. It is as if the smog inside my head has evaporated to the street outside. Maybe that will disappear too as the world awakes. Maybe the sun will come out today.

I slip on my white towelling robe, pulling its reassuring softness around me and, still in a haze, stagger to the bathroom. Funny how, just at the moment when you think you have achieved some sort of stability, life kicks sand in your face again. As I wash, I catch sight of myself in the bathroom mirror. I am looking older – and feeling it too. I am 34 already. Soon the creases around my eyes will be too obvious to miss – like the silver flecks already peppering my cropped black hair. My friends say it doesn't matter, but it matters to me. Or at least it used to: nothing seems very important any more.

Tea helps. Well, momentarily. The irony doesn't escape me – Cameron McGill, lifetime campaigner against clichés and mindless populism, grasping the mug of tea as if it represents some kind of life-sustaining force. It does help to settle the sickness in my gut, but not for long.

The more I come awake, the more I think about her. The more I remember the warm, breathing, feeling woman that was my sister. Once more, this morning – like every other morning for the last two months – hot tears well up in my eyes and a seething, blistering anger overwhelms me.

Tibby, my four-year-old tomcat, brushes against my calf. I pick him up and cuddle him, deluding myself that this soft, warm creature senses my need for affection and is generously giving it to me. Then, shedding a tear at this comforting, if unlikely, prospect, I put him down and give him his breakfast.

I sip some more of my tea, looking out at the back of the house. Everything is still green and leafy before the first frosts, but the summertime glory has gone and the garden is clearly in decline as the weather winds down into winter. I shiver, as if to shake off the melancholy that I always seem to wear these days. I am becoming so tied up with my own feelings, my own sense of loss, that my life is retreating into a greyness from which I fear there may be no escape.

Yet a part of me is fighting this slide into numbness. An Inner Self, sitting on the edge of my consciousness, telling me that I have to stop the whingeing, the self-pity and the grieving. If not now, then some time soon. How have I come to this? Other people lose their loved ones and somehow manage to put their lives back together again. Why can't I just accept Carrie's death in the same way?

My mind drifts back to September and Amsterdam. Back to the pleasant but brisk police doctor. To her, I suppose, Carrie was just another statistic in the continuing saga of drug abuse: just another junkie who pushed her luck too far, and paid the price.

I was her next of kin, so it had to be me who identified the body.

It wasn't easy. How could it have been? She was my hero. It was bad enough her being dead. But the total incomprehensibility of it all made it much worse. She didn't deserve to die, especially not like that. If it was me, it would make some sense. But it isn't, is it? Against all the odds, I have survived intact. It is her – sweet, virtuous, caring Carrie – who is dead.

I finish off my drink and put the empty mug into a sink already full of dirty pots.

I begin to weep quietly. This feels so strange; like I am viewing the world from the outside. Nothing is solid any more. It is as if my life is crumbling around me; the pieces burning up as they re-enter the real world.

I am really scared that I am losing my grip.

One

Becky, sitting cross-legged in her big squashy armchair, looked at me pensively through a cloud of steam. She was holding her orange coffee mug in both hands, pressing the side of it against her mouth.

The steam seemed to turn her big soft eyes into even bigger pools of blue and, as the dampness lingered over the line of freckles that ran along the top of each prominent cheekbone, her warm, round, country face focused on me again and she lowered her mug. Her eyes held mine as she spoke carefully, slowly.

"I'm glad you came round tonight, Cam. I've been ever so worried about you. You're not yourself, love, you seem distant somehow and … well … stuck." Becky's soft Liverpool accent landed heavily on this last word, summing up her entire train of thought, and my predicament, in one word. "It must be two months since Carrie went; yet to me, anyway, you don't seem to be any different than you were just after the funeral."

I shrugged. I didn't really want to talk about it.

"Let yourself grieve, love. I know you want everyone to think you're strong, but you're just making yourself more and more unhappy."

"Becky, that's bloody ridiculous!" I bristled. "I'm a qualified counsellor, you know: I do know something about grieving." I slumped back into the settee. "Of course I'm coping. It's just been a big shock. Some things take longer. I'll be OK, I just need more time, some space … and –" I looked at her accusingly "– some support, that's all."

She uncrossed her legs and sat upright in the chair. I don't often see my best friend really angry. "Cameron, can you hear yourself?"

Her rosy face was now even redder. "Flower, I love you dearly, but someone has to tell you; someone has to bring you back to the real world." She paused, calming herself, running her fingers through her spiky blond hair, looking worn and frustrated. Becky had put up with a lot from me recently.

More steadily, she continued: "You just can't go on this way, Cam. Carrie is dead and, however hard it is, however unfair, you have to accept that she has gone. You need to get on with your life now and start letting go of the hurt."

"I am," I blustered. "But it's not that simple. I'll be all right, really I will. Another couple of months ... just let me be." Who was I trying to convince – her or me? I sounded like one of my clients promising to start drying out next week – always next week. I tried to keep the edginess out of my voice, but it was hard, handling this on my own.

She looked at me and said nothing. I shifted uncomfortably in my seat.

"OK Cameron, then how come your manager has put you on to admin work indefinitely? You are the star of the Unit, yet she has taken you away from your clients. What's that about?"

It was getting harder to keep my cool. Damn Becky. Damn her for caring so much.

"And what about Jill? Whatever you may think, she did love you. But I don't think anyone can blame her for leaving. Cameron, do you realise how hard you are to be with? You spend all your time sounding off at people: complaining and feeling sorry for yourself. You were difficult all those years ago when we were lovers, but not like this!"

She paused and gave me one of her long, penetrating looks. Then she must have seen my face start to crumple, because she got up from her chair, came to sit next to me and took hold of my hand.

No one else could have done it. But Becky, my first partner, knew just what to do. And, gently, she cut through the thick armour of my hurt and began to release the emotional waters lying beyond.

Once I started to cry, I couldn't stop. Tears came in wave after wave, with anger and resentment surfing on their crests. She held me, she talked to me, just like Carrie had done all those years ago when things seemed equally hopeless. She sat with me as I punched the cushion in my lap; she listened as I raged; she stroked me when the pain receded for a while and then she held me tight again, anchoring me, keeping me safe as the next flood of emotions swept in.

I cried for most of that night, held captive by hurt and sorrow that would no longer be contained. Letting it out, letting it go.

It was early morning when I finally fell asleep in Becky's arms, in Becky's bed.

A dog barked somewhere in the distance and there were voices in the street outside, but otherwise it was strangely quiet, uncommonly peaceful in my awakening world.

I looked up at the window and blinked at the bright sunlight forcing its way into the room through the unlined curtains, remembering that I was at Becky's. I was alone. I turned over and lay on my back, staring at the textured surface of the ceiling, following the swirls, joining up the ridges, quietly taking stock. I hadn't slept so well for months.

I closed my eyes again, trying to concentrate in a sleepy, haphazard way on what was different. I felt tired and drained from the emotional intensity of the night, but there was something else. I felt calmer.

Becky had left me a note pinned down by a spare toothbrush. She'd gone to work. She'd rung my office to report me sick and would ring me later.

I got up gingerly, expecting to feel as bad as usual.

Instead, I felt like breakfast.

My next urge was for exercise, so, after ringing Becky to let her know I was all right, I walked the short distance to Monk Bar and climbed up on to the city walls.

York, nestling within the pale fortified walls, looked at its best in the gentle autumn sunlight: medieval, timeless. To my left, the soft, creamy stonework of the Minster, with its huge towers and its massive, elegantly engineered Chapter House, dominated the view. Beneath me, the lawns of the Deanery spread a carpet of tranquillity right up to the foot of the wall on which I stood.

I still wasn't quite sure how I felt about Carrie. Maybe after last night, I was beginning to let go. I knew that I felt different. Yet there was a tight feeling in my gut. The way she had died still seemed very wrong. I had told myself over and over again that there was no doubt, I had seen her perforated body for myself. Yet still I could not let go of the notion that the manner of her death just did not fit the woman. My sister was a health freak, she took care of her body. She would never do drugs. Yet I knew she had. Why? What had happened to her during those last weeks in Amsterdam?

Perhaps I should spend a few days there; try and adjust to what had happened, face the reality? But I didn't know if I had the courage.

A party of French schoolchildren made their way past me in a long snake: forty pre-pubescent kids chattering and laughing, enjoying their foreign adventure. I thought about me when I was that age. Carrie had just graduated from Leeds University and gone to work for the *Yorkshire Post*. She had chosen Leeds so she could be near me, even though she was no longer living at home. I spent a lot of my time at her flat in Burley. It was a place where I could be myself. A place of refuge.

Perhaps I needed to do more than just go back. Perhaps I needed to piece together her time in Amsterdam, find out what had happened – why she, of all people, had ended up doing hard drugs. Maybe if I knew how she got into it, then I could accept her death and finally let it go. Maybe doing something would be better than just thinking about her.

I thought back to the summer and her last letter: "I think I'm on to something that will make a really good story ... it's an issue that affects women ... is being ignored (hushed up?) by the authorities."

My sister was a good journalist. She liked a challenge and she took a real delight in exposing greed and corruption, particularly where it affected children, the disadvantaged, or women. She had a knack for finding out things that other people missed. The people whose issues she fought trusted her as a friend rather than a journalist. But she made enemies, of course. The politicians, the authorities, the fraudsters and the crooks disliked her and had good reason to be fearful of her success. She loved stirring things up, asking embarrassing questions, putting the establishment on the spot with her own brand of prickly reporting. I wiped my eyes and blew my nose. I missed her.

The tight feeling in my gut grew again. I had to know about her last days and why she had changed so much, so quickly. I had to have some answers. I had to make some sense of her death.

I sat on the walls for most of the afternoon, watching the squirrels in the Deanery garden and returning the polite smiles of the tourists, until the light fell.

Back in my own house, I remembered the plastic bag of worn clothes and possessions that had been returned to me when I identified Carrie's body. I still hadn't opened it, but if I was going to get through all this, I had to do it.

I opened the bag, tipping the contents on to my bed. There wasn't much apart from the clothes she had been wearing when she died, now raggy, dirty and unkempt: a pair of blue denims, a bright orange tunic top, a large T-shirt and a pair of sandals. I felt sick ... dirty or not, they were still hers. There were a few items of jewellery:

my mother's ring, a bead necklace and a brooch. There was a waist bag, passport, her NUJ card, a few guilders, her credit cards and other personal effects. The police had said this was all they had.

I returned the items to the bag, fighting back my anger. I wanted to find out who had got her involved with drugs in the first place. I wanted to know how anyone could have persuaded her to take even the smallest amount of a drug, let alone six hits of some fucking weird cocktail, which even the Dutch pathology labs hadn't been able to identify.

I didn't know what to do with the clothes. They were my last link with her and I couldn't bear to get rid of them just yet, so I stuck the bag under my arm and took it downstairs. I would wash them later and keep them for a while.

I did go back to work the next day, though not with a lot of enthusiasm. I missed my real job of counselling the users who came to me from the courts. Some just wanted to pull the wool over the magistrate's eyes until they were offered a lighter sentence – or no sentence at all. Others were terrified and despondent. Some were women, trying to cope with the gender games on the street along with all the other shit.

If they didn't care, then there was little I could do. If they genuinely wanted out, then I could help. I was passionate about my job, and I was good. Drugs almost finished me off when I was 21. I know how I felt; I know what Carrie and Becky had to go through to clean me up.

My boss must have seen me moping around, looking pissed off. I suppose I expected her to come over all managerial and tell me to get my act together. But, instead, she surprised me and told me to take a month's sick leave, to get away for a while and spend the time sorting out my feelings – so that I could be useful again.

Somehow, it sounded like a good idea.

***

As soon as I got home, I booked myself and my beautiful Harley-Davidson Sportster on to the Hull to Rotterdam ferry for Thursday night. A good blow-out would do us both a lot of good.

There were just a few things to do before I went and one of them was washing some clothes, particularly some jeans, to take with me. I emptied the wicker laundry basket and sorted out the different colours into light and dark. Then I noticed the plastic bag lying on the floor. Carrie's clothes. My first instinct was to leave them again, but I had to stop running away from reality, so I emptied the bag and distributed the contents between the two piles.

I stuffed my jeans into the washer, going through the pockets out of habit to pull out the used tissues, bits of paper and, rarely, the occasional folded £10 note in the small-change pocket. Without thinking about it, I did the same with Carrie's jeans. They had already been cleaned out by the Dutch police ... except ... I held my breath as I extracted a small piece of folded, crumpled card from the tiny pocket on the right-hand side and carefully opened it up. It was some kind of business card. The print was very faded, very washed out, but it was just legible:

THE ONLY WOMEN-ONLY BAR IN TOWN
Vrouwencafé Juno
Laurierstraat, Amsterdam
Open 15.00 'til 1.00/2.00
with pool table and cat

Overleaf there was some pale biro, almost washed away. It looked like a name – 'Pat' – and a telephone number – 020 629 42.

I knew the Vrouwencafé Juno: it was mine and Carrie's favourite bar. But I knew of no friend called Pat. Could she be a regular there? Did she know my sister? Could she explain how Carrie had got on to drugs? Could she have something to do with my sister's death?

My heart was racing and there was a truckload of different emotions driving through my brain. Amsterdam used to be my favourite city. I wanted to find out what had happened to my sister in those last weeks, but I was scared of what I might find.

Two

My Harley-Davidson purred quietly beneath me as I waited at the lights on the outer fringes of Amsterdam.

It was 10 a.m., Friday morning and, though the sky was dark, the rain had held off. The drive down the motorway from the ferry port at Rotterdam had felt so good – a clear, wide road where I could open the bike up, break the speed limit and let some fresh, cold air into my soul. It felt good to be away, good to be astride my sweet, powerful, black and gold machine.

The lights changed and I opened up the throttle, feeling the powerful surge beneath me, the big engine growling a throaty bass line as I wove my way through the trams and the traffic along Scheldestraat over the Amstelkanaal towards Wetteringsschans.

I remembered how much I used to like this place. Even the suburbs. The clean lines of the streets, the unpretentious apartment blocks, the quirky, humorous sculptures by the roadside, the colourful trams, the bridges, the canals. The simple beauty, the space and the flatness of this uncomplicated city began to soothe me again with its calm and order.

Marriette must have heard the bike as I manoeuvred through the gate into her backyard. By the time I had cut the engine and removed my helmet, she was coming towards me, a beaming smile on her face, her arms outstretched. She was a well-rounded and comfortable-looking woman, around five-foot-three, in her mid-forties, with a friendly, open face, and a personality to match. Of all the dykes I have ever met, she was the one who was perfectly suited to running a women-only guest house. All her customers liked her – you only had to glance at the visitors' book to see that – and I guess many of them were slightly in love with her too. She was welcoming and kind to everyone.

But today I knew that this was not the hotel proprietor who was greeting me so warmly, it was one of my sister's oldest friends.

"Hello darling, it's so good to see you again." She folded me in her arms and I responded, holding her close to me for a long, long time. I knew Carrie had stayed with her many times and they had been very close. Marriette had found her death hard to take.

When she relaxed and pulled back, holding me at arm's length, I could see the tears in her eyes. I was her friend's sister and, I supposed, her pleasure at seeing me was both sweet and painful. I wore Carrie's memory all about me, in my eyes, in my face and in my voice. I was part of the past – part of Carrie's past – and I was a potent reminder of her loss.

We looked at each other for a few moments, the sadness reflected in both our faces. I hugged her again, as much for myself as for her. Grief is sometimes so tangible that you can feel its crushing, paralysing weight all around you.

After I had chained up the bike and lifted the big panniers full of my gear off the back, we went down the steps and into Marriette's basement flat below the guest house. The kitchen was big and simply decorated in pale yellows and greens. Fresh flowers, yellow chrysanthemums, were casually arranged in a tall brown jug on the table, and in the hearth was an old-fashioned black stove, filled with glowing embers, warming the room against the autumn chill.

I put the bags by the door and sat down at her large pine table as she poured me a mug of strong, full-flavoured Dutch coffee. On the wall, the casement clock ticked loudly and regularly, a steadying influence on our racing emotions.

We sat for a while, becoming gradually more comfortable with each other. I'd always liked this woman. Until Carrie's death, I hadn't know her very well – I'd just stayed with her a few times over the years – but recent events had drawn us closer. She ran one of only two women's houses in the city and her guests were mostly dykes like herself. Carrie was straight, but if she had been lesbian, she and Marriette would have made a good match. Though physically quite different, they were both around the same age and Etts's quietness and natural caution would have been a nice balance to my sister's adventurous and impulsive nature. Maybe that's why they were such good friends.

"You will miss your sister," she said with her beautiful Dutch accent. "It is all so sad and all so unexpected. I couldn't believe it when I read the piece in the papers." She choked back her tears again. I nodded in agreement. "I thought, no, they've made a mistake, it can't be Carrie. Then, after you had identified her, I knew it must be true."

She shook her head in disbelief. "I'm sorry, darling, I'm so tied up with myself that I haven't asked how you are."

"I feel just like you, Etts – that's why I'm here really." I took my empty cup to the sink. "I just don't seem able to accept what's happened. It's like ... she's on my mind all the time. I know she's dead but I just can't believe she was mainlining. It doesn't fit, does it?"

She mouthed a sad "no" and I sat down at the table again, sighing. "Anyway, I thought that if I had a few days over here, I could perhaps find out why she got addicted. Then, maybe, I can come to terms with it all."

Marriette looked at me sympathetically. "It is understandable that you should find Carrie's death difficult to accept, darling, but I am sure the police did a very thorough job. I can't believe there will be anything else for you to find out. It is strange that she took drugs ... but this is Amsterdam and, well ... there are all sorts of temptations."

Part of me wanted to agree with her and take the easy way out, but I knew very well by now that, unless I had reasons for her death, I wouldn't be able to rest. I shook my head in disagreement. "Carrie might have been an adventurer, Etts, but she wasn't stupid and she hated drugs. I just don't see how she would get involved." I looked straight at her. "Not willingly, anyway."

We sat in silence for a while. Marriette had turned her head away. I thought I must have upset her. But after a few moments she spoke again, remembering back to the summer. "She only stayed with me for three days this time, Cameron; I expected her to stay longer. She said the story would take about two weeks to research properly – but then she left to stay with friends somewhere.

"Anyway, you know what she was like when she sensed a good story; she was very excited and she came in on that last day, packed and left within minutes." As the memory came back to her, she grasped her wiry blonde hair in her hand as if she needed something to hold on to. "I was checking someone in at the time; I didn't know she was in such a hurry. Before I knew it, she was going down the stairs and out of the door, shouting, 'I've left the keys on the bed, sorry to rush, I'll see you before I go home.'" A tear ran down her cheek.

"I ran to the top of the stairs, shouting, 'take care!' … But she had gone. She was very happy, just her normal energetic self. I never saw her again." Marriette looked up at the ceiling, stifling a sob. "If only I'd stopped her, maybe I could have found out where she was going. Then maybe I could have done something."

"But didn't she leave a forwarding address, Etts?" My sister was usually very good at letting friends know where to contact her. "That doesn't sound like Carrie."

Marriette didn't reply: she shook her head and gazed into her coffee, unable to meet my eyes, or simply lost in her own thoughts.

She turned around again. Now, with more strength, she said, "Cameron, I've been around, I know about these things and I can tell you for sure that your sister was not a user when she left that day. Whatever made her start must have happened in the three weeks after she left here. But she did take drugs and, whatever we think, that is a fact."

She came back to the table and sat down again. "Cameron,

darling, there is nothing to be gained from stirring things up, except heartache. I think you should just accept that Carrie has died and try and enjoy a nice holiday in our lovely city. That is what she would have wanted you to do, I'm sure."

I looked at her, laughing slightly in disbelief. "Etts, it isn't as simple as that. I can't just let it rest. I've tried that for the last two months and it doesn't work." I shook my head, appealing for under-standing. "I need to know more. That is the only way I will be able to accept what has happened."

She looked at me blankly.

"Look," I said, passing her the card from the Juno Bar, "I found this in Carrie's jeans. I presume that 'Pat' is someone she met in the women's bar. If I can get in touch with her, then, maybe, she will tell me all I need to know."

Marriette examined the card, turning it over in her hand and reading each side several times.

"It's all I have to go on," I confessed, "but it may be enough."

She shook her head. "It is less than you think, Cameron. You can't even ring this Pat – the last two digits of the phone number are missing."

I took the card back off her, cursing quietly; the last two num-bers must have disappeared when the jeans were wet. But I wasn't going to give up so easily.

"Etts, will you help me? ... Please?"

She looked at me dolefully. "Cameron, I just don't want you to get hurt any more than you already have ... But, yes, of course I will help, if I can."

"You're sure it's the last two numbers that are missing?" I asked. She nodded. "So, in that case –" I smiled patiently "– Pat's number must end somewhere between 00 and 99."

She nodded slowly. "Ja, that makes sense."

I stroked her shoulder, priming her for the next question. "Etts, this is asking a lot, I know, but... would you do me an enormous favour and ring all those numbers to see if you can find her?"

She looked stunned. "But it will take hours, Cameron!"

"Yes I know it will … but my Dutch isn't very good and I won't be able to ask the right questions. Please? If we can find this Pat, she may be able to tell me all I need to know."

Marriette resigned herself. "OK, my sweet, I can see you are not going to give up on this until you know more, so I will help." She wagged her finger at me. "But you must promise that, once you have found Pat, you will let the matter drop."

I nodded. "If she can make some sense of it all, then I will gladly let it rest there. I have absolutely no wish to go poking around Amsterdam trying to find out everything. I just need to understand, that's all."

She smiled a little, more relaxed now.

I put my arm around her shoulder and kissed her on the cheek. "Sorry, Etts, I know that it is a horrible job. But whilst you're doing that, I can talk to the police again and visit the Vrouwencafé Juno to see if anyone there knows the woman."

She looked at me as if I had got the better end of the deal. "Why don't you call at the bar first, before I start ringing round?"

"Yeah, I suppose that would be sensible. Trouble is, I need to do a number of other things first. Look, why don't you ring the Juno Bar before you begin and ask them if they know anyone called Pat?"

"OK!" she said, laughing lightly. "I can see that I'm not going to get out of this, so I might as well get on with it!"

I put my arms round her and gave her a another kiss. "You're a real love."

"Mmm," she reflected. "Well, I wouldn't do it for just anyone."

After she had shown me up three flights of steep stairs to my room, I left Marriette with her assignment.

It was already midday and I wanted to get down to the police

HQ as soon as I could. Two months had passed since I saw Inspecteur Dankmeijer and I hoped that, by now, he would have more information on my sister's death. The police station was only a mile away so I left my bike in Marriette's yard and hopped on a number 7 tram just outside the door, paying the conductor at the back and settling down into one of the many empty seats. I wiped the condensation off the window with my sleeve but the raindrops on the window still obliterated most of the view. I cursed for not bringing a brolly and then it dawned on me that I was still wearing my black leathers and boots. Not exactly the right clothing for an interview with Dankmeijer.

I'd only met him once, and in distracting circumstances, but some people make a strong impression. He was a big man – broad as well as tall – with a square-set but not unpleasant face. He looked like he took care of himself, or perhaps his wife did that for him. He was certainly a family man: photos of his kids – two girls aged around seven and eight – had been prominently displayed on his desk when I last saw him. There was nothing about him to upset anyone, yet I couldn't bring myself to like him.

Maybe it was his professional manner, or his natural reticence. Maybe he found women difficult or maybe he was just a career cop who kept his work separated from his personality. Whatever it was, we had got off to a bad start then and I was going to have to try particularly hard if I wanted his co-operation now.

I looked at my tight black leather suit and calf-length boots and knew I should have gone back and changed into something softer, more feminine. Carrie would have done. She always worked out the psychology of the occasion and dressed for it. She could be kind, warm, cold or aggressive, depending on who she was interviewing. She knew how to work her way under the most difficult skin, how to find a particular Achilles' heel, how to get information that wouldn't be given to anyone else. I could only be myself. And sometimes that didn't go down too well.

The tram screeched to a halt on Marnixstraat and I jumped off and crossed the main road to the big new police station, shielding my eyes from the rain and dodging the continuous stream of bicycles.

The interior was clean, bright and tastefully modern. What's more, I was greeted politely by a male receptionist, seated behind a large and attractive sycamore desk. The Dutch police had style at least.

I was shown to Dankmeijer's office on the first floor.

"Good morning, Miss McGill." Inspecteur Dankmeijer smiled politely and spoke softly as he stood up to shake my hand across the desk. I had forgotten his preciseness. The neat office, the well-pressed grey suit, the groomed hair and meticulously knotted navy tie. Huh, I felt put down before I said a word.

He didn't ask me to take a seat. A bad sign: he wasn't anticipating a long conversation. He also stayed on his feet, protected behind his desk. The thought crossed my mind that he might feel inhibited by my leathers, so I made an effort to be particularly pleasant.

"Hello, Inspector, how are you?"

He smiled rather thinly and didn't answer my question. "It is a surprise to see you again. How may I help?"

Forget the pleasantries, Cameron; you're wasting your breath. "I'm over here for a few days, Inspector, and I just wondered if you had any more information on my sister's death, since we last spoke?"

He shook his head, impassive and factual in his reply. "I am very sorry, my dear, but I told you when we last met that, as far as we are concerned, the case is closed. The police doctor was quite specific that nothing was out of order."

I must have looked stunned, because he hesitated, and then began again. "Regrettably your sister died from a combination of overdosing on hard drugs and asphyxiation through drowning. There are no suspicious circumstances and no evidence of foul play. So regrettably, as far as we are concerned, the case is closed."

I suppose that was what I should have expected. Police all over the world like to have an open and shut case. Why should the Dutch be any different? Even so, I tried again.

"Inspector, I know you must be very busy, but surely you can appreciate that something isn't right. My sister did not, would not, take drugs." I tried appealing to his sense of reason – surely he could understand why I was concerned. "Can't you see that something must have happened to make her do it? There has got to be more to this than just an overdose!"

This time he exhaled a little too loudly, his voice beginning to betray the impatience that he was still managing to keep out of his polite, official manner. "Miss McGill, it is understandable that you should be upset. Next of kin often find it difficult to accept drug misuse in cases like this, but the report on your sister is quite clear. I repeat: I am sorry, but the case is closed."

I was even less successful than him at hiding my feelings. I sat down. I wanted some answers before I left. "Inspector, the facts don't add up!"

He looked at me in that patient, understanding way that suggests your brain might be filled with gravy. "Then you must be working on a different set of facts to us, Miss McGill."

I gave him my 'I do not like being patronised' look.

He cleared his throat and continued, quite immune to my stare.

"Like any other city, we see a lot of deaths through drug abuse. Our pathology labs are extremely experienced. All the toxological tests in your sister's case point to a cocktail of very dangerous drugs. However unfortunate, it is quite certain that your sister overdosed and that, if she had not drowned, she would have died from heart failure."

He stopped and looked at me as if that was the end of the matter. I couldn't believe that this was happening.

"I know all of that, Inspector – you wrote to me after the autopsy report was finalised – but the situation is still not satisfactory. For a start, can you actually name the drugs she took? All I've been told so far is that they were 'dangerous' or a 'cocktail'. A cocktail of what, for God's sake?"

For the first time since I had met him, he looked rattled and the colour rose in his face. "There are a lot of drugs on the market, Miss McGill, from all over the world. Some – a very few – are pure, others are compounds containing trace elements of, say, cocaine or heroin, and a lot of dangerous rubbish. Because of this, it is not always easy to be specific about what was actually taken – and that was the case with your sister."

Bullshit. I may know nothing about pathology, but any chemist worth his salt should be able to analyse the contents of a blood or urine sample right down to the component parts. Especially with the modern computerised equipment available to the Dutch police.

"OK," I said belligerently, "let me have a copy of the pathologist's report. I want to read that bit for myself."

He tensed. I was really getting to him now. "I can't, the public prosecutor will not release it."

Yeah, only because you recommended he shouldn't.

"I repeat, the case is closed."

I stood up and faced him across the desk. "Inspector Dankmeijer, you want to know what I think? I think that you are being less than honest with me. You know, and I know, that my sister was not a user and that, for all your bland reassurances, there remains something very disturbing about her death.

"It may suit you to file this case neatly away," I protested, "but I am certainly not satisfied. If you won't continue the investigation, then I will do it myself. If you can't, or won't, get to the bottom of this, then I will!"

The room seemed to fall suddenly silent and very cold. Dankmeijer's face drained of all colour and his manner changed from non-committal to openly hostile in the space of half a second. He seemed to lean right across the desk, his big face only inches away from mine, his voice dark and threatening.

"Don't meddle in things you don't understand, young lady."
Then, very slowly, very firmly: "Go home. There is nothing you can
do here."

I sat still for one of those endless moments of time that are actually no longer than a second or two. I could feel the anger washing
through me.

The words, when they came, were quiet but sharp. "Don't you
dare patronise me, Inspector! It may be convenient for you to clas-
sify my sister's death as misadventure. But I don't believe it. And if
I want to 'meddle' then I will … and there isn't a damn thing you
can do about it!"

He flinched a little, took a step back and paused. Then, like
most men faced with a strong woman, he took the easy way out,
moving towards the door and bringing our brief conversation to a
close.

"I'll show you out …"

"Don't bother, I know the way." I turned and was out of his
office and on to the stairs before he had even got to the door.

My mind was spinning with anger, dismay and disbelief. I could
see there was no way that I was ever going to convince him. No one
in the police was ever going to do anything about Carrie's death, but
I was damned if they were going to stop me. Anyway, I hate being
told what, and what not to do, especially when I know I'm right. It
made me all the more determined to stay in Amsterdam and dig
deeper.

Angry or not, I usually look where I'm going. But not today. I
had my head down, thinking hard as I ran down the stairs, wanting
to get out of the building as fast as I could. Had I seen the woman
walking up the stairs, then I would have moved out of her way. No
doubt she would have moved too, if she had seen me, but she didn't
look up either until the very last moment. Almost simultaneously, I
looked up too. Then everything went into frame-by-frame motion.

She was about my size. Strong oval face. Slightly turned-up nose. Bright blue eyes. Blonde hair falling just short of her shoulders, brushing her face untidily. She had been reading some notes and her relaxed, studious expression changed to blind panic in less than a nanosecond.

She put her arms out to protect herself, dropping her sheaf of notes. I lunged to the left to avoid her and in the process knocked her off balance. She grabbed my right arm to steady herself and I wrapped my left arm around her back as I fell, pulling her with me. I kept thinking 'keep your head up – land on your shoulders' as I hit the steps, grateful for the protection from my leather jacket. We landed inelegantly in a heap in Reception, with her lying on top of me and my hand resting on her bottom.

Time accelerated back to standard speed as I struggled awkwardly to my feet, aware of the laughter around us. She got up as well, adjusting her sky-blue police shirt and dusting down her navy trousers as she said something in Dutch. I guessed she was swearing. I said she should look where she was going and, when she spoke to me again in English, I found I was right about the swearing. Neither of us said another word but we held each other's eyes for what seemed like an age. I could see the fire burning inside her; feel the injured pride of a woman who liked to be in control. For a police officer, she wasn't unattractive, but she was as arrogant and rude as I might have expected.

When she started to pick up her papers, I got out before I was booked for assault. I could feel her eyes burning into my back as I left.

Outside, a light drizzle was being swept around by a cold, gusty North Sea wind. I felt stupid: stupid for not being able to handle Dankmeijer, stupid for bumping into that woman and falling down the stairs. I pulled my jacket collar up and made my way down nearby Elandsgracht towards the centre of the city, trying to control my feeling of inadequacy. There was one more thing I needed to do before the day was over.

It is a long walk across the city centre to Waterlooplein, perhaps two or three miles, but this is such an attractive city that it is a pleasant, therapeutic experience, even in lousy weather – and I needed that therapy. I crossed the three canals that skirt old Amsterdam, the Prinsengracht, the Keizersgracht and finally the Herengracht. No Vrouwengracht, I thought, but then a 'woman's canal' would have no status at all in the canal-naming league of the seventeenth century.

The trees that lined the sides of each canal were clinging to the last remnants of their summer leaves. I passed one of the many male urinals and smiled as I remembered Carrie's story of the feminist protests of 1969 when local women tied up these urinals with pink ribbon, waving banners proclaiming that 'women had the right to pee as well', then baring their bums in front of the world's press to do just that – into the canal. Carrie had been there – an energetic sixteen-year-old who had slipped away from the school trip and made her first friends in the city.

Once over Herengracht, I turned right and made my way alongside the floating flower market, stopping next to a building where the 'Amsterdam Joffers' had their painting studio. Carrie had taken my photo there on my first visit to the city in 1988. I was 23 and fiercely feminist. My sister, having been through the revolutionary protests and sit-ins of 70s Amsterdam, was in a more reminiscent mood. She told me the story of the Joffers – eight early feminists who caused outrage at the turn of the century because they chose careers as professional artists, dressing in work clothes and flouting convention. Their paintings were inoffensive but their lifestyle was not. 'Be yourself. Live your life the way you want' was her message. I thought how Carrie never had any trouble being herself. Me, I still don't know who I am.

But I love the flower market. It's crammed full of the most colourful and exotic flowers – everything from strelitzias, lilies and orchids to tulips and daffodils. In summer, you can buy a huge selection of flowers for just a few pounds. Today, though, all I wanted was a bunch of purple Michaelmas Daisies, the simple 'September Flower' that had been Carrie's favourite.

I paid the man and cradled the precious bunch in my arm. Now feeling very sombre, I left the colour and the clamour of the Bloemenmarkt and made my way along Amstel towards Waterlooplein.

When I saw the road bridge over the Amstel, I braced myself. Further down the main road, I could see the bleak white Stadthuis building and remembered the Sunday trip with Carrie to the flea-market in the square next to it. We had bought a cheap alabaster statuette of Aphrodite, or some other Greek goddess. It had only cost a few guilders, but for me it had been a treasure. I couldn't remember what had happened to it and, for a few seconds, it seemed imperative that I should somehow find it again and keep it safe.

I stopped and leant against the side of the bridge. The barges, neatly moored in twos, bobbed casually up and down whilst other boats moved at a stately pace along the river. In the distance, at the Amstel's sluice gates, sixteen white barriers were raised like arms, as if in bleak tribute. Up above me, the gusty wind played hollow metallic tunes on the tram wires. The seagulls wheeled and dived as they were blown across the wet sky, wailing their mournful song. A police siren sounded somewhere in the city behind me. The damp iciness of the weather even seemed to penetrate my leathers. My head and face stung with the rain. Suddenly I felt very cold and very numb.

I started off again, turning right at the end of the bridge and walking the few yards to where the Nieuwe Herengracht canal meets the River Amstel. As I approached, the wooden road bridge across the canal was lifting to let a large tanker through into the river. I turned left along the side of the canal, oblivious to the people on bikes nearby who were waiting patiently to cross.

Just here, right below me, where the canal joins the river, under the bridge: this was where Carrie's body was found. This was where my sister ended her days. Dying from some unknown cocktail of drugs. Drowning in the cold, grey waters of the canal.

The tanker slid past me and into the river. I studied it as a way of distracting my mind. The dirty grey canal water lapped across the sea-level walkway that encircled the boat. It was so long that, when its stern passed me, the bow had almost reached the far bank of the river. Once out of the canal, it swung hard round before making its slow progress upstream. The wooden bridge lowered and the mass of cyclists and pedestrians on either side surged across, bumping and rattling the boards as they went.

I sat on the low rail at the edge of the canal, staring into the water, holding the flowers close to me, as if they were a lucky charm against the demons that were all around this spot.

I first heard about her death when the York police visited my house on the Sunday night. I had been out all day and they were waiting for me when I returned.

When I saw them there on my doorstep – a woman officer and a man – my mind flashed back to the spring evening when two cops called to tell me about the death of my father. I was eighteen years old and, when I saw them, I was sure it was a bust. Huh, my father had just been killed and I was relieved that they weren't after my dope.

Sixteen years later, when two more called, I guessed instantly why they were there – Carrie was the only close relative I had. And this time, it seemed like the end of my world.

I was asked to identify the body, in Amsterdam, on the Wednesday, after all the tests had been completed, and then to accompany it back to the UK for burial.

The wind was growing stronger now and the drizzle had turned to cold showery rain. I wrapped my arms around myself for comfort as I thought about that dreadful day.

Dankmeijer had taken me to the Free University Hospital for the identification. I supposed that it was an honour to be accompanied by a senior police officer. Now I wasn't so sure. For one thing, if the case was so cut and dried, why hadn't it been handled from the beginning by a more junior officer? Also, looking back, he was edgy. I put it down to awkwardness at the time but, in retrospect, maybe he was just keen to see a sensitive case wrapped up. Maybe he was there to make sure I didn't start asking awkward questions? Marriette came along to give me support and we sat together silently in the mortuary reception area staring at the decorated glass panels that overlooked the car park. There was a numbness about my feelings right then. Nothing seemed very real. But, still, I wasn't looking forward to seeing her.

Marriette stayed behind in the waiting area by choice when I went through the door into the identification room. I don't know what I had expected. I think that years of reading detective novels and watching American cop programmes on TV had prepared me for a stark, sterile morgue with bodies in drawers. In the event, I had walked into a warm, pleasant room to find my sister lying peacefully, her eyes closed as if asleep, dressed in a pretty cream gown beneath a crisp white sheet and flanked by two large candles which cast a soft, shimmering light over her face.

I was relieved to see that there were no signs of the autopsy, no signs of any cuts. Irrationally and for just a moment, I thought she really was sleeping and I felt elated. But when I brushed her cheek with my hand, her skin felt cold and strange. This wasn't the same warm, soft face I had embraced so many times in my life.

It was then that the chilling truth began to dawn on me: the body lying before me was Carrie's body but it was not Carrie. Her spirit, the vibrancy that had once spilled headlong out of every pore, was gone. All that remained was a shell – nice enough to look at, but devoid of the person I had loved and cherished. My sister had gone.

At first I felt strangely unmoved, as if insulated from my own emotions. Then an emptiness reached deep inside me and, suddenly, I wanted to find her again. I wanted to get the real Carrie back into my arms, into my life.

The enormity of my loss finally came home, washing over me, leaving me light-headed and faint. I sat for a few moments, recovering my composure, pushing back the tide of panic that had engulfed me. I wanted to get out into the fresh air, to be alone, to cry. I could see Dankmeijer moving towards me, ready to shepherd me out of the room.

But there was something else that I needed to see. So I ignored the Inspector and concentrated on breathing deeply until I felt calm. Then, before he could stop me, I lifted the sheet from her upper body and drew back the sleeves of her garment.

There were six needle marks covering the inside of her left lower arm. All were still showing some haemorrhaging, so they were all recent and all probably made around the same time. Three of the perforations also showed a degree of tearing – one to a great extent. I was shocked that she could have been so careless with the needle. The bruising and the torn skin were worse than I had ever seen before. Even the most hardened users protect their veins ...

Now I threw the Michaelmas Daisies into the canal one at a time and watched them as they floated about on the water. When I visited Carrie at her London apartment, I always took her flowers. She loved them – it was almost as if they were therapeutic to her. She was always on the go, always excited or stressed, hurrying to meet a deadline, or going somewhere. But at the sight of a bunch of flowers, she would melt and relax. I liked that: it made me feel good too.

I closed my eyes and I could see her arranging the irises, daisies, eucalyptus and chrysanthemums I had bought her last autumn. She held the irises in her right hand, turning them slowly as she inserted the other stems around them, gradually making an informal bouquet which she tied and then put into a vase. I had tried it too, but I couldn't do it the way she did. It was strange, but I had been quite irritated and stung by my incompetence, probably because Carrie teased me about it. I tried and tried to copy her, but she was left-handed and I was right-handed, so her technique wasn't easy to follow.

I got up and began to walk back along the side of the Amstel towards Marriette's, thinking about this. I may only have injected for a short time, but when I did, it was easier, being right-handed, to do it into my left arm. It seemed odd that Carrie, being left-handed, had not injected into her right arm – and that she had not taken more care. She was quite squeamish – even an injection at the doctor's was an ordeal – and I was sure she would not have been so rough with herself intentionally. So what could have caused the skin to tear? Movement, perhaps: injecting in a moving vehicle, injecting whilst drunk?

Or could it be that someone else pushed the needle into her arm – someone who didn't know she was left-handed, someone she was struggling against?

And if the police were so sure there was no foul play, why did they request an autopsy in the first place?

Three

The bath water was scalding hot: just what I needed.

It had been a relief to get back to Marriette's. By late afternoon, my leathers were wet and clammy from the constant drizzle; my feet hurt from walking miles in my biking boots and my shoulder felt stiff and achy from the tumble on the stairs.

I lay in the big bath luxuriating in the heat and steam, inhaling the warm fragrances of Marriette's lavender and geranium oils and absent-mindedly sponging my bruised shoulder with hot water.

I was more determined than ever to stay in Amsterdam and try and find out what had happened to Carrie. But I knew now that it wasn't going to be easy. The police weren't going to help, for sure, and even Marriette seemed reluctant for me to get involved. I still had no idea at all where my sister had gone when she left the guest house.

So far, the only lead I had was also turning into a non-starter. Marriette, after three hours of phoning during the afternoon, had drawn one big blank. She only got a reply from 23 of the numbers – it was a work day after all – and nobody, so far, had heard of Pat. She had promised she would keep trying tonight; but there was no escaping the fact that we weren't making any progress on this front. I wondered briefly if I should have given the card to Dankmeijer, but decided that he would have just filed it. He had a closed mind on my sister's death. If there were going to be any more developments, then they were going to have to come from me.

I got out of the bath and dried myself off, giving my cropped hair a quick rub with the towel. I drained the bath, wrapped the towel around me and went down to the second floor and my room.

The rooms in Marriette's Guest House were clean, neat and spacious. Mine overlooked Wetteringsschans, a wide road on the edge of central

Amsterdam and a main route. It was dark outside and, as I sorted out my clothes, I could hear the trams rattling their way along the wet street, their conductor arms peeling blue sparks from the overhead wires outside my window. The room itself was warm: brightly lit by a halogen uplighter and a small bedside lamp. The furniture was traditional. A huge spider plant cascaded from its pot on the dressing table giving a fresh and lived-in feel. I looked longingly at the comfy chair and the bed; I felt weary from a busy day and it was tempting to give in and crash out for a while. But instead I made myself unpack.

I draped my damp towel on the chair and unpacked, pausing momentarily to take stock as I caught sight of myself in the full-length mirror. I was still lean and fit, thanks to my regular gym workouts. All my friends said that I was reaching a dangerous age when no amount of exercise would compensate for the physical changes. I grunted at myself in the mirror. They were just winding me up because I cared about muscle tone. When I told them that it was important to look good, they laughed and accused me of being 'bodyist'. Bodyist? What's so wrong with wanting to feel good?

I pulled on a ribbed, short-sleeved grey top, my favourite black needlecord shirt, black jeans, and stuck my DMs on my feet. Now, bodyist or not, I was feeling better.

I hung two more shirts in the wardrobe and stuck a second pair of jeans and the rest of my tops, socks and underwear in the drawers. Finally, I unwrapped Carrie's scrapbook which contained press clippings and copies of her most notable articles. Marriette had asked me to bring it so that she could read Carrie's work. I turned over the pages, revealing stories that spread from the Home Counties to Ethiopia. Exclusives covering the greed, corruption or prejudice of (mostly) mankind and (occasionally) womankind too. I had looked through it several times since her death. It didn't seem possible that someone who had achieved so much could have gone for good.

But she had, and I needed to know why, so I hauled on my leather jerkin and stuck the black baseball cap with the red dragon logo on my head. Tucking the album under one arm, I walked carefully down the two flights of very steep stairs to the door of Marriette's flat.

She was cooking dinner when I knocked on the door and the glorious smell of the food caused my empty stomach to perform somersaults.

"Hello Etts, would you mind if I make a quick phone call – I'll leave the money?"

She folded her arms and attempted to look stern. "Cameron, you can phone who you like – just so long as I don't have to make any more calls for a while!"

I grinned at her and passed over Carrie's scrapbook to keep her quiet. She was already leafing through it when I started to dial.

Becky was home and answered almost at once.

"Hi Cameron, are you all right?" I said that I was. "You arrived safely then?"

"Becky, I had a smooth crossing and I really enjoyed the ride from Rotterdam. Etts is looking after me here, and I am having a very relaxing time. Now don't fuss!"

"Sorry, Cam." Becky knows what she's like.

"I'm just ringing really to make sure that Tibby is OK – you have remembered to feed him? And to vary the flavours – he won't eat if he doesn't get variety. Oh, and I did leave the cat flap open didn't I?"

Becky laughed. "Talk about me fussing! Cam, you've only been gone two days!" She paused for effect. "Yes, love, everything is fine. Tibby is very happy, very well fed, but missing you madly. Now relax, and have a good break. Just take care of yourself and come back refreshed."

"Huh, OK." Now I felt embarrassed. "I'll ring you later in the week, have to rush now. Thanks Becky. Bye."

"Bye flower, take care."

As I put the phone down, I sensed Marriette's quizzical look.

"You haven't told Becky about your little investigations?"

I shrugged, trying to make light of my omission. "Oh, she knows I'm here to try and come to terms with everything, but there's no need to go into details. If you knew Becky, you'd realise that she would only worry about me."

Marriette studied me, a slight smile playing around her lips.

"Cameron, we all worry about you!"

Then she relaxed and laughed, taking hold of my hand. "Thanks for the album, I'm going to look at it properly later, darling. If I sit down now, it will make me sad and then I'll never get the meal cooked." She smiled a rather watery smile and then brightened up.

"You will stay for some supper? Pork casserole, done the Dutch way – very delicious."

"Thanks Etts," I said, genuinely regretful, "but I don't eat meat, remember? Anyway, I thought that tonight I would go over to the Jordaan – is Marjan's restaurant still there?"

Marriette carried on with her tidying up, moving around the kitchen as she spoke. "Yes ... well, it was in March. That was the last time I was there. I don't know the woman very well – or her partner, what's her name? ... Jan? Jenna? Janna? ... Yes, Janna. I met them both briefly at the funeral ... Marjan and Carrie were friends from way back, weren't they?"

"Yeah, they met in the mid-70s when Carrie was covering the feminist scene here – you know, the cafés, shops and women's projects that sprang up around that time. Carrie said that Marjan was a student then, and a hard-line separatist too!"

Marriette stopped and leant against the sink, chuckling at the thought. "Well, it's hard to imagine Marjan as a radical now, Cameron, but times change and we all grow older and more philosophical. You may not believe it, but I had my moments too. Inequality, even in Amsterdam, was disgraceful, but we made some big changes with our direct action." She smiled to herself. "Ahh, good days, exciting times."

She recovered from her reverie. "You think Marjan may know something about Carrie?"

"I'm pretty sure that Carrie would have called in whilst she was

here." I shrugged. "Worth a try anyway, she may know something."
Marriette wiped her hands and then put the cloth on the table.
"Cameron, darling, I know that you want to find out what happened
to your sister, but don't raise your hopes too much, will you? It's likely that we will never know what made her take those drugs. You may
just have to accept that in the end."

I put Carrie's scrapbook on the table and gave her a wry smile.
"You may be right, Etts, but I'm a long way from accepting anything
just yet."

I had only been to Marjan's Keuken once before. I remembered
it clearly. It was a Friday evening in June – Carrie's 33rd birthday. We
were on holiday together. Partly a birthday treat, but it would never
have happened if my sister hadn't been going through a period of
enforced convalescence. She was recovering well by the time we got
to Amsterdam and, for once in my life, I was pleased to be her
guardian angel.

I shivered as I remembered how worried I had been when I got
the telegram from the British Consulate in Addis Ababa. I was on
the first plane out, of course, and went straight to the hospital to
find that she had been in a coma for nearly three days. That would
have been at the beginning of May. She was coming round by the
time I saw her, and the physical trauma and severe dehydration
caused by her imprisonment were finally beginning to recede. But it
had been close: if her weak cries for help had not been heard by a
passing boy, then she would have perished, in her hot, makeshift
prison.

I was so tied up with that vivid memory that I missed my stop.
I got off at the next and took the short walk back along Marnixstraat
and then over the canal to Rozenstraat. I was relieved to find the
restaurant was still there: a small, unassuming place with an easy,
relaxed feel to it; and excellent Indonesian food.

As I pushed open the big green door, I thought again about that first visit. The restaurant had just opened and Carrie wanted me to meet her old friend. I remembered the stories she told me when I was in my early teens. About her trips to the city and the exploits of these liberated Amsterdam women. I was entranced by her articles on their fight for equality and thrilled by their victories. As someone who also spent a lot of time challenging Authority in my small world, I was both impressed and inspired by their activities. Now times had changed, but I respected the work of all those gutsy women – and my sister and her friend Marjan had been two of them.

The paintwork around the door was no longer pristine and, as I entered, the large room was somehow duller and yellower than I remembered it. But otherwise it was much the same. And, as before, the people sitting at the tables and around the small bar were too interested in their own conversations to turn and stare as I entered. I recognised Janna, Marjan's partner, serving behind the bar, as I squeezed on to the only vacant stool. I was ignored by the two dykes on my right, who were communicating with each other using a combination of eye contact and touch, and only briefly acknowledged by the man to my left, who smiled fleetingly and then pursed his lips as he turned back to his boyfriend and continued a vitriolic conversation of the 'I said, so she said' variety.

I smiled at Janna as she approached. "Campari en tonicwater, alstublieft."

Janna hesitated in the way people do when they think they recognise you, but aren't absolutely sure. She was in her early forties: a small, dark-haired woman with a pale, finely boned face and a complexion that still retained the smooth quality of fine porcelain. Her eyes and mouth were very expressive and, with her relaxed manner, gave her the easy sociability of someone who had served behind a bar for a long time and felt very much at home there.

She continued to look at me as she poured the drink, adding

two large chunks of ice to the angry red liquid. Dropping the second one into the glass, she spoke to me in English but with a husky Dutch accent.

"I hope that you don't mind me asking ... but you look very familiar." She paused, carefully studying my face.

I nodded my head and said quietly, "You saw me at my sister's funeral, Janna. We didn't actually get to talk." I looked down, suddenly feeling self-conscious. "I'm Cameron, Carrie McGill's sister."

The colour drained from her face and, for just a moment, she lost her composure. Then she reached out and extended her hand across the bar. "Oh, I must apologise," she said awkwardly, "you know how it is when you see familiar faces in a different place." We shook hands self-consciously, as if the formality of the gesture would somehow make it easier for us, two strangers, to talk about my sister's death.

"I'm so sorry about Carrie," she said. It's what everyone says when they don't know what else to say.

We each made the sort of remarks that people make when discussing a mutual bereavement or a funeral; attempting to tip-toe through each other's fields of pain and sensitivity, trying to establish where the boundaries of grief are drawn. She said how shocked they had been when she and Marjan read about Carrie's death. "It was so sudden. She was in here only a few days before with a man friend. Carrie seemed OK – a little tense perhaps – but we presumed that was because she was in the middle of a project. Anyway, we arranged to meet the following week, the Tuesday I think. But she never turned up. We were worried about that, about not hearing from her; then we saw the story in the paper. It was a terrible shock – I never knew that Carrie was into drugs like that."

I shook my head. "No Janna, I don't think she was – that's what is so strange. She didn't need drugs – she was one of the most together people that I have ever known."

She excused herself whilst she broke off to serve someone. I looked around me. The place was much as I remembered it: small and cosy. Every available bit of space was used. The bar was at the front and a wall had been demolished to open up a back room of roughly the same size, which was filled with eight tables of various shapes and sizes and a quaint selection of wooden chairs. Nearly all were occupied – predominantly by women, but there were two men at one table and what looked like two straight couples at another. A waiter, quite obviously gay, scurried between the tables and the kitchen, fussing over the diners and exchanging jokes and small talk with the regulars, keen that they should enjoy their meal. Marjan would be at her busiest in the kitchen, but I would talk to her before I left.

I was thinking how normal and relaxed all this looked, compared to the restaurants at home, when Janna returned to me again, apologising for breaking off.

"You said she was with a man, Janna. Do you know who he was?" She shook her head. "No, I have not seen him before. But I would say he was about 180 centimetres tall." She glanced back at me smiling. "That's about six feet, I think. He was about medium weight … though quite well built, and very good looking in a roguish sort of way. Casually dressed, but smart and I would say … oh –" she stopped and pondered "– about 35 years old – quite a lot younger than Carrie. He was a black guy … also probably a Netherlander – he spoke very fluent Dutch, anyway."

I told her why I was in Amsterdam and asked if there was anything else she could tell me that might help. She looked in the diary: yes, they had reserved a table, it was 16 August, a Friday, when they were there – only two days before she had been found dead.

So I now knew that just two days before her 'overdose', my sister was still acting normally and still making arrangements for the future. I was concerned about the man and his possible involvement, though. I needed to find him, somehow.

Janna could remember nothing else. Even if she had, I felt that she might not have shared it; there is something about people who work behind the bar – they get into a habit of listening a lot and saying little. In any case, I was hungry and she was busy again, so I went across and sat at a small table, hidden safely in a corner next to a piano where a black and white cat was lounging on a pile of newspapers. Without thinking, I put out my hand to stroke it and was met by an unfriendly hiss and a raised, clawed paw. For a moment, the cat's reaction upset me, and I realised that I was feeling tired and vulnerable again. I missed Tibby and was glad that Becky was looking after him – he hates catteries.

The meal immediately improved my state of mind: brown bean soup for starters and then vegetable Nasi Goreng – a fried rice dish that tasted like heaven after my long day – washed down with half a carafe of organic red house wine. Marjan came out of the kitchen with the soup and gave me a quick hug, promising to speak to me later. I skipped coffee but, even so, it was still nearly nine o'clock when I finished. The cat was safe by now, draped languorously over the edge of the keyboard lid in a blissful sleep.

Janna was sitting on a stool, drinking tea at an empty bar, when I went over to pay. She took the money and then held up her hand. "Hold, hold," she said, "you must not go before you have spoken to Marjan! She will not be so busy now." And she scurried off into the kitchen, re-emerging with her partner: a small, round, dark-skinned, dark-haired and jolly woman in her late forties. No longer the assertive, rather fierce political figure that I had imagined her to be when I was a teenager. Marriette was right, age mellows us all.

She held out her arms and hugged me. "Oh sweetheart, I am so sorry about your sister. It is such a tragedy – and so young. It is good to see you, we did not feel that we could intrude at the funeral. It must have been hard for you, it has been hard for all of us. What can I say?"

There wasn't a lot that could be said. But I found that I could talk easily with this warm woman about Carrie and her career, her frequent trips to Amsterdam and about the days before her death which were a complete blank. She confirmed Janna's account of Carrie's last visit and we compared notes about Carrie and drugs: confirming each other's feelings that she was unlikely to have been a user. Marjan looked mystified over it all. Like me and Marriette, she was having difficulty accepting the reality.

"I still expect her to walk in through the door one evening," she said, with a tinge of desperation in her voice. "It's so hard to accept that I will never see her again. She was always so full of life."

We talked on for perhaps ten minutes, trying to exorcise the empty space left by my sister's absence. But, after that, it started to become awkward, and there were no words that were adequate enough to fill the void. I said my goodbyes and was on my way out when, even amongst all the background chatter in the restaurant, I heard my name called.

I turned round and waited as Marjan approached me. When she reached me at the door, she held on to my arm in a conspiratorial way and lowered her voice. "Sweetheart, this may be nothing at all, and Janna thought it was none of our business, but I think you should know. The man who was with Carrie was sniffing a lot. All the time he was in here. Twice during the evening, he had a very bad coughing fit." She shuffled her feet and bit her lip, obviously embarrassed. "Cameron, the signs were that he was a regular cocaine user." She shrugged helplessly. "And ... well ... Janna also overheard him say something about a police raid as well. She didn't know whether she should tell you or not." She put her hand on my arm. "In the circumstances, she didn't want you to think badly of Carrie."

I put my hand over hers. "Thanks for telling me that, Marjan. It could be important."

By now she looked quite distressed. "Cameron, I don't know what kind of people your sister got involved with, but maybe if you find him, you can find out what happened to her."

She hugged me again, tighter and longer this time. "I'm sorry we can't give you happier news. Whatever you do, take great care, Cameron. This is a pretty city, but there is a dangerous side to it as well. Be very careful, darling, won't you?"

***

The Juno Bar is only three streets away from Marjan's, but by the time I got there, I felt as if I had been in Amsterdam for a lot longer than one day. I seemed to have done a week's worth of talking and walking; yet I had only succeeded in adding to the questions in my mind. Maybe the women's bar would start to provide an answer or two. I hoped so, I badly needed some encouragement.

Laurierstraat is an ordinary, narrow residential street with apartments and houses jammed together for all of its quarter-mile length. The edges of the roadway are lined with the ubiquitous brown bollards which have become one of the symbols of this unusual city. They are meant to provide a safe margin for pedestrians on either side of the narrow roads, but the bikes which are chained along the buildings and the dog shit that litters the pavement area both provide an effective deterrent for anyone wanting to use the footpath. So like most people, I walked in the road. It may have been riskier, but if I died, it would be with clean boots.

The Vrouwencafé Juno is about halfway down. I stopped when I saw it, unexpectedly feeling a strong sense of nostalgia and a little sadness. For a women's bar, this place had been around a long time and had played quite a part in my love life and that of countless other lesbians from Amsterdam and all over the world. I had been here with Carrie, of course, but it had also been a frequent haunt on other trips with Becky, Joanne and Henny. None more than once – my relationships were not known for their longevity. But it had been a good place to be each time. I crossed my fingers and hoped, for entirely different reasons now, that the good run would continue.

I pushed open the door on the corner of the building and walked into the small, high room, with the polished wooden bar ahead of me. Behind, a large mirror was surrounded by well-stocked shelves of bottled spirits and liqueurs, with the occasional porcelain barrel for effect. A hi-fi in the corner was playing salsa and the huge fan above my head swished as it revolved, redistributing the hot air, actual and metaphorical, around the dimly lit bar. It was Friday night and the place was full. I stopped, taking in the beautiful sight before me, soaking up the noise and the laughter, glad to be back in a room full of women.

I ordered a Campari and tonic at the bar, and showed a photo of Carrie and the card from her jeans to the woman who was serving. She told me Marriette had phoned earlier. "It was very good to talk to her again. She used to come in here a lot but, well, now she has the guest house … Anyway, I told her that I didn't know of any customer called Pat; it's an unusual name, I would have remembered. I'm sorry." She looked at the photo. "But I do remember your sister, she came in regularly over the years. The last time? In the summer, I think: July or early August, perhaps. I am very sorry to hear of her death."

I thanked her for her help and took my drink to the large upstairs area with its dark wooden chairs and assorted plain tables, distributed around a plain varnished floor. Like most of the so-called 'brown bars' in the city, the ceilings and walls in this one were lacquered to a deep golden hue by the cigarette smoke and the alcoholic breath of thousands of customers. The difference with the other bars was that, here, they had all been women.

All the tables were occupied, so I looked around, weighing up the various groups of dykes, trying to decide which was the most approachable. A couple to my right smiled back at me so I asked if I could join them. Like many Dutch people, they spoke enough English to hold a reasonable conversation and they seemed pleased to have someone else to talk to. We chatted easily – about the scene in Amsterdam and the lack of scene in York, about living in the Netherlands and what England was like. Eventually they asked me if I was on holiday and I was able to show them the card and the photo and tell them the story. To my relief, Julika and Liliane volunteered to go round the room with me and ask the other women if they had known Carrie or the mysterious Pat.

There were maybe fifty women in the place, so it took a while to get round them all, but it seemed longer because we more or less drew a blank at every table. One or two of them said that the face in the photo was vaguely familiar, but none of them had talked to her. I had just about given up hope when we went downstairs to the pool room.

There were only five women in there – two playing and three watching. They all came across to look at the photo and one of them, one of the two players, said that she recognised Carrie. Her partner was taking the next shot so she leant back against the wall, one foot on the floor, the other resting against the wall. She was in her late twenties, the sort of self-possessed – sexually possessed – boyish dyke you could meet in any lesbian bar in the western world.

"Yeah," she said, nodding her head slowly. She looked at the photo, then pointedly, looked me up and down as well. "Yeah, I know this woman." She handed the picture back. "I was talking to her in the summer. We got chatting over a beer, like you do. She'd just got here and I suppose I asked her if she was in Amsterdam on business or pleasure. She said that she was a writer of some kind … no, a journalist. Seemed interested in drugs." She looked up and clicked her thumb and finger several times as she recalled the conversation, then she remembered: "Crack users – particularly women, she said."

She broke off to play her shot, sinking five balls, one after the other, and bowing theatrically to the whoops of delight from her three friends. Her partner looked rueful. My informant was someone who would be worth beating but would be a poor loser.

"Very impressive," I said, looking at her appreciatively, in the same way she had looked at me earlier. She grinned back, enjoying this game as well.

"Where was I?"

"You said that my sister was interested in women crack users."

"Oh yeah. Well, I thought that she was wanting to deal at first, so I was ready to get her thrown out. We don't do drugs in here. But then she said that she had heard about a crack scam in the city that was exploiting women, and I got more interested.

"But I couldn't help. I think I suggested she contact the drug agen cies around the city. Yeah, that's it – she said that she had already done that and that the results were ... 'interesting'."

"Did she say what the scam was?"

"Ohhh, I can't remember, but I think that she was not very will ing to tell me what she was finding out." She eyed me suspiciously "Why aren't you asking your sister about this?"

I looked down, trying to think of an easy way to tell her; I knew my answer would embarrass her. But there was only one way to say it "Because she was found dead in one of the canals two months ago and I want to find out what happened to her."

"Oh my God! Shit, no!" She clamped her hand to her forehead "Sorry, sorry; she seemed a nice lady." Then looking straight at me again, incredulous, "You think she was murdered?"

I nodded. "It looks that way to me, but the police say it was an accident."

"Huh! Police, what do they know? ... Hey, you playing detective?"

I smiled and shook my head. The directness of this woman was refreshing. "Not really, I just want to know what happened to her."

"Well, good luck, gumshoe, I hope you find out what you need to know."

"Thanks," I said, meaning it, "you've been a big help."

She shrugged. "Sorry I couldn't tell you more, it was just a casual conversation."

As I left, her eyes followed me and, without smiling, she called after me, "See you again, I hope."

I threw her a non-committal smile. "Yeah, maybe."

I made my way back upstairs and rejoined the two women at the table.

"Who was that?" I said. "You know her?"

They both laughed and Julika spoke in Dutch, lightly rebuking her friend. When I looked puzzled, Liliane smiled broadly at me.

"She's scolding me for deserting you! I'm sorry, that was Pauly she's just a bit of a randy woman, I think. I left because I thought you had pulled."

I was amused. "Nice thought, but I have other things on my mind at the moment. Still, it's good to be appreciated."

We talked a bit and I bought another round of drinks, then the two women left for Vive la Vie and the big Friday party. Regretfully I declined an invitation to join them. I was so tired. It was only 10.30, but I was ready to call it a day.

I leant back in my chair and closed my eyes, wishing I could be magically transported back to Marriette's, back to that comfortable-looking bed. I was almost asleep just thinking about it, when someone bumped my shoulder very hard. It still hurt from the fall and the knock sent a jab of pain right across my back. I nearly lost my balance as well, but managed to grab the table for support and pull the chair back on to its four legs.

When I regained my balance, I looked up, expecting at least a muttered apology, but instead, the woman looked down at me with clear contempt, head on one side, and spoke sweetly in a phoney show of remorse.

"Oh I am so sorry, Miss McGill. My fault entirely, I do hope that you are all right!" The tone was taunting and sarcastic. Her voice was a little slurred, too, from too much alcohol. "Perhaps you do not recognise me out of uniform? Senior Police Officer Hellen van Zalinge."

She sat down opposite me and I cringed, knowing that there must be more to come.

"I don't know what you do in England, but in the Netherlands, when we knock someone over and pull them down half a flight of stairs, it is customary to apologise, rather than shout abuse at them."

She was a slim woman in tight blue jeans, with a loose-fitting white T-shirt tucked in at the waist. Her body and face had an element of sensuality that owed more to a fullness of figure than to any athletic build. She was about five-foot-six, her almost shoulder-length blonde hair spilling out in waves around her strong, pretty face. The blue eyes looked just as remarkable now as they had in that split second on the stairs.

"Of course, some people are just ignorant."

I tried to be conciliatory; although my shoulder was bruised, my ego – unlike hers – seemed to be OK. Anyway, I was too tired to argue.

"Look, I'm really sorry," I explained wearily. "It was an accident, I was in a hurry. I was angry."

"You were bloody clumsy!" She exploded in my face. "Look, next time you go down stairs, just watch where you are going, will you?" She got up to go and, in a sweet voice that reminded me of cyanide-laced honey, she added, "Oh, and one other thing. If you are going to roll down a flight of stairs with me again, please do it somewhere quiet, rather than in the main lobby of Amsterdam's biggest police station."

She scowled at me. "I may never live this down!"

Four

By the time I got down to breakfast, the other guests had gone: no doubt taking in the sights, the cafés, the museums, the art galleries. I longed to join them and enjoy this beautiful city like I used to. But I didn't know if Amsterdam could ever be the same for me again.

In this contemplative and slightly depressed mood, I helped myself to a boiled egg and some Gouda from the buffet and sat down at one end of the big breakfast table in Marriette's lounge. It was a little brighter outside today and the light from the window filled the far end of the room, highlighting the bright colours on the big squashy settee and freshening up the greenery on the various side tables. In the middle of the wall, an open fire blazed in an enormous brick fireplace, giving the room a soft and comfortable ambience. I sat for a while, soaking up whatever comfort I could from the homeliness and warmth. In truth, I felt quite alone.

I sliced open the crisp white roll on my plate without much enthusiasm, hungry yet not interested in eating. Yesterday had seen a lot of frantic activity but little progress. Maybe I was being too impatient. Huh, maybe I wasn't cut out for detective work. Emma Victor, Lindsay Gordon and VI Warshawski never seemed to have any trouble getting to the heart of the matter. But, unlike my favourite fictional heroes, I was finding it hard asking questions and digging around. The real thing didn't feel very glamorous at all.

I wondered about what I was doing. Maybe Marriette was right; maybe Carrie would want me to just let the matter drop. Maybe I should go home. Maybe, maybe.

I was working myself into a nice black tunnel of depression when Marriette appeared with her big smile and a jug of steaming hot chocolate.

"Goedemorgen, Cameron. How are you today?"

"Oh, OK," I replied in a voice that sounded anything but OK.

She threw me a concerned look and poured out my drink. Then she continued in a determinedly cheerful voice.

"Well, you will be glad to know I worked very hard last night and I have got through every one of those tiresome numbers!"

"And ... ?" I asked sullenly.

She threw up her arms in mock despair and gave it to me straight. "... And I'm sorry, Cameron, there is still no sign of our mystery woman."

So, her good cheer had more to do with finishing an unwanted job than with actually finding anything useful.

"Wonderful!" I moaned. "That makes me feel a lot better!"

"Sorry," she squeaked, making out she was scared of me.

I looked up at her and smiled. I couldn't be bad-tempered with this woman for long. "Etts, you've worked really hard, and I'm sorry if I seem unappreciative. It's just that ... Well, you know ..."

She smiled sadly back. "Yes, darling, I know. It would be good to have some answers. But probably we will never know what happened." She patted my hand. "Enjoy your breakfast."

As she turned to go, I had a thought. "Etts, how many of the numbers were unobtainable?"

She turned and looked pensive. "Five of them. Why?"

"Well," I said, "if our Pat isn't at any of the 95 traceable numbers, she must have been at one of the five disconnected ones."

"So?"

I sighed in exasperation. "So, all we have to do is find the addresses for the disconnected numbers and I'll check them out."

"She could just as easily have been at one of the numbers I rang," she said sceptically. "Someone could have lied to me, or got confused over the name."

I gave her a sideways look. "Oh, come on, Etts. First of all, why on earth should anyone lie? Secondly, Pat is hardly a common name around here, so there isn't likely to be any confusion."

She put her hands on her hips. "So how do you propose to find out the addresses of five disconnected numbers?"

"The phone company?" There was already a note of doubt in my voice. I could sense what was coming.

Marriette shook her head slowly. "Sorry, Cameron, there is a privacy law in the Netherlands that prohibits any company giving out personal details." She looked sympathetic now. "Probably the only people who could get the addresses are the police – and they are bound by the same rules as the phone company, PTT." She shrugged her shoulders. "Not that you know anyone in the police who would want to help anyway."

"Well ... there's the woman I knocked down the stairs yesterday! Though, after what she said to me last night, I think she would probably rather have me arrested than help me."

Marriette looked puzzled and shook her head at me in despair, choosing to ignore the comment. "Well, I'm sorry, darling, I can't think of anyone else. It's all been a bit of pointless, hasn't it? ... Still, we tried."

"Don't feel bad, Marriette, I'm very grateful for all your hard work." Grateful, yes. But I was also beginning to think she was somehow relieved not to have found anything.

"Well, what now, Cameron? I suppose that's it, is it? Will you stay a few days before going home?"

"Hang on, Etts," I said, trying to make light of her comment, "I'm not giving up just yet. I'll have to think of something. Maybe I can find a computer nerd to hack into the telecom system; maybe I could bribe a PTT employee?"

"But that would be illegal!" She looked genuinely shocked.

"Etts, can't you see that I will do anything to get to the bottom of this, and if that means breaking some ridiculous privacy law, then so be it. I have to get some answers soon! Anyway," I said, lightening up again, "you needn't worry, you know I'm not very good at bribery and corruption."

She laughed and wagged her finger at me. "You are the one who is usually championing human rights! You should be ashamed of yourself for even thinking of breaking a privacy law!"

"Yeah, all right," I admitted, "but this is different."

It wasn't, of course; but I did need those addresses.

"Anyway, tell me what you did yesterday." Marriette brightened up, recalling my earlier comment. "Tell me about this woman and the stairs."

I told her about my visit to the police station, about the policewoman and our collision, about my visit to Marjan's and the information given to me in the Juno Bar.

She raised her eyebrows and leant towards me slightly. "So, is that why you are so fed up?" I waited for her reproach. "I'm sorry, darling, but you are being unrealistic." She stood up straight and folded her arms. "If you keep asking questions, you will get some answers. But after two months, it's not likely that you will be able to piece them all together, and that is going to make you even sadder." She gave me an uncompromising look. "It's a shame about those numbers, Cameron, but I'm afraid you'll just have to accept that there's no way round it!"

My mouth fell open. "Etts, you really can't be serious. Carrie was your friend – don't you want to know what happened to her?"

She turned away and dropped her arms dejectedly to her side, busying herself clearing the table. "Please Cameron …. just let it go." She sobbed.

"Etts, you've been looking at the scrapbook, haven't you?"

She bit her lip and a tear ran down her cheek. I stood up, turned her around and gave her a hug.

"Oh Cameron," she sobbed, "it's all so upsetting. There are some wonderful memories in the album, but they all reminded me of what a precarious life Carrie led."

"I know," I replied, slowly letting go of her and sitting back at the table next to her. "I was thinking last night of the time in Africa and how lucky she'd been to survive."

She sighed with exasperation. "But that's the whole point, can't you see? I was looking at the press cuttings before I went to bed last night and I'm scared, Cameron. Scared about you and your safety in all this."

"I know, Etts, but it's different here." I tried to reassure her. "We're in a western city with good communications and police everywhere – and I'm not trying to expose anyone like Carrie was in Africa that time. I'm just doing a little digging, that's all."

She shook her head, tears running down her cheeks which were flushed with a mixture of anger and sorrow. "Cameron, that Peter Karst was a nasty man. He intended to kill Carrie then because of what she found out about him. Who's to say that this time she wasn't trying to expose another dangerous criminal?"

"The thought had crossed my mind, Etts, but I promise that I'm being very careful."

She shook her head in disbelief and put her arms around my neck. I could feel the wetness of the tears as she sobbed into my shoulder.

"Cameron, I've already lost Carrie. She was so special, and now I am so frightened that you will get yourself killed as well, trying to find out what happened to her."

I hugged her tightly for a while, then held her at arm's length and looked directly at her. "This is nonsense, Etts. You're upset about Carrie, that's all, and you're getting everything out of per-spective. I'm not involved with any criminals, I'm quite safe and I intend to stay that way. All I'm doing – all I'm going to do – is ask a few questions, find out a little more about what happened and then leave it at that … OK?"

She nodded and wiped a tear from her eye.

***

I didn't tell Etts but, after breakfast, I set out to visit all the drug agencies in the city. There were a dozen of them, so I knew it would take a while and, from what Pauly the pool player had told me, it was a fair bet that I would be following in my sister's footsteps.

Big cities are honey pots for drug users, and Amsterdam is one of the biggest honey pots of them all. Good lines of supply, anonymity and agencies that bring some relief to a life lived on the street and in hostels. They all remembered Carrie and they all told me the same story that they had told her. Thanks to the methadone programme, the decriminalisation of cannabis, the better treatment of addicts and the heavy targeting of dealers by the police, heavy drug use had stabilised in Amsterdam. Some even said that it was falling. There was optimism, guarded optimism, but nevertheless a feeling that some corner had been turned in the war against hard drug misuse.

But I sensed that there was a cloud too. The figures spoke for themselves, but nobody seemed prepared to believe that it would last. Something was beginning to obscure the sunshine of their success. But no one would admit it directly.

By the time I finished the last-but-one call, it was still only early afternoon, but I felt tired and bored. The bruise on my shoulder was uncomfortable and my head was beginning to ache. I almost skipped the Freebase office on Spuistraat, expecting that I would only hear more of the same. But I like to finish a job properly, and so I made my way through the main pedestrian shopping street, until I reached one of the alleyways that led through to Spuistraat.

The office consisted of just one rather scruffy room on the first floor above a bar. Hans Knaapen, the co-ordinator, was the only person in there – administrator, receptionist and clerk all rolled into one slightly flabby, unshaven man in his early fifties. It was the end of his day too and, from the look of him, he wasn't feeling much better than I was. Maybe that's why he seemed glad to break off and talk. I accepted his offer of a coffee just to be sociable – though, in truth, I was longing for a simple cup of tea – and sat down in a plastic chair next to a cheap utilitarian table.

Like all the others, I told him that I was a drugs counsellor visiting Amsterdam for research purposes. Like most of the others, he was pleased to tell me about his work. He was informal and relaxed. I took to him at once.

"We are very different to other drug agencies." He threw me a grin as he put the filter paper into the percolator and spooned in an exact amount of ground coffee beans. "Some of the others don't like us because we are being totally independent and keeping our distance. We are not moralising. We just want to help users avoid health and other problems. Our staff are on the street where they belong, talking to users, keeping their ears to the ground. As far as we are concerned, people can use what they like. But we just want them to do it safely."

"That sounds good." I said, warming to his obvious sincerity. "Refreshing even."

He was quite tall and pale-skinned. The lines around his eyes and mouth might have added some distinction to other men but on his drawn face they spoke of a life that had been far from easy. His clothes were casual but neat – the standard male uniform of denims and shirt, found in most Amsterdam offices. His hair was close-cropped and he wore a single gold ring in his right ear. This was a man I felt I could relate to, and, from the smile he had given me when I walked in, I guessed that he could relate to me as well.

He poured hot water into the funnel of the percolator and set it down, bubbling and hissing on the table in front of me with two rather beaten-up mugs and a jug of the usual yellow evaporated milk. Sitting down opposite me, he leant back in his chair.

"Many users, they suffer from poor health, so simple information from us can combat pneumonia, hepatitis, abscesses, tuberculosis and

AIDS. We keep things simple and we don't disapprove. That way they trust us."

"So you get close to the users on the street?"

He poured the coffee, spilling a large pool of it on to the faded Formica between us and swearing gently in Dutch as he mopped it up with paper tissue. He continued to talk in an enthusiastic, almost passionate way, motioning to me to add my own milk.

"Ja, we are having four field workers at present in the city. They are people with personal knowledge of drug use and/or homelessness; so the users, they respect them and vice versa: they meet them regularly on the streets, at the methadone bus and in dealing places. We talk to them and give them both verbal advice and simple written advice which relates to their circumstances. We are promoting safer drug use too – for instance, encouraging them to smoke heroin rather than inject. We have lists of needle exchanges and we give special advice to vulnerable women users.

"Our approach means that we are also more aware than anyone of trends on the street. We tell all users when dealers are selling bad heroin or unidentified pills. They know that we do not bullshit and so take notice. Anyway, often this sort of information comes to us from the users themselves – we all work together."

He smiled in an ironic sort of way. "Like I said, we are different to other agencies."

Hans himself wasn't like the others either. So far today, I had learnt little. This could be my last real chance to find out what Carrie had been up to. I decided to level with him.

"Hans, I need your help."

He looked at me, holding his palms out wide. "Anything. I will tell you all I can."

"First, I should tell you more about my reason for being in Amsterdam. I am a drugs counsellor and I am interested in the drug scene over here but there is another, much more important reason for my visit."

He nodded. "Go ahead."

"My sister visited Amsterdam in the summer. She was a free-lance journalist with some kind of a lead on a drugs-related story. I'm trying to trace her movements and I believe that she may have been to see you." I pushed Carrie's photo across the table to him. He picked it up and studied it.

His face brightened visibly. "Yes … yes, I remember her. A very attractive woman with real – ah, what is the word – yes, presence." He laughed lightly. "She came in here one really hot day in August. I remember because we joked about the smell from the drains out-side. She was very easy to like, very interesting … and I am thinking about her quite a lot afterwards. I do not like journalists usually but I felt we were on the same side. She was a nice lady." He handed the photo back, looking concerned. "Has something happened – why are you asking?"

It was still distressing having to talk about her death to strangers, but it was becoming part of my daily life. "She was found dead in the Nieuwe Herengracht at the end of August, Hans. The police say it was an accident."

I could see the colour draining from his face. He looked horri-fied. "Oh my God, no. That is truly terrible." He shook his head in disbelief. "But why?" he asked. "You say 'accident' as if you don't believe it was."

I breathed out sharply. "Yeah, I think she was murdered. That's why I need your help. All the other agencies have been pleasant and accommodating to me, but they haven't told me everything. I know they haven't.

"Hans, my sister was a good journalist. She must have been on to something really big; something that made her a threat to some-one. Something to do with drugs."

He got up from his seat and walked over to the window, rubbing his hand across the stubble on his chin. He looked out of the win-dow for a few moments, gathering his thoughts, then he turned back and looked at me carefully.

"Cameron, I have to say that this would be a very good time to walk away from whatever it was your sister was involved in."

I shook my head, slowly.

"Huh, I didn't think you would." He took a deep breath. "OK. I don't know how your sister found out about it, I suppose journalists have many contacts, but she was asking questions about users who were disappearing, particularly women." He leant against the window sill. "There is always a problem with users coming and going. Of course it has never been easy keeping track of them. People move on, particularly foreigners. Huh, also some die, some OD, some are murdered."

He shrugged like someone who had seen it all. "It can be dangerous on the streets. But recently, there is a feeling amongst the professionals, especially amongst my field workers, that many more women are disappearing this summer."

"Don't the police have figures?"

He laughed cynically. "No one has meaningful figures, Cameron, especially the police. Many of the people on the street are transient and they are having a dislike of law and order. We all know something is happening – including the police – but there is no way to prove it. So we keep quiet. The last thing we are wanting to do is cause alarm over what may turn out to be nothing more than people moving on."

"But you don't believe it is 'people moving on'."

He made a face and shook his head. "No, it is happening too often. Besides, the users themselves believe that there is some kind of abduction taking place – or, at least … enticement." He opened his mouth to continue, but stopped.

There was something else.

"What? What is it, Hans?"

He looked up and spoke very firmly: "I cannot tell you anything else."

Frustrated by the sudden halt in the information, I walked around the table until I was next to him. "But Hans, I need to know. I need your help!" It was then that the truth dawned. "You told Carrie, didn't you?"

He took hold of me by the shoulders. "Cameron, I've only just met you but I can see that you are a nice woman, like your sister. I am doing what I can to help users. I am not part of some moral fight against drugs and neither are you. That is up to the authorities."

He must have sensed my stubbornness because he gripped me tighter. I thought for a moment that he was going to shake me like a naughty child. Instead he spoke with an intensity that I did not expect. "If your sister was murdered, then it was because she was getting into something that was too big for her. If you carry on asking questions, like she did, then you will be endangering your life as well. It is not worth it, Cameron. Leave it to the police ... please."

He relaxed his grip and stepped away from me.

I stared at him defiantly. "The police aren't doing anything!"

He shrugged again. "There is no way you can know what the police are doing. I am sorry, Cameron, there is nothing more that I can tell you."

"Yeah. You mean there is nothing more that you will tell me."

"Put it how you like. But please, take my advice and stay out of this. Please, whatever it is."

I was with Hans for only half an hour, but when I left, I needed a drink and a little time to get my thoughts together again. The Vrouwencafé Juno was only ten minutes walk away, so I headed there, the exercise occupying my limbs whilst all the information in my brain sorted itself out. I felt really sore that Hans had clammed up after such a promising start, but by the time I got to Laurierstraat, I was beginning to make more sense of what I had, and hadn't, heard.

The pump delivered its glassful of pale amber beer and Agnes, the woman who had served me the previous night, scraped the froth off the top with a wooden spatula.

"Did you find out anything about your sister?"

"Yeah, thanks, it was useful and I'm slowly tracing her movements, but it's slow and I'm not really sure if it will lead anywhere."

I didn't go into detail. Hell, I didn't have any detail to go into. Just the certainty that, somewhere along the line, Carrie had upset someone. I didn't feel like being sociable; I needed to think, so I sat down at one of the tables upstairs. The place was a complete contrast to the night before. There were only six women in the bar and two of them were at the pool table. I recognised k.d.'s Ingénue album coming over the speakers and sat back, prodding my brain into action, as she asked where her head had gone. Yeah, I could relate to that.

I took the notepad out of my jacket pocket and started to make a list of what I knew about my sister's death.

I knew that Carrie had left Marriette's after only a few days, presumably because she was on to something.

She had contact with a woman called Pat but I still hadn't been able to find her.

I knew now that Carrie's sources had probably been right – women were disappearing off the streets – but what had Hans told her that he hadn't told me?

What exactly was the drug that had killed Carrie? Furthermore, why kill someone with six injections rather than one big one?

Also, why were the police being so unhelpful – was there a link with Hans's secrecy?

Finally, who was the man with Carrie at the restaurant?

I read and re-read the list whilst I sipped my beer and listened to k.d. After Hans's warning, I wondered what I was getting myself into. Whatever it was, I couldn't stop now. The self-doubt I had felt that morning had gone, replaced by a determination to get to the bottom of this. For one thing, I was fed up with being told to go home, be careful, leave it to the police. Everyone seemed too concerned with my welfare.

But determined or not, I still had nothing to go on. I had to find out more – and one way of doing that was to talk to some of the users directly.

I finished off my beer and put my leather jacket back on, wrapping my long, grey woolly scarf around my neck, ready for the damp cold of the late afternoon, and headed downstairs, stopping at the bar on the way out.

Agnes put her head on one side and gave me a sympathetic smile. "Pretty tough, huh?"

"Yeah," I said. "I don't know what was going on with my sister. I'm looking for answers but all I seem to get is more and more questions."

"It will become clear in time, I'm sure."

I wasn't convinced, but I nodded anyway. I had to believe I could get to the bottom of this.

"Leave your phone number with me and if anything else turns up, I'll give you a ring."

I gave her Marriette's number and thanked her for her trouble.

"Tot ziens." I smiled my goodbye, as I opened the door.

"So long, Cameron, take care."

Five

I slept for an hour when I got back to my room and would probably have slept into the evening if I hadn't been woken by a knock at the door.

I got out of bed, still fully dressed, yawning and trying to focus my fuddled mind. It was Marriette: she was excited about something but trying hard not to show it. Her transparency, though sometimes worrying, was an endearing quality and it was good to see her feeling better.

"Hello, sweetheart – oh sorry, have I woken you?" Sorry or not, she wasn't going to be put off. "Lieveling, I have something really good to tell you. Come downstairs and have a coffee with me."

I let my amusement and my curiosity show. "What?" But she turned her back on me, mischievously, and scurried down the stairs into the kitchen. I followed, quizzing her all the way, but she didn't say a word until I had sat down and she had the ubiquitous mug of coffee in front of me. It crossed my mind that, if I stayed in the Netherlands for too long, I was more likely to OD on caffeine than any hard drug.

When she finally sat down, her face twitched as a big smile tried to force its way out from behind her thin mask. There are times when you just know someone is winding you up.

"What? … Marriette, tell me!" I shouted.

She grinned. "I think I may have solved the telephone problem."

"You've been to bed with one of the women at the phone company?" I asked incredulously.

She shook her head, laughing. "I was prepared to do anything to help you Cameron, even that! Well, especially that! But in the end I didn't need to." She paused. "No, we have a new guest, a German businesswoman, Dr Helga Wassenheim: she's in Amsterdam for a few days for some meetings. She rang up earlier to check that I had a room and now she is here – on the second floor, the room next to you. A very smart lady indeed." She gave me a deep, meaningful look.

Somewhere along the line she had lost me. "Etts, I may be dense but I can't really see any connection."

"Ah! Well –" she blushed a little, embarrassed "– you see, I was talking to her when she arrived, only about an hour ago – you know, just chatting – and she asked me about the other guests, as she is likely to be on her own on an evening. Well, everyone one else is in couples, so … well, I told her about you and … well … about Carrie and about the missing numbers."

Thanks Etts, tell everyone about me, maybe I could go on TV as well.

She saw the disapproval pass across my face. "I know darling, I can see what you are thinking, and you are quite right: I shouldn't have said anything. But anyway, I did, and she said she had a friend at the telecom company who she was sure would help. So she has taken the numbers and I said that you would meet her later on tonight."

My face lit up again. "To get the addresses?"

"No, she won't have them by then. I just thought you would like to meet her. She is certainly rather keen to meet you!"

Oh Jesus. Just what I needed; a blind date with a German businesswoman, probably straight. Almost certainly boring.

"Honestly Cameron, you'll really like her, she is very attractive."

I wanted the information badly but I wasn't thrilled at the prospect of an evening with anyone who was called Helga Wassenheim.

Etts wasn't giving up. "She doesn't eat meat," she coaxed.

"Oh great!" I moaned. "We can discuss our recipes for lentil soup!"

Marriette smiled indulgently and put her hand on my arm. "Oh come on, Cameron, she does seem very eager to help. And you did say that you wanted to find this Pat, didn't you?"

"Yeah," I conceded, "you're right! Thanks for your help, Etts, you're a real brick."

"Brick! Is that a compliment?"

I laughed. "I just mean that you really are a big support to me." I gave her a little hug and a quick peck on the cheek. "Anyway, I must fly. I only came back for my bike really, I need to catch the methadone bus on its early evening rounds."

She gave me a funny look.

"No, no, it's not for me ... oh, I'll tell you later."

"OK darling, but be careful." She went and got her rucksack and took something out of one of the pockets. "Here, take my mobile phone, I want you to be able to ring me if you need any help. Promise?"

I laughed good-naturedly. "Yep, I promise."

Outside the narrow streets of the city centre, Amsterdam's main roads are wide and straight, so it didn't take me long to get to Vondel Park, where, I had been told, the bus made its most popular stop.

As I drove, I remembered the huge urban park in all its summer glory: lawns filled with sunbathers and people relaxing, smoking their joints, sleeping or watching the buskers and jugglers practising; the stalls selling cakes and clothes; the musicians and bands; the cafés and ice-cream stalls; the tarot readers sitting under the trees; the old men fishing in quiet hidden ponds that were covered in green algae; secret paths through the shrubberies; brightly coloured parrots in the trees and the smell of roses, cut grass and dope all around.

Today it wouldn't be like that at all – just wet and bare, waiting for the seasons to turn again.

I took a left off Overtoom, on to the short stretch of Katten Laan and saw the green and white bus ahead of me, pulled in to the park entrance.

The men and women around the bus were much like any bunch of users – they looked perfectly ordinary as they milled around waiting their turn. I guessed they would be people from all walks of life: some were smart, some scruffy, some weird; there were young and older people; people who were clearly homeless and one or two so well dressed that they looked out of place. They were predominantly men, but some women too. Maybe forty people were queuing at the bus or talking in small groups around the parking area.

I didn't know where to start, so I just pitched in and walked around showing the photo and asking everyone if my sister had talked to them in August. Most people shrugged or shook their heads, either unable to help or unwilling to. It was one of the women who recognised Carrie.

"Yeah, she spoke to me." She was small and shapeless in her thick, grubby tweed overcoat. Her spiky ginger hair and her pierced eyebrows and nose made her look fierce, but her eyes held more mischief than malice. She looked 40, but I guessed she was probably nearer 30. Drugs and life on the street have that effect. She spoke with a raw, gravelly voice, probably the result of smoking too much heroin.

There was a directness about her that was honest rather than offensive. "Yeah, I remember her." She looked straight at me. "She gave me money after I answered her questions."

I took the hint and held up a 25 guilder note. She smiled and took hold of one end. I held on to the other, insisting she earned the right to it. She shook her head good-humouredly, let go and sat down on a nearby tree stump. "You police?" she queried, head on one side, studying me.

"Me? Hell no!" I said, shocked. "I'm just over here trying to find out what happened to my sister."

She nodded approvingly and smiled. "Naah, you don't look like police."

"Thanks, I'm pleased about that."

She looked up at me again and spoke with the same directness.

"So you're looking for your sister?" She pulled a face, showing a degree of sadness that punctured her tough exterior. "Happens a lot – people disappearing off the streets – people come and go for all sorts of reasons. Sometimes they OD, other times they move on. Sometimes no one knows. You learn to live with it." She looked at me meaningfully. "You learn not to ask too many questions."

"Was that what my sister was doing?"

"Yeah." She looked serious. "She was asking questions about women disappearing."

"And?" I prompted, waiting for more.

She didn't hear me because she had spotted some guy a few yards away. She stood up and started waving and shouting, "Kom is hier, Karl!" (Come here, Karl.)

Karl, a slightly built six-footer of a man with a wispy beard and of indeterminate age, broke off his conversation and ambled across to join us.

"Karl, do you remember that woman –" she took the photo from me, showing it to her friend "– this woman. Remember? She was asking questions about people disappearing, ja?"

He sat down on the tree stump and took out his Rizlas and his pouch of Drum tobacco. "Yeah, I guess so." He spoke with a thick Dutch accent. "Some kind of reporter after a story. Who is she?" He waved his hand in my direction.

"The woman is her sister, Karl. She's looking for her."

Karl shook his head at me. "She was asking some dodgy questions, lady." He started to roll a cigarette. "Users do disappear these days. No one acknowledges it too publicly, but it happens. Mostly women, too. I keep a close watch over Bella here; don't want anything to happen to you, babe, huh?" He gave her a squeeze and turned back to me, tapping the photo.

"Look, I'm sure this isn't what you want to hear," he said, sounding awkward and a little embarrassed, "but if I was you … well, if I was you, I would not count on finding her. I am sorry … but people who ask questions like her –" he paused "– and you – well, they scare other people."

I declined his offer of a smoke. "What do you mean?"

He looked around a little nervously and then looked at Bella. "She OK, you think?" Bella nodded.

"OK, you seem sound, lady; so I'll tell you what I told your sister." He lowered his voice. "We had two friends who vanished early this year: one in April, one in May. They were both nice girls, fucked up, but sweet with it. The first one just disappeared one night – never came back. The second one – Joany – told us that she had first been given free supplies of crack; then she had been offered an unlimited supply and a place to sleep in return for a few hours' easy work each day. She turned it down the first few times, worried about what had happened to her friend. But they told her that her friend was having a great time and kept giving her free samples, encouraging her to go too. They would never tell her what the work was, though it doesn't take too much imagination to guess.

"She resisted for a few weeks. Then they gave her what she said was a 'special'. It wasn't crack, she didn't know what it was, but it blew her mind. She told us it was ten times better than crack – a real psychedelic trip as well – she couldn't wait to get her hands on some more. The next night, he came back and she left with him. That was it, we never saw her again."

"She left with a stranger – just like that?"

He shrugged. "She was a crackhead like her friend. So normal rules don't apply. Look ... people who have any sense keep away from crack." He shook his head angrily. "Man, it seems cheap and you get a big buzz all right; a real fuckin' A1 feeling – just like when you fuck. But it lasts a few minutes only, so you need another hit ... and then another, until you are using big-time. By then it's too late; the habit has got so fuckin' expensive, it's a nightmare."

"So, anyone taking crack is vulnerable?"

"You got it, lady, 'specially the women. We guess our two friends found something that gives them an even bigger high. And, if it was free, why would they resist?" He whistled through his teeth. "Shit man, it must be something if it's more addictive than crack ..." He shook his head in disbelief.

"Hey –" he narrowed his eyes and peered at me suspiciously "– you sure you're nothing to do with the cops?"

I put my hand on my heart. "Honest."

He didn't look entirely sure, but then he noticed that the queue by the bus had gone and a look of mild panic crossed his face. "Yo! It's our turn, Bella. Come on sweetheart, let's get some of that fuckin' honey, darling."

At that, he was off, loping across the grass and into the bus with a smile on his face. Bella paused and I gave her a 50 instead of the 25.

"Thanks."

She smiled at the sight of the note. "Cool." Then, slightly embarrassed, "Sorry about the police thing; it's just that the cops keep coming round and hassling us for information. We don't trust them, so we –" she drew her fingers across her mouth "– we keep it zipped." She touched my arm. "Look, just take care, OK? Be careful who you speak to." Then she ran after Karl, turning as she went, almost running backwards as she shouted, "Hey, I hope you find your sister!"

I followed the bus to its five other stops and heard a similar story from three others – the dates and the names where different, but the circumstances were the same. There was always crack involved, always the lure of free supplies of something 'special' and, ultimately, the promise of unlimited supply for easy work. And ultimately, they had all given in.

They had all been women.

It was after eight by the time I pushed my bike into Marriette's yard. The dark night air had become thick with a wet blanket of fog. My head and body were dry, thanks to my leather jacket and helmet, but my jeans were heavy with water and my feet were squelching in my DMs as I chained up my bike. I should have worn my full biking gear. Etts was out, so I had to walk round to the front of the house to use my key in the guests' door.

Cold and wet physically, but even more chilled mentally, I went straight up to my room and threw off all my clothes, reflecting that it never seemed to stop raining for long in this city. Then I got into the deep red silk robe that Marriette had lent me and made my way upstairs to the bathroom. Within minutes I was under a stinging hot shower, but I couldn't relax. The evidence that large numbers of women were disappearing off the streets was frightening; the link with Carrie's death undeniable. She had obviously been on to something big when someone stopped her. I wasn't going to jump to any conclusions just yet – but I was scared about what I was beginning to uncover.

At least the shower warmed me up and released the tightness in my shoulder. I towelled myself dry and, throwing on the robe, wandered out of the bathroom and back down to the second floor, ready for a quiet drink and then a blissfully early night ...

"So you must be Cameron."

The woman standing at the lounge door and blocking the way to my room had a German accent ... Helga!

I acted cool and smiled a hello, like I had remembered all along. "I'll just get dressed," I said lightly. But she made no effort to move out of my way. Instead, she looked me up and down and gave a broad, sensual smile.

Every inch of Helga Wassenheim exuded style. From her neatly coiffured blonde hair down to her neat Gucci heels, the woman was perfectly turned out. She was about my size but in her heels she looked down on me slightly. She wore make-up, but modestly: enhancing her natural highlights without being too obvious. Her complexion was still unblemished and her skin firm for a woman who, I guessed, was pushing her late thirties. Tidy eyebrows hovered above piercing, dark brown eyes which shone out in a challenging way from her sophisticated and angular face. Her earrings were gold and she wore an expensive-looking chain necklace. Her black Armani jacket contrasted with the cream blouse underneath and the matching skirt almost reached her knees, which were encased in sheer pale beige tights.

Not my type at all.

I really needed to get out of her way: or rather she needed to get out of mine. Usually I try not to meet tall imposing strangers without my clothes on. So, when I made a move to walk past her, I expected her to step back and let me by.

But she stood her ground and put a hand on my shoulder. Her voice was soft but there was a firmness there that was difficult to argue with.

"Oh no, my dear, there's no need to change, you look so comfortable." I didn't much like the sparkle in her eyes as she put her arm around my waist and steered me through the lounge door. "Come with me, there's a nice warm fire in here and I have a full bottle of cognac and two glasses. There are no other guests around tonight, so you can make yourself really comfortable. Let's have a nice chat."

After what I had discovered about Carrie, the last thing I needed was a romantic tryst with Helga Wassenheim; besides, she made me feel like a fly who has just been invited to relax on a particularly sticky web. But, damn, I needed this woman and her friend at the telecom company, I needed those addresses! So I smiled meekly, making for the only armchair – rather too slowly. Helga was a woman who planned her tactics in advance and she had moved ahead of me effortlessly. Already standing by the chair, she poured my drink and invited me to sink into the large settee.

It was warm and cosy in the lounge. The big fake-log fire glowed realistically, pools of soft light were overflowing from around three large table lamps and mellow jazz was oozing its way out of the hi-fi. It all made me feel very uncomfortable: my borrowed robe was big and long, but I was all too aware of my naked body hiding apprehensively beneath the thin material.

I wasn't surprised when she settled beside me: her knees turned towards me; her back straight, projecting her breasts forward; her arm resting on the back of the settee, close to my left shoulder. Her body language was deafening me.

I tried to concentrate on looking cool but, inside, my adrenal glands were working overtime, priming my body for a fast escape – or something else. Right now, I didn't know whether to be scared, flattered or excited.

"So Cameron, Marriette tells me that you are in Amsterdam to try and find out how your sister became addicted to drugs?" She touched my arm with her hand and kept it there, her fingers playing with my sleeve. "I am so sorry she died in such distressing circumstances." She was soft, sympathetic. "It must have been very hard for you, my dear. What was she like?"

I shifted on the settee, turning to face her and moving a little further away as I did. "She was very special, my only living relative, apart from a few distant uncles and aunts." I wasn't going to mention my mother. "We were close. Her death was – still is – a blow."

She took hold of my hand. "It is terrible, liebchen. To lose a sister like that is hard. I too lost a close friend some years ago."

"Really?"

"Yes," she sighed, "he was like a brother to me. A friend, that's all, but a close friend." She fell silent, gazing into the distance. The cognac was excellent. I felt calmer; maybe I was warming to her.

"What happened to him?"

"Ach, it was a long time ago, liebchen, and very complicated. Let's leave it at that."

We sat quietly for a moment. Helga spoke first: "Did Carrie ever take drugs before?"

"No, never. I'm sure that she would never have willingly taken them. That's why I'm so puzzled."

"So, that's why you want to trace her friend Pat."

I nodded. "Yes, though I don't know if she was a friend. I just hope she can tell me what Carrie was doing during those last two weeks."

"Marriette tells me that your sister was a reporter; you believe her death may have had something to do with her job?"

"Well she was a journalist rather than a reporter ... Oh, I don't know, but that's why it is so important to find Pat." I found myself touching her arm. I'm not sure whether it was out of gratitude or desire. "Thank you for your help – it means a lot to me."

She smiled reassuringly, taking my hand in both of hers. "Yes, of course; anything I can do to help. I make a lot of contacts in my line of business; I do people favours. Sometimes it is good to ask a favour in return."

Even if that favour meant obtaining confidential, private information by illegal means? Unlike the rest of me, my Common Sense had not been seduced by the alcohol, but it was rather distant, relegated to the edge of my consciousness, quietly worrying over what sort of businesswoman had access to such privileged detail; and why anyone would be prepared to risk their job and several years in jail for a simple favour.

"What is your line of business?"

She made a dismissive sort of noise and waved her hand, modestly, but rather obviously, playing down her position. "We do a lot of things, my dear; I am a director of a large international corporation with interests all over Europe. We do a lot of import and export – it's all deals and more deals. It is very boring, let's talk about you."

I was happy to talk; it seemed a better option than not talking, just at that moment. She filled my glass with more cognac and I began the story of my sister's death and my belief that she had been forcibly injected with the drugs and then dumped in the canal. I can't really believe that I said so much. It must have been the relaxing surroundings, her Teutonic charm, the cognac; maybe all three. In truth, I told her too much: about Hans at the drug agency; about my conversation with Bella and Karl by the methadone bus. She sympathised and it made me feel good. When she moved in closer, I let her, glad of the warmth of another woman. It must be so hard losing a sister, she said; she was going to be around for a few days – perhaps she could help in some other ways too. Right then, at that moment, it felt nice. I suppose that Helga made me feel less alone, safer somehow.

By then it was quite late. The cognac bottle was nearly empty and my head was nearly full. I felt mellow and relaxed. Perhaps I was wrong about Helga. I looked at her. I couldn't imagine her being lesbian; perhaps she was bi, or maybe just away on business and curious. She was certainly giving all sorts of signals, but I couldn't work her out. I must have looked for too long and given a signal that I hadn't consciously intended, because then she moved closer, took my head in her carefully manicured hands and kissed me full on the lips, her wide red mouth first covering mine then moving around, kissing my bottom lip, then my upper lip.

I responded in spite of myself. It had been a long time and I needed some love, some release.

She slipped her hands inside the robe and, parting it, slid the material away from my shoulders, revealing my breasts and my hard, welcoming nipples. She kissed me, taking each one in turn between her lips whilst I struggled inside myself: my Need fighting against My Better Judgement; my Better Judgement losing heavily. I could feel her hand stroking my thigh, moving gently, just above the surface of my skin, sending streams of pleasure pulsing through my body, making me wet, making me want more.

I unbuttoned her blouse and slid my hand inside, caressing her breasts, kissing her neck, inhaling her perfume … Chanel … Number … 5 …

Carrie's favourite.

My breathing stopped. The warmth of her body, a turn-on just a second earlier, no longer seemed so erotic; the touch of her hands, so enticing moments before, turned to irritation. Suddenly her mouth was roaming in private territory. Right now, I didn't want to be here on this settee with my hand in this stranger's blouse and her fingers between my thighs.

Helga must have felt my body stiffen.

"What is it, liebchen?"

I pulled back. "Not tonight," I said, shaking my head, the perfume lingering between us: Carrie's memory held firmly in my consciousness. "Not now, not here."

"Oh liebchen, and you were so enjoying my touch." She was disappointed. "What is it, darling?"

"I'm sorry, Helga, you are very nice, but this isn't the time or the place."

I let her stroke me for a while and then she disconsolately lifted up my robe and draped it back around my shoulders. "I'll go and make us a nice mug of hot chocolate, darling, and then we can go to bed." I had to get out of this without upsetting her too much, I still needed those addresses. "Helga –" I said it gently, as if I meant it – hell, maybe I did mean it "– I'm sorry, but I'm really tired, you know … and … well …" My brain was racing, trying to come up with the very best of all excuses. I tried to look embarrassed, which was easy because I was: embarrassed at the way I had let go so fucking easily. "Well … I'm menstruating and, well … it's rather heavy … so I would rather not, not tonight anyway."

My instincts had been right, Helga was a woman who didn't like messy bodily functions and, to my relief, she capitulated at once. I relaxed a little – this excuse could be stretched for at least two more days and by then she would have left.

"All right, darling, I'll see you tomorrow, perhaps?" I nodded, which was the easiest way out just now – I desperately needed to sleep. And, quite suddenly, I needed to cry.

She was going to kiss me again but I got up and made it across the room before she could. I stopped by the door. "When do you think you will have the addresses, Helga?"

"Didn't Marriette tell you?" I shook my head, confused. "My contact works nightshift," she said in a reassuring voice, "and they will be on Marriette's fax by the morning, I promise you."

"Thanks, Helga, you are very kind."

She came across and kissed me again. This time I was too tired to object.

But I wasn't too tired to realise that Helga now knew a lot about me – and that I knew virtually nothing about her.

Six

It may have been my relief at escaping Helga's clutches or the effects of the cognac, but I I slept like a baby that night and only woke when Marriette came into my room with a morning cup of tea, waving a piece of paper above my head.

"Hello sweetheart, I've got some good news for you ... My! You're still asleep and it's almost nine o'clock!"

I grunted something unintelligible and struggled to focus my eyes. She drew back the curtains, letting in the grey dullness of another autumn day, then turned up the halogen uplighter so that something resembling daylight finally flooded the room. I sat up to sip the sweet, hot tea, blinking in the strong light, rubbing my forehead to ease the cognac-induced headache that was muddying my thinking. I scowled at Marriette and she turned the light lower.

The tea had the desired effect and I was soon studying the details of the five phone numbers printed on the fax. Opposite each number was a potted history, giving the address, the name of the subscriber, the date connected, the date disconnected and the reason for termination. Of the five numbers, four had been cut off long before Carrie arrived in Amsterdam, but the fifth was only disconnected on 3rd September, due to non-payment. The subscriber was a P Breckelman; better still was the subscriber's address – De Nieuwe Molen in Westpoort. One of the city's most famous squats.

I looked up, hardly believing our good fortune, and met Marriette's beaming face.

"Goed, ja?"

"Zeer goed, Marriette!" I put my arms round her neck and gave her a great big kiss. "Dank u wel! You're a wonder!"

She shrugged her shoulders and made a face in an exaggerated display of mock modesty, but I could tell she was pleased. I re-read the list, feeling delighted.

When I looked up again, Marriette was more serious. "There is just one thing, sweetheart. I seem to remember that the squat was evicted last summer – there was a lot in the press about a stand-up fight between the police and the squatters, and I'm fairly certain it was at the Molen ... so, be prepared, it will probably be empty."

My heart sank a little, but I wasn't going to let Marriette put me off just because of her own worries. Empty or not, I finally had a link with Carrie's last few weeks and it felt like a real step forward.

"Keep smiling, Etts," I sang as I swung my legs out of the bed, "this is good news – and there may be more information in the Molen building, even if the birds have flown. I'll go and have a look right after breakfast."

Marriette smiled as she left, but it seemed a little forced.

I was concentrating on peeling my hard-boiled egg when I heard Marriette talking to Helga on the landing.

"You were up very early this morning, Helga!"

"Ja, it is very difficult sleeping in a strange bed so, rather than just lay there, I decided to go for a walk."

"In the dark?" Etts sounded incredulous.

Helga replied in a matter-of-fact tone, "Nein, it is not so strange, the street lights were on!"

At this point they both came into the room and Helga greeted me with a smile. "So, I hear that you have the information you needed." I nodded, thanking her for all her help, explaining my intention to visit the site of the squat this morning.

Helga frowned and shook her head. "Keep away from the Molen, my dear. My friends in Amsterdam tell me it is a dangerous place. The building is not safe, the squat has been evicted and there are bad characters around there now."

I pulled a face, indicating that it made no difference.

Helga turned to Etts, her voice taking on a harder pitch. "This is not sensible, Marriette. I obtained this information to put your mind at rest." She looked at me again. "If you go into that building, Cameron, you will be putting yourself in great danger. That is not why I helped you. You must hand over the information to the police now, as Marriette said you would."

I looked up at Etts, surprised.

Marriette nodded. "She is right, Cameron, please be sensible." My hangover had gone but the warning bells in my head were giving me a headache all over again.

"I can't go to the police, and you both know it." I felt angry at the way the two of them were attempting to manipulate me. "They will want to know where I got the address from before they do anything." I looked first at Etts, then at Helga. "And I can't tell them, because the details were obtained illegally."

I carried on eating, making it clear that the subject was closed.

"Well, you must do what you think is best –" Helga's voice was cold "– but I do not think you will be welcome there." She made her way to the door, turning back just before she left the room. "I think you are very unwise to interfere in such matters."

Marriette put her hand on my arm, pleading, "Don't go, Cameron. It is too dangerous."

I was exasperated. "You know I have to go. This is personal. I have to know what happened to her."

She looked at me with her big, pale green eyes. "Well, if you must, please let me come with you; it sounds dangerous."

I shook my head. I definitely didn't want Etts with me. "No, sorry, this is something I have to do on my own."

She turned away and busied herself clearing the table, but I could tell she was distraught.

I looked at the fax again. I still couldn't work out why Helga was so keen to help last night and so anxious to deter me this morning. I had told her a lot – far too much – last night, but I couldn't fathom why someone like her should be so interested in the first place. For that matter, why was such a high-powered businesswoman staying in a small guest house? And the contact at the telephone company ... why would anyone risk being sacked and possibly imprisoned, just to do a favour for a friend? Maybe it was all about sex: maybe she was trying to impress me last night. Maybe this morning she felt rejected. Anyway, I had the information. That was what mattered.

Marriette was concentrating a little too diligently on her jobs, so I got up and went over to her, taking hold of her shoulders and turning her round to face me.

"Marriette, I know you're worried, but I really have to do this. I will be careful, I promise, but I am a strong woman, I can handle myself. You musn't worry."

A tear rolled down her cheek, but she tried to smile. "I am sorry that I am being so silly. But when Carrie died, I felt so bad, so guilty ... if anything happened to you ..."

I hugged her tightly. "Nothing is going to happen to me, Etts. Helga is just being over-dramatic. All I am going to do is visit an old building. If it is empty, I'll have a look round; if it isn't, then I'll try and talk to whoever is there. That's all."

She began to look a little calmer. "You will take great care won't you?"

"Of course. Look, I've still got your mobile phone. I'll only be a couple of hours anyway but, if I have the slightest problem, I'll give you a ring. I promise."

I smiled reassuringly at her and she relaxed.

"Thank you, lieveling. That makes me feel better." Then more firmly, "But if you are away too long, I will call the police."

I smiled at her persistence and took the small phone out of my jeans pocket to show I had it with me. She didn't look totally convinced, but I gave her a peck on the cheek and headed for my room before she could start arguing. I slipped on my leather jacket, grabbed my helmet and gloves and was on my way out, shouting as I left: "Bye, Etts – and don't worry – I'll be back very soon."

Outside, the Sunday morning roads were quiet. Even the weather was in limbo: no breeze, no rain, no sun, just a dull greyness that seeped everywhere. I turned on my bike's electronic ignition and started the engine, working the throttle to burn off the damp. Sitting astride the deep leather saddle, I thought about what might lie ahead that morning. I was excited at the prospect of discovering more about Carrie's last few weeks, of doing something, at last. I felt good, in control again.

I never gave another thought to Helga's warning.

Since it was so quiet, I decided to take a shortcut through the city centre, driving by a subdued Dam Square – almost emptied of its sightseers, buskers and pickpockets – then along Damrak, past the tourist restaurants and gift shops, finally skirting round the side of Centraal Station and on to the road that leads to the Western Docks.

A cold northerly wind met me as I rounded the station and emerged by the edge of Het Ij – Amsterdam's inland sea. It swept off the vast stretch of water to my right, peppering me with sharp, bitterly cold drops of rain, stinging my ankles and making the legs of my jeans flap wildly.

I was still almost a mile away when I saw what I took to be De Nieuwe Molen ahead. Even allowing for the less than imaginative architecture of a docklands area, it was a severely dull and unattractive building. Perched on a narrow promontory of land, the rectangular, windowless structure was over two hundred feet high and maybe a hundred feet wide; a dirty grey eyesore jutting out into the sea on a concrete platform.

As the Molen came closer, I passed derelict railway lines crisscrossing the scrubby land to my left and working barges moored in tandem by the quaysides on my right. When the road swung slightly to the left, I pulled off to the right, just in front of a pair of heavy black iron gates. A crude hand-painted sign announced in bright red that I was now entering 'De Vrije Molen Squat'. I stopped and looked around me. The place didn't look dangerous, but it did look creepy. High up on the dirty grey structure, facing the road, a huge home-made banner was slung across the building, flapping in the wind and declaring in bold red lettering: 'B S FREE S U CAN.'

Clever. Said in English with a Dutch accent it made a perfect sentence – and an admirable sentiment in whatever language.

But this ugly concrete structure was not the 'New Mill' after all. It was built from pre-cast concrete, probably around the war and, though less than sixty years old, it really did look derelict and dangerous. It was the older, brick building immediately next to it, erected in the 1800s, that I guessed was the actual 'New Mill', no doubt replacing some smaller structure during the Industrial Revolution.

This four-storey brick building was quite attractive in its own dark Gothic way and, though much older than its close neighbour, it still looked solid and safe. It was much longer than the concrete structure next to it but nothing like as high; though scarred and damaged from over 100 years of industrial use, it still looked proud and functional.

There was no sign of any life. After I turned off the ignition, all I could hear was the constant lapping of the sea and the sound of the wind buffeting against the buildings. I put the bike on its stand, fastening my helmet to the handlebars, and walked along the side of the building.

The Molen stood alongside its concrete neighbour. There was a gap, about six feet wide, between the two buildings, through which I could see a small platform, a quay perhaps, at the back of the buildings above the sea. A rusty railway track ran along their front, leading on to a low narrow embankment which jutted out for over a hundred yards like an ugly finger into the sea. On the landward side of the embankment was a small dock, now empty and mostly silted up. The older building had around a hundred windows on this side, most of them dirty and broken. An old loading bay stood on a raised platform at the road end, its wooden canopy disintegrating and its faded blue paint peeling away. Rusty oil drums and rotting pallets were still stacked untidily alongside. More recent litter – plastic bottles, torn polythene sheeting and empty soft drink cans – blew around in the windy turbulence created by the high buildings.

I made for the double doors in the middle, walking between the rusty railway lines, stepping over the loose bricks and pieces of iron-work that littered my path. A rat scuttled across the lines further up, making for the shelter of some old canvas sheeting. The big windows on the ground-floor level were all boarded up, but the door itself appeared untouched.

I knocked hard and waited. Nothing.

I knocked again. Silence.

I turned the brown Bakelite handle on the right-hand door and to my surprise it swung open, revealing a large open space behind, with yellowing, whitewashed walls, lined with rusty old industrial shelv-ing. The inside was gloomy, the only light leaking into the building through gaps in the boarded-up windows. To both my left and right, a long corridor ran along the entire outside wall, fading away to noth-ing in the darkness at each of its two ends. Every few yards, a door indicated the existence of another room constructed from makeshift panelling in what would once have been a huge open storage area.

It was quiet and it looked empty so I decided to search the place and see if there were any traces of Carrie, or of Pat for that matter. I switched on my torch and tried the first door on the left-hand corri-dor. It opened easily and I went in, catching my breath as the damp-ness of the room hit my nostrils. I shone the torch around. It was very untidy but looked as if it had been occupied recently.

Pop art posters covered the walls in a pastiche of the hippie 70s; papers were piled haphazardly on a makeshift table which had been painted in a bright yellow. Clothes were carelessly slung across the back of an old brown winged armchair in one corner of the room and, in the other, a single metal-framed bed, with an orange sleeping bag spread out on its mattress, was pushed against the wall. Next to the bed was an up-ended wooden box with a table lamp made out of an old wine bottle.

I was about to try the next room, when I heard the outside door slam shut and smelt the damp heat of another body right behind me. I turned, my nerve ends tingling. But, before I could react, his big hands were on me – one over my mouth, the other clasped around my body and arms, pinning me to him. I could feel his hard muscular body through my clothes. I could smell the tobacco on his breath. He bundled me, struggling and kicking, into the darkness of the room. I desperately tried to release an arm so that I could defend myself, and my torch fell out of my hand. His grip was so strong, his arms so much bigger than mine. I couldn't break free; I could hardly breathe.

He set me down on the bed and held me in a vice-like grip with my hands pushed behind my back. Another, smaller silhouette came through the door and, without speaking, tied my hands securely together. Even in all the turmoil, I thought to myself that nobody carries a rope around on the off-chance. I had been ambushed.

When I was released from his grip, I tried to jump off the bed, but they had secured my wrists to the metal bedhead and I couldn't move. I was trapped. Totally vulnerable. I cursed my stupidity, my arrogant belief in my own invincibility.

The door snapped shut and blackness enveloped the room.

I couldn't hear or see them, but I knew that they were still in there – just a few feet from me. I tensed my legs, ready to kick the guy in the balls if he attempted to lay another finger on me. But, instead, there was a click and a searingly bright light shone directly in my face. I lowered my head to protect my eyes from the glare and squinted into the brightness, trying to make out my attackers. But all I could see were blotches of temporary blindness, swimming about in front of me like giant red and yellow amoebae.

"Let me go!" I screamed, frightened and angry at the same time.

"Shut your mouth, lady. No one is going to hear your shouting here." His deep, rich voice was level but resonating with anger. "Very clever, sending an English woman; but you don't fool us, lady, we know where you are from and what you are you trying to do."

"Oh yeah? Well you have one up on me, mister – I haven't a clue who you are – or why you are being so unfriendly. Anyway, I'm British, not English." Incredibly, the detail seemed important at the time.

There was silence. Then a woman's voice, bleak, scornful, and loaded with a heavy Dutch accent, said, "Do you think we are stupid? We know why you are here. If you were hoping to ruin things for us, then you are going to be sadly disappointed. We have friends out there who keep us informed."

A chill ran down my back. Helga had been right, I should have listened to her. I had bitten off more than I could chew.

"Look, whatever you think, I'm not here to cause trouble –"

"Shut the fuck up, lady. We just aren't interested."

The light was suddenly eclipsed by the outline of the man as he walked towards me. I tensed again and angled my body, ready to kick out, but he grabbed me from the side and held my flailing legs whilst the woman frisked me, removing Marriette's mobile phone and my keys.

Then he was forcing my mouth open and she was pouring a vile-tasting liquid into it. I struggled and tried to spit it out, but he clamped my mouth shut, just like I did with Tibby's tablets, and made me swallow.

When they stepped back, the lamp was extinguished and all I could see were the red and yellow blobs. A rectangle of grey light opened in the wall behind the giant amoebae as they left the room. The woman first, then the man.

He stopped and turned round to look at me, his silhouette filling the doorway. "Don't worry, lady, it's just a sleeping draught. Just to make sure you stay quiet whilst we decide what to do about you.

"Sweet dreams!" he mocked, then he closed and locked the door.

Seven

I came round in the blackness feeling muzzy, sick and totally disoriented. It took me some time to remember even where I was, let alone how I got there – a strange and frightening sensation when you are tied up. I realised I must have been out for some time because my bladder was reaching bursting point. On top of that, I felt stiff all over and my shoulder was aching again. I twisted and pulled at the thin rope round my wrists in an attempt to loosen it. It made me sore as hell but, slowly, I could feel more and more give, until I had enough extra hand movement to get my fingers around the knot that tied me to the bed.

But it was tight and it would take more time to loosen it. I played mind games to distract me from the pain.

I thought about Carrie. She used to tell me about her investigations. Mostly they weren't dangerous because the people involved were too frightened to show their hand. Instead they relied on the coercion and blackmail of colleagues and contacts. Everybody had a price, everybody had something to hide. Most bullies could find a way of keeping the lid on their activities – freezing out any investigator.

But Carrie knew how to counter the pressure from the top. She covered her trail so carefully that nobody had ever discovered her contacts. She knew that whistle blowers would always be targets, even if – especially if – they had right on their side. So she collected only hard evidence – photos, documents, recordings – and was careful to erase any connections with her source. She was even jailed for contempt after refusing to reveal a source. She had a reputation for being very thorough. I had been so proud of her.

My nails hurt and my finger ends were raw, but I could feel the knot slowly loosening.

I gritted my teeth and thought again about Carrie and about

Marriette's concern over the scrapbook. Etts had been right to worry after all. This was like déjà vu.

It was just over eleven years since my sister had been kidnapped and left to die. She had uncovered a massive fraud racket involving the illegal switching of food aid consignments during the Ethiopian famines of the mid-80s. Whilst western consciences were being pricked by Bob Geldof and others, a small time Belgian crook, Peter Karst, posing as an aid worker, was quietly creaming off some of the grain shipments and reselling the food on the black market.

When Carrie exposed the racket, she was abducted by Karst and left to die in a filthy cellar, without food or water, whilst he fled back to Europe. The little boy who heard her cries became a local hero; but the experience shook Carrie's confidence and it was months before she began to recover from the mental effects of her ordeal ...

The rope that held me to the bedhead came loose at last. My hands were still securely tied behind me, but now I was able to lean forward and relieve the stiffness in my back.

I enjoyed the feeling of partial relief for a few seconds and then swung my legs on to the floor and felt around for the wine-bottle lamp. When I finally located it, I managed to twist my body and angle my hands around its base, locating the electric cord and then the switch. Awkwardly, I pulled out the light fitting and the cord, and then smashed the bottom of the bottle against the metal bed frame. It was hard to put enough force into it and, at first, the bottle was too tough to break. I made six attempts before the glass finally shattered, leaving a bottle neck and three inches of jagged glass in my hand.

I listened for a few moments, fearful that the noise would have alerted my captors. But all was quiet.

Sitting on the edge of the bed again, I manipulated what was left of the bottle. It was tricky, angling the broken neck against the rope, but eventually I managed to squeeze a piece of the glass between my wrists, gingerly moving the bottle and severing the strands, one by one. I could feel the broken bottle grazing against the surface of my skin as I worked; feel the warm stickiness of my blood as it trickled down on to my hands. I held my breath and prayed that I could avoid cutting a vein: in here I would bleed quietly to death without anyone knowing.

Bit by bit, I could feel the rope fraying and my hands becoming freer.

By now, the muscles in my wrists and hands were screaming with pain as I twisted them, at unnatural angles, backwards and forwards, cutting at the rope. I couldn't tell how badly cut my wrists were, but I knew for certain that the pain in my bladder was getting to crisis point. So I leant forward, contracting my stomach muscles, to try and ease my desperate need to let it all out. I must have been in the room for a long time, without light or food or drink, and I felt anxious, groggy and thirsty.

I couldn't have kept it up for much longer but, thankfully, the rope finally gave way and I was able to pull my hands free of the remaining strands.

I was about to drop my jeans and achieve a state of bladder-emptying bliss when I heard voices. A woman with a familiar voice was shouting angrily in Dutch, and I could hear the man who had attacked me talking back defensively to her. The voices got louder, then there was silence when they reached my door. I heard a key in the lock and picked up the broken bottle again, feeling my way across the room and positioning myself behind the door, ready to catch him off balance when he came in.

The handle rattled and, as the door swung open, I tensed myself, raising the weapon high above my head; feeling the buzz of adrenaline as I focused all my energy, clasping the neck firmly, ready to swing it hard at the head of the man who was about to come through the door ...

At the very last moment – a nanosecond before I reached the point of no return – the figure behind the door spoke.

"Cameron, are you all right? It's me, Hellen."

***

Life has a series of priorities and, after the relief of being freed, I had the equally pleasurable relief of finally emptying my bladder.

I sat for a while on the toilet, trying to compose myself and regain my equilibrium. I had lost all sense of time or day but Hellen had told me that it was nearly 5pm – I had been tied up for nearly six hours. I was confused and disoriented. I still didn't know who had attacked me or why. I recognised my rescuer as the policewoman I kept bumping into, Hellen van Zalinge, but what she was doing here – apparently off duty in casual clothes – was still a mystery. Marriette was here too, for some reason, in a state and fussing around me. I'd had to insist on being left alone in the toilet – it was like being a child again.

My hands trembled as I bathed my wrists in the chipped wash-basin, sponging off the blood with wet toilet paper. Luckily, the grazing was only superficial. I splashed water on my face in an attempt to clear the ache in my head, then dried it with more toilet paper in preference to the grubby hand towel on the side. I felt stiff and sickly.

I was angry, scared and disoriented as I made my way back to the big room next door.

It seemed to be a café of some kind: decorated in a Gothic-meets-Oxfam-meets-Medieval-Castle post-hippie style. There was a bar in one corner and a primitive heating stove in another. Around twenty tables of all shapes, sizes, condition and colours, each with an equally varied selection of chairs, littered the floor. Above me, a huge propeller-like fan blade revolved slowly, creating a strong down-draught as it pushed the warm air back from the high ceiling. The windows on my right, which extended almost to the roof, looked out over the sea. One had doors which opened on to a balcony. It was nearly dark outside, but I could see the lights of cars and buildings on the far shore.

There were four of them in there, sitting at a table. Marriette was white with relief and very subdued. Sitting next to her, Hellen looked tense and was conducting a heated conversation with the man and woman opposite her. I didn't recognise either of them. I wasn't even too sure where I was.

The man stood up as I entered the room. He was good looking, in his mid-thirties, about six-foot tall; a well-built black guy with dark skin, a thick-set face and a wide jawline. I took in his clean white T-shirt and blue denims as he approached, deeply embarrassed, hands outstretched.

"I'm sorry, lady …"

I recognised the voice of my attacker.

Part of me panicked. And I would have run, if another part of me hadn't been so angry. As it was, I just stood there, confused, until Hellen came across and helped me to the table.

"Everything is all right, Cameron," she soothed as she took my arm, "but these two have got some explaining to do."

Hellen sat me down between her and Marriette, who took hold of my arm and held it tightly. The man sat down opposite, wincing. "Look lady, I'm really sorry – it was a case of mistaken identity, that's all."

I looked at him through narrowed eyes and then at the woman next to him. The room fell silent; the only sound, the swish of the big fan and the occasional crackle from the stove. When I did speak, I was trying hard to keep my anger in check.

"'Mistaken identity?' Just what the fuck do you mean, 'mistaken identity'?" I blurted out. "You've assaulted me, you've tied me up, you've drugged me and imprisoned me for six hours; you think that's acceptable – even if you get the identity right?"

He shuffled his feet awkwardly. "Hey, lady, just calm down. I'm trying to explain."

I glowered at him as I held my right wrist which was still really sore. "Will you please stop calling me lady? I'm no lady – to you or anyone else. My name is Cameron."

Hellen looked at me, then at the two of them. I really hoped she hadn't said anything about being a cop. "Go on then; tell her what you just told us."

It was the man who spoke again, a pissed-off expression on his face. "Lady ... huh, sorry, what's your name? ... huh, Cameron ... All I can tell you is that we've been set up by someone – I don't know who – but, whoever it is, they're giving me big problems." He took a swig of his beer and sniffed. "Look, I don't know why you came here. All I know is that we made some kind of mistake. Your friends have made that much clear 'specially –" he waved a hand dismissively at Hellen "– her." He sounded genuinely hurt.

Hellen glared at him. "Under the circumstances, I think we all have every justification for being upset, don't you, Meneer Breckelman? Your conduct has been –"

"Wait a minute." I interrupted Hellen and looked directly at the man, feeling suddenly better. "You mean to say that you ... you are Pat Breckelman?"

"Sure, what's the big deal?"

I must have looked totally perplexed. "But you're a man!"

He closed his eyes completely for a few moments. "Jesus, this is hard work."

Hellen looked at me, curiosity written all over her. Marriette just looked relieved, so I used the moment to release my arm from her grip.

"Look, Cameron," he said patiently, "I'll do a deal with you. I'll tell you why I tied you up, then you can tell me what you were doing here in the first place. OK?"

I nodded. I was still on guard. Carrie must have been at this squat around the time of her death and, so far, I had no guarantee that the man and woman sitting opposite me were not implicated.

"OK. From the beginning. This is a normal, peaceful squat – or it was until about 6 a.m. this morning, wasn't it Emma?" The woman nodded and touched his arm in a show of affection. Pat Breckelman lifted up his T-shirt to reveal a chest wrapped in bandages. "There were three of them; big guys with a real attitude problem and they all had guns." He stared at me to underline his next point. "This was serious shit, Cameron – they broke in and dragged me from my bed to inter-rogate me. Asking all sorts of questions. What I was doing in August, who I was doing it with, why I was doing it. I told them what I could – shit, there were no secrets, man, we were just fighting the owners, trying not to get evicted."

As he talked, I watched Emma. She looked just as cold and hard as she had sounded in that darkened room. But I could see the way she was giving all her attention to Pat and I wondered what else was going on in her head.

"Christ, man! Fuck knows why they picked on me. I thought at first that they were the owner's thugs, but why would they just pick me out from everyone else?"

Emma touched his arm. "Maybe they see you as our leader."

Pat, somewhat startled, protested: "But we don't have a leader here, you know that, Emma."

"Maybe not," she said, looking at him with admiration, "but if we had, it would be you."

Pat looked embarrassed. "Yeah, maybe, but they still-didn't seem like the property developer's men."

"Why?" I asked.

Pat rubbed his face. "Not sure, different sort of style, I guess. I didn't like them, but these guys had class: they seemed like big-time hoods, rather than a property developer's thugs. Anyway, they took me outside, between the two buildings, and worked me over. Then they stuck me in their car, on the floor at the back, and started to ask me questions. After I told them all I could, they told me to beat it, to leave the city, otherwise I would get hurt even more."

He looked confused. "Why me? Just who the hell feels that bad about me?" He shifted his beer bottle, rattled. "Well, whoever they are, the bastards aren't going to get rid of me that easily. Nobody's running me out of town."

Hellen might be off duty, but she responded like a true investigating officer. Her formal questions made her seem the paragon of correctness and it was hard to believe she had been so rude to me last night.

"Have you seen any of the men before?" she asked Pat. "Can you describe them? Were they Dutch?" She fired the questions one after another and I could see her filing away the answers in her head in case she had to write a report. But she slowly built up a picture of the three thugs, two white, one mixed-race. Only one had spoken and he sounded Dutch but Pat gave a detailed description of them all. He had never seen any of them before, but they knew who he was. Hellen was particularly interested in their guns.

"Do you know what they carried?"

"Shit no, I don't know anything about guns; what's that to you anyway?"

Hellen, just back off, will you? If they realise you're a cop, you'll be out on your arse.

"Well, were they all carrying the same type of gun?"

"Man," Pat was exasperated, "they were beating the shit out of me at the time. You think I'm going to stop them and say 'oh, excuse me, would you mind if I examined your pieces?' Jesus, woman, give me a break!" Then he thought a little. "Yeah," he mused, "maybe they were all the same. Smallish, black."

He sniffed and leant back in his chair, running his hands through his short, curly black hair, rubbing the side of his dark face. Something in my head had been fighting its way out for the last ten minutes, but I still couldn't get a handle on it. In any event, I didn't know if I believed him. Pat was a big man himself, it was hard to imagine him as a victim. For all I knew, the bandages could be just for our benefit. I interrupted to get Hellen off his back.

"So, what has all this to do with the way you treated me?" I asked. He half-smiled now, more relaxed with me but plainly embarrassed again. "This has been some morning! After the thugs left, I had a phone call from a woman, an American who described herself as one of our political supporters. She said that she had information. She said the owners were going to infiltrate our squat with a spy, who was going to start a fire in the building. We know that those crooks will go to any lengths to get us out, so, of course, we believed her."

"So someone, anyone, rings up out of the blue and you assault the first person who comes along!" I was still belligerent.

He shook his head. "No, it's not like that at all, lady ... sorry, Cameron. For a start, the squats are a big political movement. We get all sorts of help from each other – and from people who support us. So the phone call wasn't unusual. The real reason that we were worried about you was that you fitted, exactly, the description she gave us." He raised his eyebrows. "Can you really blame us for being careful?"

I felt my stomach heave. Either Pat was lying or someone I knew had deliberately set me up. "Pat, what time did you get the telephone call?"

He pulled a face. "Ohh, I don't know. I should say it was about an hour before you arrived ... round about 9.30."

"And how would they know your number?"

"Like I say, we have a network, lots of people in the movement know it."

And one or two others at the telephone company, too.

I glanced across at Marriette. She looked impassive, as if she hadn't heard. But it struck me instantly that only two people knew that I was on my way to the squat – the phone call had to come from one of them.

"You have to understand our situation." It was Emma speaking now. She was a small, serious-looking woman with tight, curly brown hair; no more than five-foot tall and stocky with it. I guessed that she was around forty-five and had been on Amsterdam's political scene a long time. She had that tired, worn-out look of someone who has fought a lot and never been pleased with the results.

"You have to understand our situation." She put her head on one side, adopting an intense, studied expression. "This is a re-squat. The original squat was here for over seven years with as many as a hundred of us living and working here at any one time. We were mostly artists, writers, actors and artisans – famous for our sculptures, paintings, crafts and drama. We had an alternative theatre. We also had a successful café that operated five nights a week in this room. All this brought in much-needed income to make the place habitable and to enable us to continue our fight against a corrupt council and its establishment friends."

Pat coughed and wiped his nose for the third time in as many minutes. Now I knew what I had been trying to figure out earlier, and it did nothing to increase my trust in this man.

"I want you to understand. This was not just a place to live and work, it represented far more than that. The Molen was a national symbol of revolt against Amsterdam's betrayal of the homeless. Our fight was, and is, against the council's complicity in the development of luxury housing for the privileged."

She talked angrily and with a lot of bitterness. Principles I like, but hard-line cant is hard to take. And I definitely didn't take to Emma. I looked across the table at the others. Marriette was looking bemused; Hellen, unimpressed; Pat was bored.

Emma must have sensed the mood because she let him carry on with the story. Pat leant forward and I thought I saw a smile play across his lips. "Emma was one of the original squatters," he said, as if to excuse her. "I joined about two years ago, just as things started to get rough. The first five years here were peaceful enough. The occupation was more about making a statement than creating a revolution. The property had been empty for a long time before occupation so, under Dutch law, we were entitled to squat. Then about eighteen months ago a new owner bought the buildings and that's when the trouble started. He wanted us out, preferably without going through the legal procedures. So for months we had to endure the bully boys who tried to scare us with their threats."

Emma couldn't contain herself for long, "Yeah, we fought well. There was more of us than them and we stuck together. One night we were waiting for them and, when they tried to frighten us, fifty of us scared the shit out of them instead. You name it, we used it – stones, eggs, water hoses, paint bombs, lead shot and catapults, baseball bats. We sent them running that time and they didn't come back."

I was impressed, despite my antipathy towards her. I don't like bureaucracy and big business either. Hellen was listening intently too but, I assumed, disapprovingly. I was having to remind myself that, regardless of her presence here, she was not a friend, she was a cop.

Marriette just looked uncomfortable – confrontation was something she avoided at all costs.

"So you won," I said. But Emma looked dejected, bitter.

Pat shrugged. "We won a battle but lost the war. They went to the courts, claiming that the site was to be redeveloped, and an eviction order was granted to take effect in August –"

I interrupted: "And that was around when Carrie joined you."

There was a stunned silence.

Emma spoke first. "You knew Carrie?"

"My sister," I said quietly, looking straight at Pat Breckelman. "And your lover, I presume?"

I watched Pat. His eyes closed momentarily.

"That's why I'm here. That's why I came to the squat today," I explained.

"How is she?"

I looked at him, surprised. "You mean, you don't know?"

"Know what?" His look of puzzlement was quickly replaced by one of concern.

"Pat," I said, in the kindest way I knew how, "Carrie is dead."

Eight

It was nearly 10 p.m. and every table was full. The Molen Café had been well known for years and most of the customers were regulars from the days of the old squat. Now, as it only opened twice each week – Sunday and Wednesday – it was usually full.

I was sitting with Hellen at a small table near one of the heavily curtained windows. We were set in a sea of colourful people – about sixty of them – men, women, young and old, sharing tables with complete strangers, chatting (mostly in English), moving around the room and joining other friends, shouting across tables at each other. A glorious, disorderly, hurly-burly mixture of people, dressed in all their different ways. Some had that neat casualness that suggested a life of conformity (and that this was their night off), but most were waving two fingers at straight society with their various hairstyles, piercings and tattoos – a wonderful 'fuck you!' fashion show.

Pat had been kind of quiet all evening. He seemed shocked over Carrie's death and the circumstances surrounding it. But he hadn't said much about her investigation, so I guessed that he either didn't know, or wouldn't say. I wasn't sure which.

Marriette had gone; she had guests to attend to. The whole episode had been a big ordeal for her and confirmed her fears about my safety. I was going to have to be careful with her over the next few days. I hoped she wasn't going to be difficult.

Hellen and I stayed for the meal – a delicious beet soup followed by vegan-friendly potato pie, salad, nuts, dates and cous-cous, washed down with several bottles of Kik beer. Not surprisingly, we were uneasy with each other. Pat had left us after he learnt about Carrie and this had given us a chance to talk. I wasn't sure whether this was a good idea, but, at least, I was able to ask her how she came to be at the squat in the first place.

She shifted in her chair; clearly though, her discomfort had nothing to do with the furniture. "God, this is embarrassing." She mumbled and then sighed deeply before she could bring herself to speak again. Even then she couldn't meet my eyes. "I got Marriette's number from the Juno Bar, from Agnes. I suppose I wanted to speak to you because ... well ..." She hesitated, colouring up. "I suppose I felt bad about my behaviour last night ... Anyway, Marriette answered and when I said who I was, she started to tell me how worried she was about you." She looked up at me now. "Did you tell her about that incident on the stairs?"

I nodded guiltily.

"Huh, thanks! Anyway, she kept on about you being in danger. I thought she was exaggerating – to be honest, I thought she was being hysterical and I didn't take her very seriously. Well, anyway, she was so persistent that, in the end, I agreed to come here with her."

"I'm glad you did," I said, adding, "but I would have got out by myself if you hadn't."

She grunted contemptuously. "Oh, sure; you're the real big shot, aren't you?"

"I didn't mean it like that."

We sat in awkward silence for a while. Hellen spoke first. "Anyway, you're lucky I came. The state she was in, Marriette would never have got you out. You'd have both ended up in there – so just count your blessings, Cameron."

"Thanks," I said, eating humble pie, "I really do appreciate your help, Hellen."

"OK, it's no big deal." She tried a smile and failed. "I guess I just hate messing up my day off, that's all."

Some people have a talent for getting up my nose and right now Hellen van Zalinge was taking first prize. All I wanted was to relax. If she disliked me so much, why didn't she just go home and leave me in peace? Then again, she had put herself out for me – someone she didn't know. And, yes, it was true – I had messed up her day. I should try to be pleasant.

"Well, perhaps I can make it up to you somehow?"

"Oh yes, and how are you going to do that?" she demanded.

I shrugged. "Oh I dunno, maybe I could buy you dinner one night or something?"

She grunted contemptuously again.

"OK –" my patience was exhausted "– forget it. It was a lousy idea anyway."

We ate mostly in silence but the food and drink helped. By the end of the meal, we were at least making polite conversation. But, even with my reservations about him, it was a relief when Pat reappeared.

Now he was smiling, thank goodness. He appeared to have recovered from his initial shock, helped, no doubt, by a line or two of coke. "Hi girls, you enjoy the meal?" He set three steaming coffee mugs down on the table, then, feeling around in his denim jacket, produced a joint and a lighter. "Hindu Kush," he said. "Good shit, man, very smooth, not too strong, so we can chill out and still talk."

The smell of dope had been drifting past us all evening and I was beginning to think no one would ever offer us a spliff. For me it felt strange that getting stoned was legal, but for them – even Hellen – I supposed that it was a normal part of Amsterdam life, if you wanted it. Pat lit the joint, inhaling deeply before passing it to me. I took a deep drag and passed it to Hellen, holding the acrid smoke in my lungs for a few seconds before letting it out, and feeling the soft and heady sensation of good marijuana spread around my body. One third of a joint would be enough – I still had a lot of questions to ask.

I had wanted to talk to Pat about Carrie all evening. Now, as the dope worked its magic, I felt able to broach the subject more easily.

"Pat, I need to know more about Carrie. I know it's difficult, but I really need to know what she was doing here."

I waited whilst he drew on the joint again and passed it to me.

"OK, Cameron, I guess I owe you that." He closed his eyes, composing himself before he continued. "I met her towards the end of July. We had to go to court – the new owners of the Molen wanted us out and were trying to get an eviction order passed. She was there sitting on the reporters' bench. An attractive woman. She looked self-possessed, somehow. But there was something else as well, I don't know what it was, but I couldn't take my eyes off her. She seemed very intense, I suppose, concentrating hard on the proceedings and on Pel in particular –"

"Hang on, who's Pel?"

"Oh he's the guy from the property developers. A bad man, Cameron, ruthless. It was interesting that your sister seemed really drawn by him."

"You mean she was attracted to him?"

"Shit, no. It was quite clear she didn't like him. She just couldn't stop staring at him, that's all. Anyway, Pel's lawyer produced a plan showing the work that they wanted to do to the Molen – turning the place into twenty luxury, loft-type apartments – and they got the eviction order, giving us a month to get out.

"After the hearing, I went over and talked to her, thought I might get to know her." He had the grace to look embarrassed. "She was really confident, y'know. Seemed to know exactly what she wanted and how to get it. Usually a woman like that gives me the shakes, but your sister was different."

"What about Pel? Tell us more about him." Hellen was relaxed now – and interested.

Pat shook his head. "I don't know much more. He's a short guy with a big ego, I can tell you that. A big shot in property development. We only came across him this summer when the Molen changed ownership, and, as far as we're concerned, the less we see of him the better."

I looked at Hellen – I was interested in Pel too. "You said that Carrie kept staring at Pel. Can you think of any reason, Pat? Huh, do you think she knew him?"

He screwed up his face, thinking hard about that. "I can't be that certain, Cameron, maybe she was just trying to freak him out ... but, one thing ... it was really odd the way Pel reacted to her. It was almost as if she made him nervous."

Hellen looked up. "Nervous? Why would a big-shot businessman like Pel be nervous of a reporter?"

Pat shrugged. "Maybe he doesn't like reporters. Anyway, he kept glancing across at her and looking none too happy about it."

"OK, so when did Carrie come to the squat?"

"Just a few days later," he chuckled, "I thought it was my magnetic charm. But actually it was the chance of covering our eviction." Hellen asked him how he felt about that.

"Oh, it was cool. Squatting is political and politics is nothing without publicity. So we were pleased. Man, I was pleased, I liked the woman. She even impressed Emma, with her determination to help us. It was peculiar. There we were, about to be thrown out of our home, feeling angry and upset. Yet your sister, a total outsider ... she was like a bright light in the darkness. She was so positive, so certain that we could win."

"Anything else?"

"That's about it really," he said quietly. "Carrie kept very much to herself. She was out a lot, especially at night, sometimes into the early hours, and other times she'd stay in her room for hours. Some of it could have been to do with the squat story but I'm sure she must have been working on something else as well."

Pat faltered; quite suddenly, he looked smaller, and his voice became quiet and unsteady.

"I tried ... to get close to her. Shit ... I really ... liked her, man. But it was so hard ... it was like ... she was so focused on whatever it was she was doing ... I offered to help her ... but she was so fucking independent.

He wiped a tear from his eye and breathed deeply for a moment.

"Huh, it wasn't just me, either; other people were fascinated by her, but whenever anyone asked what she was up to, she'd just smile and say that she was doing her job."

That sounded like Carrie. She was the ultimate professional and it wasn't always very comfortable for other people. Once on to something, she kept the details very close to her chest; she knew from experience that careless talk by others could destroy any story.

Pat stood up and mumbled that he'd be back shortly, heading off into the squat, rather than towards the toilet. Hellen looked at me quizzically.

"He needs another hit," I said, forgetting she was a cop and then biting my tongue.

Hellen shook her head and actually laughed. "Don't worry, I'm off duty!"

I smiled back, thankful for the more relaxed atmosphere. "His last lot will be wearing thin and he probably needs it right now. I think he feels bad about Carrie."

Without thinking, I touched her arm, concerned. "You haven't told them you're police, have you?"

"Of course not!" she shrieked. "You think I'm stupid?"

We both laughed. Me out of relief, her at the thought of walking into a squat and announcing she was a cop.

After that we sat quietly, comfortably, for a few minutes.

Hellen touched my hand. "Cameron …"

"Yes?"

"I think you're right to question your sister's death. It doesn't add up, does it?"

I shook my head. Thank goodness someone was agreeing with me at last.

She smiled encouragingly. Her blue eyes seemed almost luminescent in the half-light of the café. She seemed less resentful now. It was almost as if she had been here out of some sense of duty and now she was beginning to enjoy herself.

"Sorry if I was a bit … you know … hostile, earlier on."

"That's OK. I wasn't too friendly either. I'm glad you stayed and listened to what Pat had to say."

"Me too, but I'd better go soon, it's getting late."

We both started to get up, just as Pat reappeared, weaving his way through the tables towards us. We sat down again and Hellen giggled, nudging me. "You were right – here he comes, recharged and raring to go."

"Hey, you guys, you can't go yet! I haven't told you about the big battle."

Hellen and I looked at each other. Hellen spoke. "OK Pat, but we need another coffee."

He waved good-naturedly to a woman behind the bar and pointed at the empty mugs. She smiled and gave him a thumbs-up sign.

"Where was I? Yeah, the eviction order ... Well, we knew we only had a few weeks, so we had to act, like fast. Fuck, you should have seen us: stockpiling weapons, ready for the day when the riot police arrived. We collected smoke bombs and fireworks – some from other squats – and bricks and stones; then we made catapults to fire them with. Other people heard about the coming battle on the grapevine or on Radio Free Amsterdam, and they started to join us – some even brought gas masks with them which was good because it was likely we would need all we could get."

I turned to see how Hellen was taking this and caught her staring at me. She turned her head at once, pretending she had just been looking around.

Pat was getting quite excited. "Within two weeks, we had nearly one hundred people here from all over the city. We erected barricades outside the building, just near the gates. We boarded up all the windows on the ground floor so the police couldn't get in, or fire tear-gas through them. We even had barricades ready to put behind the main doors so that, even with battering rams, they wouldn't be able to force entry."

The young woman from the bar came across with the coffees. She had long black hair tied back in a ponytail, dark eyes and a warm, generous mouth. Pat introduced Claar to us. She smiled and we exchanged a few words of polite conversation. Hellen smiled at me as Claar left, a big friendly grin that said 'I like you'. Maybe some cops were OK after all. Well, Dutch ones anyway. Well, Dutch, lesbian ones anyway.

Pat looked reflective but there was a spark in his eyes as he remembered the events of those weeks. "Yeah, so we were all ready. But man, it was hard. We only had so much food so we had to be careful – it wasn't so much a question of living; more of surviving. Normal social life stopped and we all took each day as it came, waiting for events to unfold, sleeping where and when we could, often in shifts so that there were always people on watch. There was a great feeling of common purpose. We were stockpiling food and water, living out of cans. The tension was massive but, hell, they were exciting times!" He paused for a moment and then looked at me. "Your sister did more than her share of the work."

I couldn't put that question off again, I really needed to know. "Pat, were you and Carrie … an item?"

He looked pleased with himself. "Huh, we … er … got it together a few times. She was some wild woman, your sister." He smirked at the memory of their liaisons then, aware of my discomfort, he became serious again. "But no, there was never any chance of anything more permanent. She didn't like me sniffing coke. She was funny that way; didn't give a shit about dope, but she was really against hard drugs, almost to the point of paranoia."

"So," I asked, recovering some of my composure, "do you think she would have taken cocaine and heroin herself?"

He shook his head. "Nah, not a chance. Besides, I know she was clean until the day she left here. You say she was found a few days later – shit, that's not long enough to develop a habit. Anyway, I think the only way Carrie would ever have taken drugs is if someone had tied her up and forced them into her."

Hellen interrupted: "But how could you be so certain that she wa clean?"

Pat nodded pensively. I could tell that he had taken to Hellen "Good question, but I can't answer it. I just knew. If you're a user your self, you do. There are all kinds of signs. But also, like I said, we go together a few times and I can tell you that there were no track mark on her anywhere. She could have been snorting, but her moods wer stable. She didn't act like she was on anything." He shook his head sadly. "Man, I would have known for sure."

I couldn't believe that this was the man who'd been so rough with me. Now I almost wanted to hug him.

He paused for a while, lost in his thoughts, before continuing qui etly. "The night before the eviction, we'd been out to a little restauran in the Jordaan. We wanted a break, we needed to get away from th strain. When we got back, she shared my watch with me. We guessed that the attack must be imminent – it was several days after the dead line. We were both tired and stressed. Then we had a row. We fell ou 'cos I was using coke to keep me going and I wanted her to take some She refused point blank and we started arguing." He closed his eye tight and bit his lip as he remembered. "It was just before dawn, jus as the riot police arrived.

"Once it started, we forgot our differences and worked together. He talked faster now as he remembered the action. "They came in force, about a hundred of them, some on horses. There was a water cannon too and a big mechanical digger. We were surprised how seri ously they were taking us. I felt scared as hell, but your sister, man She was so cool: making notes and taking photos as if this was jus another day's work!

"By this time we were all high on adrenaline and started to throw the ammunition at the cops, who were advancing in a pack with their riot shields above their heads. Then we noticed some of the owner' thugs standing around, further away, smirking. Pel was there with them – he always seems to be around when there is dirty work to do

Anyway, as soon as we saw them, we started aiming everything we had at them and the bastards were forced to run for cover."

I could tell from Pat's expression that Hellen was doing something distracting. More than that, I could feel her eyes on me. He stopped talking and waved his hand across Hellen's line of vision, grinning as she turned, slightly startled, to look at him. "Hey, pay attention, woman, this is the most exciting bit!

She smiled. "Sorry, I was distracted. Go on."

He looked at both of us in turn, smiled and continued. "Then a surprising thing happened: the cops all seemed to retreat. Naively, we thought we had won and we came out cheering. Damn, we should have known better! They were only regrouping and, as soon as we opened the door, they started to fire tear gas. First through the doorway, then through the upstairs windows. Before we knew it, the mounted police were back and the digger was ramming the main doors. It was chaos, people were running everywhere – half of us were still outside the building. Smoke and tear gas filled the air and I lost touch with Carrie. I hoped that she had cut loose, gone to get her story on the wire. That wouldn't have been surprising – most of us were trying to escape by then, realising that we had lost.

"Anyway, about twenty-five of us got arrested, the others got away." He shrugged disconsolately. "We got off with a warning in the end."

I turned to see Hellen's reaction and caught her eye. She smiled back, reassuringly.

The three of us sat in silence for a while.

Hellen spoke first. "Pat, what do you think happened to Cameron's sister – is it possible that Pel and his men could have taken her?"

"Yeah, looking back, they could have."

"So how come you are back, living here again?"

He looked angry again. "Jesus, Cameron, I hate being beaten. We decided to come back here a few weeks ago. I don't think the owner ever had any intention of redeveloping – he just wanted us out. Sure, he had the builders in for a while – probably something to do with the squatting laws. Or maybe if they do some work, they can hold off for a while on the main development. Shit, I don't know, man. We just wanted to get back."

"Where did they do the work?" I asked. The building I had seen didn't look as if it had been cared for in years.

"Down in the basement. Huh, it's just beautiful! They've replastered the walls and painted – new electrics, the lot. It's the best bit of the building, but so cold and bare that no one uses it."

I didn't say anything but it struck me as very odd that anyone would refurbish a basement and ignore the rest of the building.

"Anyway, so now we are going to make a last stand. There is enough greed and corruption in this city. This squat represented something good, something wholesome for seven years. Over a hundred working people lived here a few years ago. If it is converted to apartments, it will house maybe thirty yuppies – we have to try and keep it."

"How long have you got?"

He shrugged his shoulders. "You guess. We have no legal right to be here any more. The owner has occupied the building since the eviction and under Dutch law it needs to be empty for a year."

"So who does own the building?" Hellen asked.

Patrick shrugged. "A company called Eigenschappen; a really big property developer, apparently, with connections all over Europe. But as far as we are concerned, it makes little difference who they are. They're all the same – greedy and ruthless. We know that they'll come very soon, so we are preparing our defences again: we will not be so easily fooled this time. What we don't know is who we will be fighting – the police or the thugs. Frankly, we would rather have the police."

"Well," said Hellen, good-naturedly to Pat, as we got up to leave, "I'm very pleased to have revised my poor opinion of you since we first met." He beamed back. "It's not often that I rescue women in distress either," she joked, "but, all in all, it's been an interesting experience for me."

Pat grinned mischievously, looking first at Hellen, then at me. "Yeah I did notice."

Maybe it was the heat in the room or the dope, but Hellen looked distinctly flushed.

Before we left, Pat showed us the room where Carrie had slept. It was pretty bare now and there were no traces of her occupation. It seemed odd to think she had spent some of her last weeks there. It was different to the room where I had been imprisoned, mostly because of the big window that looked out over the sea. I went over and took in the view. It was nearly midnight but cars were still coming and going on the far shore and shipping was steadily making its way past, en route to and from the North Sea. I don't know how long I stood there, lost in my thoughts, before I felt Hellen's hand on my arm. She nodded in the direction of the door, where Pat was waiting for us to follow him.

The corridor along the squat was long and we had to walk nearly the full length of the building before he unlocked another door and took us into his room. It was neat and tidy, with few personal items. He went over to a small table, resting his hand on a green and blue holdall. I recognised it at once. It was Carrie's.

"When I was released by the police, I came back here with a cop to collect my belongings. I half expected to find Carrie in her room, but of course she wasn't there, so I took her things with me as well, intending to give them back when I found her. I knew they couldn't be left here – especially the electronic notebook." He unzipped the bag and produced Carrie's laptop.

"Pat, you are brilliant!" I said, beside myself with excitement. I knew how meticulous she had been about keeping notes.

Pat looked sad as he handed me the bag, making me feel awkward about my delight. For the first time since her death, I was not going to pieces at the sight of her possessions. Unlike him. He looked numb, still adjusting to her death. Now I gave him a big hug as I thanked him, more concerned with his grief than my own.

I looked questioningly at Hellen as we walked out of the building towards her car. I was unsure whether we would meet again but, after our earlier conversation, it wasn't going to be me who would broach the subject. It was dark and windy in the wilderness around the Molen. Clouds scudded across the half moon, casting moving shadows all around the derelict site. Eddies of damp wind ruffled our hair and stung our faces as we walked in silence along the old railway track to our vehicles. When we reached the big concrete building, she turned to me, hesitating for once.

"Look Cameron ... I was really unpleasant to you last night and ... well, I really haven't been a lot better tonight ... er –" she touched my arm "– come back to my place for a coffee, will you – so that we can make peace?"

I nodded. "Yeah, that would be nice. I'll follow you on my bike."

I strapped Carrie's bag to the back of the Harley and followed her through the Westpoort suburbs, back into the Jordaan, eventually pulling up in Willemstraat beside a small bar. She signalled for me to wait whilst she parked her car in a nearby garage, then she unlocked a door next to the bar and I followed her up the stairs into her flat.

It was warm and cosy inside. Her lounge was decorated in a plain, relaxed style. Pale yellow walls, contrasted by bright prints in clean, modern frames. The well-filled bookshelves, the sideboard and the large coffee table in the centre were stained in an attractive mid-blue, a little lighter than the comfortable three-seater settee. A modern chair with a springy beech frame and a deep red cover was to one side. The floor was genuine old parquet, stained to a dark brown, mostly covered by a huge, pale grey rug with what looked like a red and yellow Kandinsky design woven into it.

She made us both a mug of hot chocolate and sat cross-legged on the floor whilst I kicked off my DMs and stretched out on her long, squashy settee.

"Make yourself at home, Cameron!" Hellen was smiling in disbelief.

"Thanks," I said absent-mindedly. "Fuck, I'm worn out; it's really hard work being tied up and abused."

She smiled ruefully. "Mmm, well I think I'll take your word for that."

I looked across, pleased to see that she was smiling. Maybe she wasn't so bad after all. Anyway, her settee was heaven.

Her smile faded, replaced by a look of concern. "I know that you'll think this is the cop talking Cameron, but you do realise what you are getting into, don't you? Whatever Hugo – I mean Inspecteur Dankmeijer – may have said, your sister must have been on to something serious. You should be careful."

"You know we didn't hit it off, don't you? – me and 'Hugo'," I said pointedly.

"Yeah, I know. His reaction reached level nine on the Richter scale! No one has ever spoken to him like that – well, not a woman anyway." She giggled. "He's OK, though. Just very straight. I wouldn't have expected the two of you to get on."

I looked up. "Do you think I should go and see him again?"

"Yes, I do. Are you going to?"

I shrugged. "I don't know. I might, maybe if I've got enough to get him to re-open the case. You think I should?

"I'm a cop, sweetheart, I'm bound to say yes. That's what the police are for."

"But, if I don't, you won't say anything about tonight, will you?"

"No. Not if you don't want me to – and as long as I'm not asked. But I won't lie."

"Thanks, Hellen ... what do you think about Pat – is he on the level?"

"Yeah, I guess, but I wouldn't trust his friend Emma." Hellen looked down into her drink and paused.

I waited.

"Cameron." She looked up at me. "You know ... well, I was wrong about you. You're OK. But I think you should go easy on this idea you have of investigating your sister's death."

It had to come, of course; it was only a matter of time. But, somehow, it hurt a little that she too was joining the 'let's persuade Cameron to stop this foolishness' brigade.

"Hellen, I'm not even going to talk about that, right? I thought I had come back here to make peace, not get involved in an argument."

"OK, OK! I'm sorry, just be careful, huh?"

She came across and sat on the floor by the settee, an act of reconciliation. "Cameron, I hope that you can find out enough to get Hugo to re-open your sister's case – but you understand that I can't get involved, don't you, that I can't condone what you are doing?"

I nodded.

"I'll do what I can to help from the sidelines, though I shouldn't even do that. I have to be careful not to get mixed up in anything that might prejudice the position of the police. Besides – and I know this is selfish – I'm up for promotion soon and I have to be doubly careful not to prejudice my own position."

"Promotion to what?" I asked.

She looked a bit embarrassed, "Sergeant."

I raised my eyebrows, impressed. "So you're a career cop, then?"

"Sorry, did that sound pretentious?"

"No, it's good, there should be lots of senior women in the police."

"There are quite a few in the Politie."

"Yeah, well good for you. Christ, most of the British police still find it hard to treat straight women as equals – dykes don't have a hope in hell."

She looked offended. "Who says I'm a dyke?"

"I just thought ... I mean ... you sort of ..." I noticed her forcing back a smile. "You're winding me up!"

"Yeah, sorry." She grinned mischievously. She really did look good. Maybe if I tried hard I could get to really like her. "Yeah, there are lots of us in the Politie. I've been out in my job since I started. It's OK. No worries."

I grunted, "Huh, there are lots of dykes in the British police as well, they just daren't come out, that's all."

"Well, in that case, I'm glad to be Dutch, as well as gay."

We chatted for a few minutes more, but it was late, so I made a move, picked up Carrie's bag and slung it on my shoulder. Hellen walked down the stairs with me to the outside door, where we both hesitated slightly. I was wondering just what form our goodbye should take; maybe she was too.

She put her hand on my shoulder. "When I rang Marriette this afternoon, it was really to invite you to dinner. Would you like to come round tomorrow? I'm on days all this week, so about seven?"

I said that I would, trying hard to sound as cool and matter of fact as I could. But, in truth, my heart was racing at the thought. We both looked at each other a little nervously for a few seconds, recognising that there could be, might be, something between us.

In the end, I put my arms out and we gave each other a big hug.

Nine

I was desperate to check out Carrie's computer as soon as I got back to my room, but it was nearly 1 a.m. by then and my Better Judgement was telling me to forget it. For starters, I didn't even know whether the battery would be charged. The last thing I wanted was to wipe the memory by mistake. Also, I was so tired that, even if the battery was fine, I could easily have done something really stupid. So I stuck my hand in her bag and rooted around until I found the charging unit, then plugged it into the wall socket before falling into my bed.

Now, at 8 a.m. on Monday, the laptop would be fully charged and my brain would be more capable of concentrating.

I decided to check out the bag first and, recalling how I had felt when I opened her other belongings, I braced myself. But there was precious little in there – a few creased T-shirts, some underwear, a spare pair of jeans, a crumpled jacket, and a few toiletries. Even these few items spoke volumes about her. For someone who travelled a lot, she had hated packing and seldom took the trouble to fold her clothes carefully.

I spread everything out on the bed and went through the pockets in the holdall and those in the clothes. The bag and its contents still carried her smell and brought a tightness to my throat and a burning to my eyes. But, in purely practical terms, there was nothing of any importance. I folded the clothes carefully before I put them back – something I had done a lot when I had travelled with her – and felt somehow comforted by this small act of caring.

I put the laptop on the bedside table with baited breath before I lifted the lid and slid the switch into the 'on' position. Black type hit the LCD screen as the computer went through its booting-up procedure and, after what seemed like ages, the Windows screen finally appeared and a box flashed up asking for the password.

I winced. Damn! Of course Carrie would have some security: all her information would be in the laptop; she wouldn't want it falling into the wrong hands.

I fell back on the bed, frustrated. I know enough about computers to find my way around but that's where it ends. When it comes down to the clever stuff, I'm out there in the wilderness like most other people. I closed down the system and stuck the laptop into my rucksack. It seemed that every time I took a step forward, I came up against another brick wall. Now I needed to find someone who knew about computer operating systems. There must be a way of bypassing that password.

Maybe Hellen could help. I pulled myself up sharply at the thought. She was a cop. She didn't want to be involved, and, sure as hell, I didn't want her to be. It was only a short step from Senior Police Officer van Zalinge to her friend Hugo Dankmeijer and I felt sure that if he got wind of what I was doing, then he would be furious. I could do without that.

Even so, the thought of her cheered me up instantly.

Things felt strangely different at breakfast. All the other women guests were talking excitedly about their plans for the day as normal, but Marriette seemed subdued.

I had just finished eating when Helga appeared in an immaculately tailored, long black coat, holding a suitcase – one of those expensive grey crocodile-style jobs that are so popular with the terminally ostentatious. It made me wonder again why she was staying at a place like this. There were a lot of things about Helga that made me wonder. However, I was relieved that she was leaving. Now I could afford to be a little less defensive. I waved and smiled, expecting her to come across and talk to me in her pushy way but she only looked at me as if I might be a carrier of some rare disease. Then she turned and went to the other end of the table, where Marriette was clearing the breakfast things, to say she was leaving for Hanover. Marriette looked annoyed and went off to get the bill.

It had to be one of those two who had rung the squat, as only they knew that I was going there. However hard I tried, I couldn't see Marriette making the call. It was plainly ridiculous – and, anyway, she wouldn't have a hope in hell of being taken for an American. So it had to be Helga. Helga who had booked in just at the right time, with just the right contacts, and to whom I had blurted out everything I knew. I felt foolish. I also felt puzzled.

She didn't say goodbye. Just a scowl in my direction as she went through the door. Maybe I had compromised myself, but I knew a damn sight more today than I did twenty-four hours ago. And I knew too that at least one other person, apart from Dankmeijer and Hans, was uncomfortable about what I was doing.

Marriette came back into the room, looking much more herself, and started to clear the table again. She looked at me and groaned. "Some people have no manners, Cameron. They think others exist just to run around after them."

She rested her hand on my shoulder and kissed the top of my head. "The main thing is that you are safe, darling – but I do wish I hadn't let Helga persuade me to give her those unobtainable telephone numbers. Then none of this would have happened."

I looked up, surprised. "But I thought you asked her to help."

Marriette blushed. "No, lieveling, I was intending to let the matter drop, so that you would give up on your wild ideas. But Helga somehow wormed it all out of me and made me feel like it was me who had asked her to help. She just seemed so generous at the time. I wish I'd never set eyes on the woman!" She looked at me guiltily.

I shook my head glumly. "Don't feel bad, Etts, Helga knew exactly what she was doing with both of us."

***

It was over a week since I had last worked out at the gym and I was getting withdrawal symptoms. My legs felt twitchy and the rest of my body was on a go-slow. A brisk walk around the city might perk me up a little – and I had some research to do.

It was the sort of day that lifts the spirits, cool but sunny. Amsterdam was looking pretty again and I felt glad to be here: sure that I was doing the right thing, even if it did worry Marriette.

I walked along the side of the Reguliersgracht and through Rembrandtplein with its outdoor cafés and bars, then on towards the city centre. I eventually found the internet café I had been looking for, just off Rokin.

I took my coffee and an almond croissant over to a free screen and, with a little help from the assistant, began to search in English for anything to do with 'squat'.

Even I was surprised at the amount of material on the web about squatting – some was American, some German, but the majority was Dutch. There were details of individual squats, squat cafés, squat produce, as well as a wealth of information about evictions and conflict with the police. I read the whole story of the Molen again on screen and it tied in exactly with what Pat had said – not surprisingly, since he had written it! But he was right – this was a big movement.

It was all interesting enough, but even after some forty minutes of reading, I still hadn't found any reference to Eigenschappen, the property developer, apart from the one in Pat's piece. So I searched again, this time using both 'squat' and 'Eigenschappen'.

The list that appeared on-screen gave me a number of sites. The Molen site was one of them, but there was another headed "Nordmag – the struggle will continue". I clicked on the title and a plain typewritten file appeared. It was eighteen months old and hadn't been updated.

At two pages, it wasn't as long as many of the others, but it detailed a now familiar story: building is empty for years; squatters move in and assert legal right to be there; they eventually face pressure from the developers; they resist; an eviction notice is sought and granted; they resist and ultimately they are thrown out. All part of the fight against Emma's Establishment. The strange thing was, though, that, like the Molen, the Nordmag was also re-squatted; it was also owned by Eigenschappen, and this web page also talked about a refurbished basement. Also, just as the owners were trying to evict the re-squat at the Molen, they had succeeded in evicting the repossessed Nordmag just before this report was written.

The document might promise that "the struggle would continue", but however much I searched, I couldn't find any other reference to either the Nordmag or Eigenschappen.

I logged off, paid my bill and walked back out into the sunshine. I hadn't got all the information I needed – but I knew where to get the rest.

The Kamer van Koophandel – the Amsterdam Chamber of Commerce – is about twenty minutes' walk from Rokin, situated behind Centraal Station on the other side of the city centre, beyond Dam Square.

Since it was still so pleasant, I took my time, stopping with passing tourists to admire the 'human statue' on Damrak: his face and hands painted like white marble, his hair covered with a white skullcap and his body robed in flowing white cloth. He stood stock-still on his plinth, looking for all the world like a sculpture dedicated to some long-gone Roman senator. A little girl gingerly put some coins in his box and suddenly the statue came to life, bowing gracefully to her with a serene smile on its face, much to the surprise and fascination of the child and the amusement of other onlookers, including me. It was good to smile again.

I moved on and took a short-cut through Centraal Station, picking my way through the crowds of travellers, passing the guys selling *Z* (Amsterdam's version of the *Big Issue*), the winos, and the homeless, all enjoying the warmth of this huge railway station. Carrie used to be mesmerised by all the colour and clamour of this place, but then she loved all airports and railway stations. They symbolised travel which, to her, meant freedom. I felt a shiver of guilt at enjoying something that was now beyond her. Poor Carrie.

I walked down one of the long, wide corridors, passing the instant food shops, which smelt deliciously of doughnuts and pastries, and re-emerged into the sunlight on the road that led to the Westpoort. A few minutes later, I reached the modern glass and metal building that was the Chamber of Commerce.

This time I didn't have to use a computer myself. The woman behind the desk did it for me – and in less than two minutes, she extracted the information from the Chamber's database.

It had been a late night at Hellen's and I was beginning to wilt, so I made for the nearest brown bar. I sat down at a table overlooking the Singelgracht canal with my cappuccino, nibbling at the biscuit which accompanies every coffee in the Netherlands; watching the sun reflecting off the water; enjoying the colourful tapestry of people cycling and walking along the narrow road by the canal. Two police officers strolled casually by – a woman and a man – and I wondered why they always looked so much more relaxed here than at home. I thought about Hellen again and felt a pang of concern about the frequency with which she crossed my mind.

Eventually, I shook myself out of my reverie. Maybe it was the late autumn sunshine that was relaxing me, but I needed to concentrate; this was not a holiday.

In the Netherlands, every business must, by law, register with the Chamber of Commerce in each area, and Eigenschappen was no exception. The details in front of me were short and factual.

Eigenschappen BV was classified as "a property company, specialising in prime residential developments". The company was formed two years earlier from an offshore trust; so far, no accounts had been filed and there was no evidence that the company was trading at all. If that seemed odd, then the name was even odder. Unless they had a separate, snappier trading name, then 'Eigenschappen' wasn't going to impress anyone – as far as my limited Dutch was concerned, it meant nothing. The directors were listed as H E Schmidt (German), 6 Pelder Strasse, Hamburg, Germany; J Shepherd (UK), 297 Churchill Road, Altrincham, Cheshire, England; and S Pel, 1046 Henri Porrel Straat, Amsterdam.

Stefan Pel really existed then, in public records as well as real life – and he wasn't just a 'heavy'.

I walked back towards Marriette's, still enjoying the day. I needed to check out Pel's address and have a look at Nordmag. I would need my bike for both, but I had plenty of time. I took the narrow side streets with their small, quirky shops and walked back over the three central canals until I came to Prinsengracht. It was midday and the bells of the nearby Westerkerk chimed happily above me with the clear, sharp, clarion ring that is so familiar in this city.

Then I turned left along the canal and stopped outside Anne Frank House, where the Jewish teenager hid with her family and wrote her famous diaries. Her greatest wish was to be a journalist, and I knew that Carrie's passion for her job had started when she read Anne Frank's account of her two years in hiding. We spent almost two hours in there, Carrie and me. I remembered her telling me how amazed the young girl would be with the success of her writing – now regarded as a significant historical work, highlighting the tyranny of the Nazis and fulfilling her ambition to "go on living, even after my death". Maybe, I hoped, a little of Carrie would survive in the same way.

Cutting behind the Westerkerk, I came to another important shrine. The three large, triangular, pink granite slabs that descend from the church square to the Keizergracht canal represent the symbol used by the Nazis to persecute gay people. Amsterdam's Homo-Monument is dedicated to all those in the lesbian and gay movement who have been persecuted because they dared to be different. Today, like most days, the slab with its point at the water's edge was covered with flowers of remembrance for people who had died from AIDS.

I walked down on to the shiny marble and stood near the water, the flowers at my feet, thinking about intolerance. This monument was evidence of some success in the fight for equality – here, at any rate, supported as it was by both the Dutch Government and the city council and built next to the most prestigious church in the city.

One day maybe we'll have one by St Paul's ... huh, don't hold your breath, Cameron.

I carried on along Prinsengracht and made my way to Leidseplein, easily the most entertaining square in the city with its jugglers and acrobats, street sellers and open air cafés. As usual it was packed, with a few excellent buskers working crowds that were large for a November's day. A few winos were there too, attempting their own pathetic cabaret acts in an effort to extract money from the café patrons in their neat rows of chairs.

The sounds of Leidseplein are something else – the clank and rattle of the trams as they constantly pass through this busy intersection, the hum of the crowds, the cries and exclamations of the buskers and the music seeping out from the cafés. A bountiful, non-stop bedlam of noise.

I could have stayed there for the whole afternoon but deep down a restlessness was jabbing me in the ribs, reminding me why I was there. I needed to get on, so I hopped on to a number 6 tram and was back at Marriette's within a few minutes. Ten minutes later, I was leaving on my Harley.

It had already occurred to me that the directors of Eigenschappen were an odd bunch, living in three separate countries. It seemed strange too that there was no evidence of trading after they had applied for the Nordmag eviction two years earlier.

Henri Porrel Straat – Pel's registered address – was a nondescript street in the south-western suburb of Slotermeer. Though it was pleasant enough, it was predominantly a low to middle income area. It didn't look like the kind of place where a property developer would choose to live.

I motored slowly down the street, starting at the bottom with the lower numbers. As I drove, I began to get the feeling that the street was not long enough and, by the time I reached the top, the building numbers had only reached to 806. Pel's number 1046 did not exist.

I rang Becky on Marriette's mobile.

"Hi Beck, it's me again."

"Ohhh, hiya Cam. You've just caught me, I'm on my way out. What is it? You in trouble?"

"No, course not. Just want a favour that's all. Can you check on an address in Altrincham for me?"

"What?"

"It's 297 Churchill Road, Altrincham, Cheshire."

"You want me to go to Cheshire!"

"No, of course not. I just want to know if the address exists, that's all."

"Cameron, how the hell am I supposed to find that out?"

"Try the voters' list at the library, Becks, or ring the local police. I'm sorry, but it's important!" I knew I was being tetchy. "Can you leave a message with Marriette?"

"Right, OK flower." I could feel her good-natured resignation through the ether. "Cameron?"

"Yeah?"

"What are you doing? Why do you need to know about this address?"

"Not much, Becky. Just digging around a little." It sounded weak, even to me.

"Cam, you aren't just having a holiday, are you?"

There was a long silence.

"I knew that there was more to it than just 'coming to terms with Carrie's death'! Cameron! What are you up to?"

"Becky, I'm just following up on a few things, that's all. Honestly, there's nothing for you to get all anxious about!"

"You promise?"

"Yeah ... Of course."

"Mmm ... Well do take care, love. I know what you're like. If you get an idea in your head, you won't let go. Just remember you're on sick leave and you are supposed to be convalescing."

"Yes I know – and I do feel much better."

"Yes I can tell – and that's what really worrying me!"

I changed the subject. "Will you get that information for me?"

She sighed heavily. "Course I will Cam. I'll ring Marriette's tonight. Now, you take great care, OK?"

"Yeah, OK Becks, I will."

"And Cameron ..."

"Yeah?"

"Give yourself a break. Relax, love, please?"

Nice thought, but things had gone too far now.

I took out my piece of paper again, looking at the questions I'd written down in the Juno Bar and adding the new details. Amid all the unanswered questions, one thing stood out like a beacon – no one seriously believed that Carrie had died by accident. Not Marriette, not Pat, not Hans, not Hellen and certainly not me.

So how come the police were still treating her death as a drug-related accident?

Time to pay Hugo Dankmeijer another visit.

"Sorry, the Inspecteur is in a meeting all afternoon," said the man at the desk, putting down the phone. I looked at him. We both knew he was lying.

"Fine, so who is his superior officer? I'll see her instead."

The man fidgeted. "It's Hoofd Inspecteur Vrieling, but he is out of the office for the moment."

"OK," I said, pleasantly enough, planting myself down in one of the nearby easy chairs with obvious stubbornness. "Tell Inspector

Dankmeijer that I will wait until either he or his superior becomes available." I could tell he recognised trouble when he saw it and I was pleased when he disappeared to another room, presumably so that I couldn't overhear his comments to the Inspector.

It only took ten minutes before Dankmeijer found a convenient break in his 'meeting'. He came down to the reception area himself and shunted me into a nearby room. To say he wasn't pleased to see me would be an understatement.

"Miss McGill, you are trying my patience. I see little point in talking to you. I have already told you that the case is –"

"Inspector, I just want to know what is going on."

"The case is closed, nothing is 'going on'!" he said, exasperated. "Please, I have other work to attend to …"

I stayed cool. "Yes, I'm sure you have, Inspector. So, please, just answer a few questions, then I promise, I'll leave you alone."

He sat down impatiently on the edge of the interview table. "All right, go ahead."

"If the death of my sister was a drug-related accident –" I held my hand up and counted off the questions finger by finger "– why has she only got six needle marks on her arm; why were all six made on the same day; why is there extensive haemorrhaging around most of them; why were they injected into the wrong arm for a left-handed woman? And why does everyone who knew my sister in those last weeks say the same thing: that she was against drugs and would not use them?"

He looked non-committal.

"Come on Inspector, if you have carried out your investigation properly, and I am sure you have, then you must be aware of all those questions – and of at least some of the answers."

He didn't move a muscle.

"Finally, you say that you cannot identify the exact substances that she took." I paused, I wanted him to think I was certain of this. "I think you know very well what those substances were, Inspector.

They are the same as those that are beginning to circulate on the street; they are the same substances that are connected with the women who are going missing."

If he was trying not to give anything away, he was very good at it. But, however calm he tried to appear, he couldn't hide the alarm in his eyes or the nervous, unconscious movement of his feet.

"I'm sorry, Miss McGill, but your imagination is getting the better of you. We have reached our conclusions. The case is closed."

"Inspector, I'm sure that you are a decent man and a good police officer, but you are being less than frank with me." I softened my voice. "I know when something is real – you're never going to convince me that it's all in my mind. So please stop patronising me, OK?" I reasoned with him. "Look, this isn't easy for you either. So why don't you just tell me the truth? Maybe then I really will go home and leave it to you."

He paused for just a few seconds too long. I could see that he was tempted. If what I suspected was right, then he would do almost anything to get me out of his hair. Almost anything but tell me the truth. I thought back to Carrie's last letter: "I think that I'm on to something ... It's an issue that affects women ... is being ignored (hushed up?) by the authorities."

Dankmeijer stood up straight again. "Miss McGill, I think that you have a very active imagination. Your sister's death was very sad and must have been a great shock to you. I think that, if I was in your position, then I too would be looking for acceptable reasons for her untimely end. Unfortunately, I can't tell you any more than you already know. I must ask you to leave it at that."

We looked at each other for a moment. Now I knew for certain that there was more to Carrie's death than a drug overdose. What's more, he knew that I knew.

I turned to go, speaking quietly as I opened the door: "Thank you, Inspector. You have told me all I need."

At last, I was beginning to get the picture.

Ten

It took me half an hour to get from the police station to the Northern Docks. I thought that it would be easier to avoid the city centre and use the ring road instead. But I was wrong: it was mid-afternoon and the motorway traffic was already beginning to build towards the rush hour. The road tunnel under Het Ij was awful: the traffic pollution seeped into my helmet, restricting my breathing and poisoning my eyes. By the time I emerged at the northern end, my head was throbbing and my eyes were watering.

I thought about Helga. Who was she? It seemed too much of a coincidence that she had booked into Marriette's the day after me. And why had she first helped, then interfered? There had to be some connection with Carrie. I thought about who I had talked to when I first arrived and was surprised at just how long the list was. The police, Marjan and Janna, all the women in the Juno Bar and most of the drug agencies in Amsterdam. I had seen them all before Helga appeared at Marriette's. I had really announced my arrival in a big way and, in truth, she could have been tipped off by almost anyone.

It was a relief to get off the main roads and breathe cleaner air, but it still took me another twenty minutes to locate the Nordmag building and by then the light was beginning to fade.

For a building that had been up for development two years earlier, the Nordmag looked in a particularly derelict state. The huge three-storey warehouse had few windows and those were roughly, but solidly, blocked up. Each floor had a set of loading doors which looked in a poor state too. Only the roof looked sound. The surrounding area within its high brick walls was littered with rubble and waste. It stood near the edge of Het Ij, almost opposite Eigenschappen's other building – the Molen – about a half-mile across the water.

The area around the warehouse was also derelict. There were a number of old buildings in much the same condition and a few modern ones which also appeared to be empty: a regeneration that had run out of steam some time ago. Old jetties languished at the water's edge, no longer of use in these days of container ports. On the water, oil tankers and huge barges passed, ferrying their wares to and from the North Sea, Rotterdam and Germany. The roads were full of potholes and grass was beginning to grow between the cobbles, but a big black Mercedes was parked neatly amidst the dereliction. Someone, somewhere, always makes money out of others' misfortune.

A strip of land, only about twenty feet wide, ran in front of the Nordmag building, with a short wooden jetty extending out into the sea, the water lapping against the half-rotted timbers underneath. From here, I could almost see into the Molen's squat café – and more significantly, into Carrie's old room.

I walked along the side of the building, looking for signs of life and seeing none. The main door was securely nailed shut and it wasn't until I walked back to the road end of the building that I noticed the smaller door set back in the wall, near the corner.

I went closer and saw the signs of recent usage – a door handle polished by regular use, and letters hand-painted in white on the dirty red door saying: 'SQUAT – KEEP OUT.'

Strange. According to the web page, the re-squat had been evicted. It seemed it was back, but the web report hadn't been updated.

I knocked hard and stood back. There was no way I wanted to go inside by myself after my experience at the Molen, but I still wanted a good look round. After I hammered on the door for the second time, I heard voices and a panel opened in the top of the door to reveal a thin-faced man, probably in his thirties, with long black matted hair and a tattoo of a spider's web to the right side of his forehead. I wondered if he had 'hate' and 'love' on his knuckles as well.

"Hi!" I smiled. Nothing.

"Er ... I've just arrived in Amsterdam, and I'm desperate for a place to crash out tonight – any room in your squat?"

He looked at me contemptuously. "No."

OK, so maybe charm would work. "Please, its getting late – just for tonight will do." I felt sick doing the 'little girl lost' routine to such a creep.

He gave me a black look. "Just fuck off, will you." Then, suddenly, I was looking at the woodwork again.

I can tell when I'm not welcome. Of course, I wanted to see inside even more now. I've been to a few squats over the years, but none as hostile as this. However, it was 3.30 p.m. and getting dark. There was nothing much I could do, unless I broke in, which didn't seem like a very good idea. So, reluctantly, I walked back to the road and started my bike. This time I headed back along the northern shore to the car ferry that would take me back to Centraal Station, avoiding another unpleasant journey through the tunnel.

The ferries cross continually and I only had to wait a few minutes before driving on to the big raft-like structure and parking near the bow. The journey was a short one so I stayed on the bike, reflecting on Eigenschappen. Various things were puzzling me. Like, why get an eviction order on a building and then do nothing with it? Why evict a squat at Nordmag, refurbish a basement, evict a re-squat, then give up and let another re-squat stay? Was it significant that Eigenschappen's two buildings were virtually opposite each other? And that only the basements of both buildings had been refurbished? … And whose was the black Merc that had just driven on to the ferry behind me?

I studied the car in my mirror. I couldn't see anything of the driver through the tinted glass, but the car looked like the one parked a few yards from the Nordmag. Huh, probably a coincidence. All this detective work was beginning to make me paranoid.

The journey across only took a few minutes and I was soon back at Centraal Station. In no hurry to get back to Marriette's, I drove through the Westpoort suburbs and made my way to Laurierstraat again for a quick coffee in the Juno Bar. Since it was nearly empty, I spent most of the next half-hour talking to Agnes and sipping two cups of her strong dark brew.

I hoped that Marriette would feel more settled again this evening and, on impulse, I bought a bottle of sparkling wine before I left, as a present for her. It was dark when I came out. I still hadn't put the panniers back on my bike, so I fastened the bottle to the back seat with an elastic retainer and set off, through the Jordaan, towards Wetteringsschans, hoping to cheer her up.

I like the roads in the Jordaan. They are long and narrow, running parallel with each other and linked by a network of side streets. Some of the long streets have canals running their entire length, crossed here and there by humpback bridges, whose arches are lit each evening by hundreds of small white lights. I was taking my time, motoring slowly, enjoying the prettiness of Amsterdam after dark, when I began to feel uneasy. Something didn't feel right.

My Harley sounded good, the weather was fine and the roads were OK ...

It took a few moments before I registered the constant, throaty sound behind me and realised that it had been there since I left the bar. When I looked in my mirror I saw him. A big man wearing leathers and a black helmet, driving a powerful BMW motorbike. He was only a few yards away, close enough for my rear lights to be reflected in his mirrored visor. It looked like I was being tailed.

I turned left sharply along one of the side streets; he turned left. I turned right; he followed. I went to the top and turned right again along the canalside; he was still behind me.

I began to feel threatened: he seemed to be moving even closer. I sped up a little to try and leave him, but he accelerated hard; coming right alongside me on my left and lunging out at my shoulder with his hand. I wobbled erratically as I struggled to balance my heavy machine, dropping my revs at the same time and falling back behind him. He did the same and, before I could do anything, he was alongside me again, pushing at me. I lashed out with my left hand and he grabbed it, trying to pull me off my bike. I moved closer, so that our machines were almost touching, giving him as little leverage as possible. Then I pushed back, leaning towards him slightly, using the weight of my machine and putting him off balance for a vital few seconds. He let go.

I was desperate by now. A calmer inner voice was trying to keep control, confident that I could get out of this. But my body was shaking with panic and my driving was becoming more and more reckless as I tried to get away.

I accelerated hard again, but he stayed with me, reaching over, trying to grab my jacket, trying again to unseat me. I yelled out at him over the roar of the two engines. "You bastard! What the fuck do you want?"

He just kept lunging at me.

There was a junction ahead, so I tensed, ready to turn at the last minute and, hopefully, get away from him. But, before I got there, he hit me hard and I mounted the kerb with a jolt, just missing the bollards and careering along the footpath. Recovering my balance, I came back on to the road at the junction and turned sharp right, heading off down a long street, gunning the Harley as I went. He went straight past the end and I lost him for a few seconds. But then he was back behind me again, accelerating like hell.

I could feel the sweat on my back and the panic in my gut as I tried to calm myself down so I could think. I waited until the last possible second and then turned right again, leaning hard into the corner, steadying myself with my right boot scraping the road, pulling my back wheel round speedway style, accelerating hard off the turn.

I shot along the short street and over the bridge beyond, taking off at the top, landing with a thump just before a sharp left turn along the other side of the canal. My back tyre squealed in complaint as I pulled the machine round again. I turned right along another side street, then sharp left within yards. Thank God the roads were quiet.

Every time I turned, I pulled ahead a little more. I glanced over my shoulder; he was still with me, but I was twenty feet ahead of him now. My bike was smaller, lighter than his, I had some advantage on the corners. He had the advantage on the straight. I tried to keep to the corners, praying that no one got in the way.

My heart was trying to tear its way through my ribcage by the time I hit the next side street. I turned right, just missing a man on a bike. A delivery wagon was parked a hundred yards ahead of me, taking up the entire road, its amber lights flashing. There would be just enough room for a pedestrian – or a motorbike – to pass on the pavement to the left, inside the brown bollards – but only just. I slowed down, checking that nobody was walking through the gap, letting my pursuer get closer to me again. When he was only a few feet away, I pulled the wine bottle out of its restraints on the back seat with my left hand, accelerating hard with my right.

As I shot through the narrow gap, I raised the bottle above my head and tossed it behind me.

I didn't hear the bottle smash on the road but I heard the squeal as his front wheel connected with the broken glass. I dropped my revs and glanced back to see his bike skewed across the gap, the back wheel wrapped around a bollard, the front pressed against the wall. The driver was a black shape in the road, several yards further on.

I turned another corner, slowed my speed and tried to drive responsibly again. Jesus, I needed to stop. But I had to put some distance between us first, so I drove along a number of side streets and across a few more canals before pulling in to the side, sweaty and faint – a mixture of fear and relief tearing at my insides. I thought I was going to throw up.

I took off my helmet, breathing in the cool evening air, concentrating on relaxing my shaking body and reducing my heart rate. I was startled at the sudden violence and very relieved that I had been able to get away. It took me a good ten minutes to calm down to a reasonable level, then I put my helmet back on and set off slowly up the street, to the junction at the top, and the road back to Marriette's.

I was shivering with a mixture of relief and cold. The sweat on my back had cooled and my heart rate had slowed. Even my leathers couldn't keep me warm now. I felt totally drained. All I wanted was to get back to the warmth, comfort and safety of my room. A left turn at the top of the street and I would be home within minutes.

When I reached the junction, I paused, putting my feet to the ground. My legs and arms ached from adrenaline withdrawal, so I took a few moments to stretch, working my tired limbs. Then I opened up the throttle and slowly began to turn left.

I heard the screech of the wheels first, then I saw the big black Merc accelerating from its hiding place only a few feet to my right. Before I could react, its bumper hit the back of my bike and I felt the whole machine lift off the road. I was thrown against the car bonnet, whilst my beautiful Harley was despatched, scraping and clattering along the cobbles. The impetus of the collision sent me slithering across the windscreen and over the other side, hitting the road as the car drew quietly to a stop.

Instinctively, I came straight up into a crouching position, hands in front of me, facing the car and ready to fight. But I was grabbed from behind, my arms pinned painfully behind my back. The passenger door opened and a stocky man in a balaclava got out. He walked slowly, calmly up to me and studied me for a few seconds, pursing his scaly lips, then wetting them with his tongue, as if in anticipation of some imminent pleasure.

"Get your fucking hands off me, you bastards," I yelled, kicking out with my heels at the legs of the man behind me. I felt him wince and step back out of my range as I connected with his shin. But he pulled my arms further up my back, making me cry out with the sudden pain.

The man with the balaclava reached out coolly and grabbed my neck with a leather-clad hand, squeezing my windpipe and making me gasp noisily for air.

He pulled my face close to his: so close that I could feel his stinking dog's breath crawling all over my skin. His voice was deep and guttural and he spoke slowly, dispassionately. "I am not going to kill you this time, McGill. But unless you stop sticking your nose into things that don't concern you, you will get hurt … badly hurt …"

He pulled my head even closer, so that our faces were touching: all I could see were the anaemic blue pools that were his eyes; I could feel the rough dampness of his balaclava against my nose; I could feel his lips brushing against my own as I fought for breath. His voice became low and menacing. "Do you understand? If you don't leave Amsterdam by the morning, you will get terminally hurt."

He released me and got back into the car. The other thug threw me sideways to the ground and got in the driver's side. I staggered to my feet, limping painfully off the road, coughing, holding my bruised throat, concerned in case they intended to run me down.

Dogsbreath opened his window and stabbed a finger in my direction. "Just remember what happened to your sister. One death in a family is unfortunate, two would be careless." Then there was a squeal of tyres as the car sped off, leaving only the smell of burning rubber, a battered Harley-Davidson and a very bruised ego in the quiet canalside street.

This time I did throw up.

Eleven

As soon as the thugs had gone, I sat down on a nearby bench shaking all over. I moved my arms and legs. Nothing felt broken – my leathers had protected me – but my ankle felt sore and I guessed that I would have some colourful bruises on my side from hitting the car. The physical harm was relatively minor; right now, I was just scared out of my mind.

I couldn't imagine who the men in the black Merc could be. It would have been better if I could have seen their faces. The balaclavas made them even more alarming.

I was trying to get my thoughts together when a woman ran out of a nearby house and asked if I was all right. She didn't speak any English but I understood she was angry at what she thought was a hit and run. I had all on, given the state I was in, to persuade her not to call the police or an ambulance.

"No, honestly, dank u wel, I'm fine." I protested, gesturing that she should calm down. "Ik ben OK. Geen Politie, geen ambulance alstublieft. I sit, quietly … Stil dankje."

She ordered me to wait, and disappeared indoors again.

I got up with some effort and limped across to my bent and battered Harley. The front wheel was buckled and the bodywork gouged and dented. It didn't look like a write-off, but it was certainly unrideable. With some effort, I managed to drag it the short distance to the side of the road, away from any traffic, and sat down again on the bench.

Now I had absolute proof – if I needed it – that I was on to something. First Helga and now these thugs.

One way or another, I was being warned off. 'They' wanted me out of the country.

The woman reappeared from the house, bearing a brandy and a hot coffee. I thanked her profusely and signalled, with my limited Dutch and some mime, that I would leave my poor bike chained by the side of the road for collection later. I also asked if she would call a taxi. She nodded and smiled weakly, still concerned about my condition.

"Dank u wel. Ik voel me OK!" I made a supreme effort to look as if I really was OK, standing up and twirling round in a show of OK'ness, grinning at her, concentrating on keeping my face wince-free.

"Goed!" she smiled, satisfied. And, asking me to leave the cup and glass outside her door, she returned home.

The coffee and brandy felt good. I seemed to remember that stimulants were not good for shock, but they felt fine to me, and soon I was feeling both warmer and calmer. I started to weigh it all up again as I rubbed at my sore ankle.

Over the last few days I had really put myself around and, at some point, I must have been seen by, or talked to, someone who was connected, however tentatively, to Carrie's death. As I sat by the road, rubbing my sore ankle, waiting for the taxi, I went through all the possible suspects in my mind.

I still daren't trust Pat; Carrie had got very close to him and he could have been at the heart of her investigation. He was certainly one of the last people to see her. Emma could have been jealous of Pat's relationship with my sister. She was, after all, obsessed with both him and her political dogma. Then there was Hans; I had told him a lot and I still couldn't swear that he was genuine. There were the users I had talked to around the methadone bus ...

But the most obvious suspect was Helga; a wealthy woman staying in a small bed and breakfast. Someone who had been a little too eager to help – and a little too keen to get to know me. Someone who had asked too many questions. Someone who had, almost certainly, set me up at the squat. Why had she done that? To frighten

me, to warn me off? Was that incident a taster for the threats made
by Dogsbreath just now?

I couldn't rule out Dankmeijer either. He had not been helpful
and I knew now that he had been lying to me about Carrie's death
– or at least skirting around the truth. He could be covering up,
holding back for some reason – he could be bent. Bad cops are every
where, even Amsterdam.

But, if Dankmeijer was a crooked cop, then what about Hellen?
She was, after all, on first-name terms with the man. Hell, I didn't
even want to think about that – there had to be someone I believed
and, out of them all, she was the one I most wanted to trust.

The taxi pulled up – ironically a big white Mercedes – and I got
the driver to help me move my bike to some nearby railings where
I chained it securely.

Hellen was taken aback when she saw me. I know I looked ter
rible: white with shock, dirty leathers, stiff and limping badly. She
wanted to take charge and look after me (I seem to have that effect
on women – Becky, for instance) but I wouldn't let her. Instead, I
told her what I was going to do. She didn't like it. But she stopped
trying to dissuade me when I made it clear my decision was made.

I stayed just long enough to borrow some of her clothes and
have another coffee. I didn't say much. I wasn't in a mood for con
versation.

Etts, already stressed from the squat incident, hardly knew how
to cope when I arrived home. I couldn't help her much either. It's
hard to be reassuring about your personal safety when you're scared
out of your wits and you feel like shit. I told her about the chase,
keeping the heavier details back, but she's no fool, she must have
guessed what the score was.

"Cameron, sweetheart, I'm so sorry ..." she said, with tears in her eyes.

"It's not your fault, Etts." I stroked her arm. "We were right about Carrie's death, weren't we? It didn't fit. She was murdered – and now someone, who is frightened of being exposed, is targeting me."

I held her in my arms: stroking her hair, comforting her. I felt emotionally and physically drained, scared of what lay ahead.

Marriette pulled back and looked at me with dread in her eyes.

"Cameron, you will leave tonight, won't you? I just couldn't stand it if they got you as well."

The nightmare was happening all over again. She'd already lost one of her best friends and now she could lose that friend's sister. I hate lying, but in the circumstances, there was no way I could tell her what I was going to do. I knew it would make her ill and I couldn't put her through that. Besides, like Carrie, I realised that, if she knew what I was really going to do, it could compromise me. Carrie was good at her job and she still got killed. I had to be even more careful if I was going to survive.

"It's OK, Etts," I reassured her, "I'm leaving. I've booked the flight already, I got the last seat on the 8 p.m. flight to Leeds/ Bradford.

"Oh, thanks to the Goddess, Cameron." She hugged me with relief.

"Etts," I said with a little concern, "can I ask you a favour? Will you sort my bike out for me?"

She smiled weakly. "Don't worry, lieveling, I'll see to it. There's a local garage I know that will collect it and do the repairs. I'll ring them in the morning."

By the time it got to 5.30, we were both calmer and more relaxed. We sat, waiting quietly for the taxi.

"What will you do when you get home?"

"I've got some friends in Leeds; I'll stay with them for a while.

I don't want to be on my own, so don't try and ring me at home, I won't be there." I looked at her to make sure she understood. "And please, Etts, don't mention any of this to Becky if she rings – I wouldn't want to frighten her. Just say I'm OK and I've gone off on my bike for a few days away. Tell her I'll be in touch. Please don't say anything about me leaving. I'll ring her and you in a few days. All right?"

She nodded, then her hand went up to her mouth. "Oh, I'm sorry, Cameron. You just reminded me: Becky rang this afternoon. She said to tell you that the address you gave her doesn't exist. She said you would know what she meant."

"Yes, I do, don't worry, it's nothing important." So, at least two out of three Eigenschappen directors had given false addresses ...

"Cameron, what about your date with Hellen?"

"I'll ring her from the airport."

The taxi arrived and we hugged again. She was still crying. "You will come back and see me when this has all settled down, won't you?"

"Of course I will."

I smiled my strongest, most confident smile and gave her a long, last hug.

But, inside, I felt guilty as hell. I was walking out of Marriette's house into real danger – just like Carrie had.

It wasn't hard to spot the other car. I knew it would be there and, sure enough, when the taxi drove away from Marriette's, a silver-grey Toyota pulled out from the kerb behind us. They, whoever 'they' were, wanted me to know I was being watched. They were making sure I left. For my part, I made it clear that I had spotted them by constantly looking out of the back window as if scared to death. This wasn't difficult.

The car followed us right to the airport drop-off zone. I got out, slung my holdall on to my shoulder – wincing as it contacted my bruised muscles – and paid the taxi driver.

People from all over the earth were milling around Departures with suitcases, children, ageing parents, lovers, relations, friends ... Schipol is one of the busiest hubs in the world and, though spacious and typically well organised, the area was pandemonium, with huge queues of passengers. I studied the departure screen to locate my check-in desk and was soon threading my way around a long snake of people and luggage, checking in for a flight to Tenerife.

When I stopped to shift the weight of my bag to the other shoulder, I saw them. Two men were following me – and they were making no effort to be subtle. One was big and swarthy with dark hair, deep-set eyes and a moustache, the other was smaller with a shaved head that shone under the airport lights, as if it was freshly polished. They were watching me, but someone else was watching them. I thought at first that it could be a coincidence, but a dark-haired woman in jeans and a sweater averted her eyes as I looked towards her.

I joined the queue at the Air UK check-in, looking over my shoulder several times in their direction, letting them see I was anxious. I answered the usual security questions, and took back my passport with the boarding pass, watching as my holdall made its way along the conveyor with the other baggage. My shoulder bag was staying with me – Carrie's laptop was in it.

I went through the gate to the departure lounge, showing my boarding pass and passport to the officer on duty, and glanced back. The two men were deep in conversation, each glancing my way as they talked. Then Shiner turned and took the down escalator, leaving the Moustache to watch the departure gate, whilst he, presumably, was going to make sure I didn't reappear in Arrivals.

But they were so tied up with me that they hadn't noticed their tail. The Woman was following Shiner down into Arrivals. Now I would have two of them to deal with. Lucky I was prepared.

It was now 6.35 p.m.; boarding was at 7.40. I was beginning to feel better. My ankle felt nearly all right and, though my side still ached from the hitting the Merc, the adrenaline was coming back into my bloodstream, kick-starting me as I put my plan into action. I rang Hellen from a phone in the departure lounge, reassuring her that all was going to schedule. Then I found the nearest toilet and went into one of the cubicles.

I took off my jeans and shirt, pushing them into the flight bag, and started to put on the outfit that Hellen had lent me from her 'plain clothes' selection. Good job I had time to spare, it wasn't easy. I managed to pull on the tights without putting my finger through them but they felt really hot and uncomfortable, clinging to my legs, the waistband digging into my midriff. The pretty shirtwaister was easy to button up but my legs and knees looked weird, encased in nylon and exposed below a hem that felt at least twelve inches too short. The flat shoes weren't anything like as comfortable as my DMs, but at least the beige jacket felt more normal – even if it was short and fitted.

After I flushed the toilet, I came out of the cubicle and, in one revealing moment, caught site of myself in the mirror, walking towards the washbasins. Somehow, I really had to try and move differently, otherwise my total lack of deportment would stand out a mile.

I found Hellen's make-up kit and applied a small quantity of claggy foundation all over my face with a sponge that was already full of the goo. It felt like I was wearing a greasy mask that was blocking off every pore on my face.

I began to wonder whether I could really go through with this, but with Shiner and The Woman waiting for me in the arrival area, I really didn't have much choice.

The mascara felt all right, it was the way I kept poking myself in the eye with the brush that hurt. I put on some grey eyeshadow with a dirty-looking applicator, then some blusher and, finally, I greased my lips with a deep red lipstick that tasted of animal fat. It all felt horrible and I wanted to wash it off and clean up my face again.

I winced at my new image for some minutes, but I had to admit that the person before me did not look at all like Cameron McGill. I stuck out my tongue at the new me, put Hellen's black floppy hat on my head and made for the departure gate, trying to remember to keep my knees together and my shoulders back.

I usually have trouble with officials so I was surprised and secretly triumphant when the airline staff were so kind to me. The woman behind the desk at the departure gate was very concerned and the man became all protective when I wiped a tear from my eye and told them that my Dutch aunt had just had a relapse and that I had to return at once to Amsterdam.

"You will need to return through Arrivals, my dear," he explained, calling another uniformed man who escorted me back, where a very helpful Customs official waved me through.

It took them half an hour to locate and reclaim my luggage and it was a relief when I saw a porter walking across the baggage area with it. So, by 8.15, I was coming through Dutch Customs and into the arrivals area, looking for all the world like a respectable hetero-sexual: my feminine helplessness still intact after all those years. Interesting how power can sometimes exist in the most unlikely guises ...

As I emerged from Arrivals, I looked around for Shiner and The Woman but the huge concourse that links the airport with the rail station was virtually deserted. It was good to be on my own again and out of immediate danger. In fact I felt quite exhilarated now, as I walked across the huge covered concourse, swinging my hips and fielding admiring glances from the few men who were around. Even my ankle seemed better and the bag on my shoulder was quite bear-able. Ah vanity, thou art such folly!

I should have known better. First my mobile rang. Then, as I answered it, I saw him: he was lounging behind a pillar just a few yards to my left, gazing languidly in my direction.

I flicked the phone open, holding it to my left ear, hiding my face as much as I could and trying to stay calm. "Hello?"

"Cameron? It's me, Marriette, aren't you on the plane yet?"

I kept on walking, relieved that it was at least a familiar voice. So far, Shiner hadn't shown any interest in me. I still couldn't see The Woman.

"Marriette! Why are you calling me?"

"Because, darling, you still have my mobile phone."

I breathed a sigh of relief. "Sorry, Etts, I completely forgot – I'll mail it on in a few days, I promise." I thought quickly, I didn't want to get into a conversation with her right now. "The flight's being called, I'll have to go."

"All right darling, take care, have a good trip. Ring me, won't you?"

I glanced round carefully. Shiner was still leaning against the pillar, looking towards Arrivals.

"In a few days, Etts. You take care too. Bye."

I still couldn't see The Woman. Either she had gone, or she was much better than Shiner at staying hidden. Anyway, it was too late to worry now.

Feeling good again, I stopped at the rail counter and bought a ticket for Centraal Station, smiling salaciously at the middle-aged man behind the counter, who shifted uncomfortably and went bright red. Then, posing as elegantly as I could, I descended via the escalator to the platform.

By the time the taxi had dropped me off at Hellen's door, I was becoming accustomed to my temporary image and to the difference it made to the way I was treated. When she opened the door there was a pause.

"Erm, excuse me," I squeaked in my best Marilyn Monroe style, "I'm looking for a Miss van Zalinge."

Hellen's face lit up with gleeful surprise, before she broke into laughter.

"Cameron! Is that really you!" Then she went all serious and husky. "Oh, do come in my dear, I just love straight women. Are you curious, *bi* the way?"

I stuck my tongue out at her and walked up the stairs.

The hot bath water brought out the bruises from all over my body. My right shoulder, where I had hit the car bonnet, was the worst, but they were all over the place. I was going to be sore for a few days. I lay for a while, letting the heat warm and soothe my tired muscles, enjoying feeling clean again, enjoying being free of the make-up.

The door opened slightly. "Dinner will be ready in fifteen minutes, Cameron. Are you all right?" Hellen was being very discreet.

"Yes, I'm fine thanks, I won't be long, just having a soak."

I got out of the bath and patted myself dry with the towel. Now that I had recovered from the shock of the attack, I was feeling much more positive – I was also feeling very hungry. I slipped into Hellen's big white towelling robe and made my way into her lounge.

She was laying the table and came across to me with a big glass of red wine. "Here you are," she said, smiling affectionately, "get some of this inside you, it's the best medicine in the world."

I smiled. She took a step back and studied me.

"Well, you look much better than you did a few hours ago," she declared mischievously, "but I think maybe the make-up suited you."

I made a face at her.

"Anyway, Cam, it's nice to see you've got your colour back. You feel OK?"

"Yeah, I feel good," I said, really meaning it, "there's nothing physical that won't go away within a few days ... I just feel bad about lying to Etts."

She stood there in her red T-shirt and Levis: legs apart, head on one side and arms folded, looking sexy as hell. But I sensed that what she was about to say was serious.

"Cameron, I've already told you that I don't approve of what you are doing. I know you won't listen but I said earlier that you should have gone home and left this with the police. What you are doing is too dangerous." She sounded stern, censorious. She sounded like a cop.

I sat down on the big settee and scowled. I hoped she wasn't going to push it, I wasn't in the mood for a debate.

She sat down next to me, putting her hand on my arm and softening her voice. "But if you have made up your mind to stay at the squat, I think that you're right to keep Marriette out of it. For one thing it's safer for her; for another, if she doesn't know that you are still in Amsterdam, then no one can trick her into giving you away – you said yourself what a gossip she is." She smiled at me again and I felt my insides melt to butter. "Back in a minute."

Now I was ready to eat.

"Dinner is served!" Hellen came back into the room with a flourish and a steaming casserole dish. I picked up my glass of wine and sat down at the table. The meal smelt wonderful.

"Swordfish in a garlic and tomato sauce, OK?"

I nodded appreciatively, helping myself to the fish and accompanying vegetables, whilst she lit the candles and turned down the main lights. I felt so relaxed, pleased that, at last, I knew where I was going. The wine soothed my bruised body making me feel mellow, safe. I smiled at Hellen as she sat down, wanting to let her know how much I appreciated her support but still too embarrassed to say it.

The hi-fi was playing a soft jazz-funk album. The lights were low, the room was cosy and warm. The whole ambience was soft and romantic, almost as if I was being seduced.

***

The meal was delicious, ending with the sort of rich, full-bodied coffee that you only get in the Netherlands. We had already drunk a bottle of wine, now we sat on the floor and started on the port.

"You are a courageous woman, Cameron," she said, with what sounded like admiration in her voice. Then she spoilt it: "Even if you are foolish."

I shook my head and looked away, feeling a small wave of emotion sweep over me. "I loved my sister, Hellen. I simply can't ignore what happened to her, and, since someone is so obviously getting nervous – first threatening Pat and now me – I know I'm on the right track."

"That's the strange thing, you know, Cam. The more I think about it, the harder it is to link the two together."

"But we were both threatened by thugs; we were both told to leave. It must be the same people and it must involve Helga."

"Sure, on the face of it. But let's look at the hard evidence: Pat said that the thugs who beat him up 'had class', didn't wear masks and threatened him only with violence. You said that the two men in the Merc, on the other hand, were dressed in jeans and sweat-shirts, were coarse, wore balaclavas and threatened you with death. Also, your attackers didn't use guns, Pat's did, and the suspects' descriptions are totally different. There are similarities, Cameron, but the M.O. of the two is completely different."

"So, what are you driving at?"

"I think you and Pat have upset two completely different factions."

"What!"

She shook her head. "Between the two of you, you've certainly shaken things up!"

"So where does Helga fit into all this?"

Hellen screwed her face up. "Who knows, she could belong to either … or neither."

She moved closer and took hold of my hand. "Cameron, be very careful. It looks like your sister upset some powerful people. Now you are doing it too. I know you won't go home. But for goodness sake, lay low for a bit. Keep out of trouble."

"Yeah, well I've no intention of getting myself killed, that's for sure." I squeezed her hand and leant back against the settee, sipping my port. "Don't worry, I'll be OK. I know how to look after myself."

Helen smiled ironically. "Yeah, I know, you've told me that before."

I raised my eyes heavenward. "Don't let's get into that again." I took a chance and stroked her arm, looking into her blue eyes. "Let's be friends tonight, huh?"

She laughed with real pleasure and returned my touch, leaving her hand on my arm. "Tell me about your sister. Why was she so special?"

"Ooh, it's a long, long story. I don't usually talk about it." But I looked briefly into her eyes and continued. "Carrie was my mother's first child. They weren't just mother and daughter, they were best friends as well. My father didn't like that: he wanted to control them both but he couldn't break their independent spirit."

"Your mother and father didn't get along?"

"Not in Carrie's memory, anyway. My father was a social climber, a snob. He wanted my mother at home, in her 'proper' place – huh, having his babies. This was the early 60s and it must have been difficult for women to have a separate career, especially when they were married to a reactionary Scottish Presbyterian like my father."

"Cameron, that's awful, my parents were always very supportive of each other's lives. Your mother must have been very strong."

I nodded. "A brilliant cellist too. She wanted to go back to playing professionally when Carrie was a bit older."

"How wonderful! My parents were very ordinary, I would have given anything for a glamorous mother!"

I cleared my throat, feeling awkward. "Yeah, well, she gave up the cello in the end."

Hellen looked disappointed. "But why?"

I hesitated. "Because she got pregnant with me instead."

Hellen squeezed my arm. "Well, I'm sure you were an equally wonderful alternative."

I grunted. I didn't like the way this conversation was going any more. "What about your parents – you said they were ordinary. Does that mean you didn't like them?"

"God, no, Cameron. They were lovely – just not very remarkable by way of achievements, that's all." Hellen sighed. "I guess I was lucky. I never appreciated them, of course, not until it was too late. But they loved me. Funny how you often take the good things for granted."

"Not always," I said, taking hold of her hand.

She moved closer and put her head on my shoulder, then continued. "I was a late child, my mother was nearly 45 when I was born; a surprise addition to my two brothers who were fourteen and eighteen." She giggled, "I got spoilt terribly."

"You still on good terms then?"

She shook her head dispassionately. "No, they're both dead now. My father passed away five years ago, my mother last October. I miss them. Your parents still alive?"

I topped up our glasses. The fire was glowing, the lights low and the sweet sounds of Mathilde Santing were coming from the hi-fi. For once I felt like talking.

"My father died suddenly when I was eighteen; my mother, well …"

I must have looked wounded because Hellen put her hand on my thigh, stroking my leg in sympathy. "You don't have to tell me if it's too painful."

I shook my head. "It's not that; it's just that it always feels like self-pity." I frowned and looked into Hellen's eyes. "Huh, maybe it is."

She took my head in her hands and kissed me lightly on the lips. "It's OK … tell me."

I leant into her, enjoying the comfort of her body next to mine. The only other person I had talked to about this was Becky.

"You said that your mother and Carrie were close. You must have been close to her as well then."

I shook my head sadly. "I was never close to her. She resented me for ruining her career and she lost no opportunity to remind me."

"Cameron, that isn't fair!"

I shrugged. "Fair or not, it's the truth."

We were very close now: lying there against the settee, the warmth from the fire, the soft music and the port all combining to wipe out our inhibitions. I felt like I had known her for ever.

I took a deep breath. "My mother's still alive, but she is severely ill." I turned to look at her. "I mean mentally ill. It started with severe depression when I was very young." I shrugged. "There's no 'care in the community' for my mother. She was well past that by the time I was seventeen."

Hellen snuggled even closer. I could feel her heart beating.

"Sorry. I'm getting maudlin," I said, surprised that I'd been able to talk about it at all. "Anyway, the point I'm making is that Carrie was the most important person in my life. Your parents loved you. Mine never loved me. But Carrie did. She became my substitute mum, my sister and my best friend all rolled into one. It was Carrie who made my childhood a happy one. It was Carrie who played with me, loved me and made me laugh. It was Carrie who was there with words of encouragement when I needed them and Carrie who helped me through all the anger and defiance of my adolescence.

"Her love was unqualified. She never stopped being my friend, even when I was on heroin, even when I was sleeping around and going wild. Carrie just kept on loving me, helping me to find myself, helping me to let the anger go. I owe my life to her. So, you see, I have to repay some of that debt: I can't let her down now."

We talked a lot more, until the early hours, sitting close together on the floor, touching, holding each other close, kissing more and more as the time passed by. We talked about our adolescent protests and our early relationships. She talked about her last girlfriend and the pain when she left her for someone else. We compared love affairs, laughed over our coming-out stories.

As the minutes passed, the talking became less and the touching increased. The mellowness evaporated as our sense of excitement rose. Now we were stretched out on the floor, facing each other. I put my hand out and stroked her face gently, feeling the clean, soft lines of her cheeks. She leant into the caress, expressing her pleasure, squeezing my other hand. Then she leant forward and stroked the back of my head, running her fingers along the nape of my neck, moving under the robe and on to my shoulder, caressing me all the time.

I could feel the buzz between my legs, feel the juices in my cunt as my body responded to her touch. I pulled her head towards me and kissed her full and long on the lips; she returned my passion, kissing my face, then my neck. Our lips met again and then our tongues, each relishing the sweet taste of the other.

She looked wonderful in the warm, subdued light. Her blonde hair tousled, her face flushed with excitement, her lips full and inviting. I unzipped her jeans and pulled them from her legs, revealing her soft brown belly and silky hips, crowned by a mound of pale golden hair.

I felt the robe fall from around my shoulders and gasped with pleasure as her fingers moved across and then under my breasts, pausing at each nipple before continuing down, exploring my stomach, stroking my hips and finally losing themselves in the wetness between my legs.

Twelve

It was still dark. Hellen moved closer to me in her sleep, her warm, naked body pressing against mine. It should have been perfect. I should have felt wonderful. But I was irritated. I turned over to find some space of my own. My head was full of Carrie again. The sound of her voice, the colour of her hair, her love and affection, her friendship. I could feel the tears welling up in my eyes as I buried my head in the pillow and curled up away from Hellen.

I dreamed. Long, muddled dreams of chasing and being chased; men in balaclavas relentlessly pursuing me; I was running, stumbling, unable to lose them. I stopped and ripped off their balaclavas, so I could see their faces. But under each balaclava was another one ... and another. I turned, panicked and fell down a deep black hole, flailing and twisting, trying to grab at the sides, get hold of anything to save myself. Suddenly I was caught; arms secured me, stopped my fall, held me prisoner. I struggled to free myself but they were too strong. I was trapped.

I felt her hands on my skin, her lips on the back of my neck and heard her voice, soothing, calming, telling me it was only a dream. My shoulder hurt again, my ribs were sore and my head was pounding. I turned over and buried myself in her arms, dazed and confused, smarting with fear.

"Shh, just a dream." Hellen's voice was soothing, safe, and I drifted into a troubled half-sleep, intertwining my legs with hers, pressing my body against her soft breasts. I felt a pleasant ache in my cunt as she pressed her thigh against me and I fleetingly remembered the joy of our love-making. But, as I woke again, I started to remember other things.

Hellen opened her eyes and smiled at me in a warm unfocused

sort of way, blinking several times before waking properly.

"Hi, lover." She reached down and kissed me on the lips, before cradling my head back against her breast. "Do you want some coffee?" she muttered, her voice still muzzy from sleep.

"No, I gotta go soon," I said, a little too impatiently, moving away from her.

She sat up, awake now, concerned and uncomprehending. "What's the matter, Cameron? You're all tense."

I got out of bed and started to dress. "Nothing's the matter, I just need to get on, that's all. It's seven o'clock already and I have things to do."

She laughed incredulously. "Cam, it's early! You know that there will be no one about at the squat until around nine and I'm not on duty until then either, so we have loads of time." She looked at me beguilingly and patted the empty space next to her. "Come back to bed, sweetness. For just a little longer."

"I shook my head and pulled on my T-shirt. "No ... no, I can't, Hellen. I'll go and make some coffee. You stay there if you want."

She sighed theatrically as I left the room.

I went through to the kitchen and put a fresh filter into the coffee percolator. My stomach was churning. I felt pissed off. Why the fuck couldn't I just enjoy whatever pleasures came along?

Hellen came into the kitchen wearing her dressing gown and an expression that didn't look very friendly any more.

"What's with you, Cameron?" she demanded. "I do all I can to help you. We have a pleasant evening and a wonderful night together. Then suddenly, this! What in God's name is the matter with you?"

"Nothing's the matter," I muttered. "I just have to get on, that's all. Carrie is dead and I need to find out why."

She threw her hands in the air, clearly angry with me. "Jesus, Cameron, if you could just hear yourself! You keep saying that like it's some kind of mantra. For goodness sake, give yourself a break ... huh, give me a break! ... I feel like I'm competing against your sister."

I turned on her at that. "Well, go right ahead and compete if you want. You certainly won't win!"

She backed off, gasping in disbelief, and leant against the kitchen unit. "Cameron, you have got a real problem!"

I filled the percolator reservoir with water and switched it on. I didn't know what to say. Inside, I was burning up with something. I had to go back to the squat and sort this thing out before those thugs found me again.

Her voice softened a little. "Cameron, I just don't know why you are doing this to yourself. There is no need for you to get so stressed. This is something the police should handle."

"Well, you would say that, wouldn't you?" I replied scornfully. "Look, you've already said that you can't help me, so just let me get on with it, will you?"

"I didn't say that." She took a deep breath, calming herself. "I know what this is about. You're scared, aren't you? Go on … admit it … Well, so am I. I just wish you'd be sensible. This is so dangerous."

"Don't you think I know that?"

"Aaargh!" she exclaimed. "You are so bloody obstinate! Look, finish your coffee and I'll drive you down to the Molen."

"It's OK, I can walk."

She sighed in exasperation. "Cameron, if you are going to do this, for goodness sake get your head together or you will get killed. You are not supposed to be here, so you must keep a low profile. I don't actually want to take you to the squat but I will, because it's the safest way. If they see you, they may not give you a second chance."

"Yeah, OK … thanks."

I poured out the coffee and we both sat down in the lounge. Me sullen and preoccupied; Hellen, I guess, angry and hurt.

Still, the boundaries had been drawn now. I was sorry about screwing up something that could have been fun. But that's the way it was. We left around eight in her beat-up old Skoda. It was cold outside but the atmosphere in the car was even frostier. I stuck the floppy hat on my head again, since it obscured a large part of my face, and slid down low in the passenger seat, whilst she drove the short journey to the Westpoort. Neither of us said a word.

She stopped the car by the main door to the squat and turned off the engine. We looked at each other for a while. She must have felt as uncomfortable as I did, but she didn't show it. Her voice was tight. "Well, here we are ... Take care ... Don't let them get you, Cameron."

"Yeah, I'll be careful, don't worry."

"Look ... I know we haven't got on so well this morning. But ... well, I meant what I said about helping where I can."

"Thanks ... I'm sorry about ... well, y'know."

"Yeah. Well ... it was nice last night."

I nodded and smiled self-consciously. "You've got my mobile number?"

"Sure, I'll ring you if there is anything you should know ... You keep in touch, you hear. I still want to know that you're all right."

"I'll be OK," I said, beginning to bristle again.

She moved towards me as if she expected us to embrace. But I could feel myself getting wound up all over again. I leant forward and gave her a light kiss, then I got out of the car, slinging my holdall over my bruised shoulder, not caring that it hurt.

She turned the car round and stopped again as she drew level with me.

"Cameron, there is more to the death of your sister than a drugs overdose and there are powerful people out there who will stop at nothing to protect themselves. Find out what you can, then hand the information over to Inspector Dankmeijer straight away. Please don't put yourself in any danger."

"Sure," I said, as I remembered for the umpteenth time that Hellen was a cop. "Sure, I'll watch out."

***

Maybe it's a personality fault, but I admit that I felt better just as soon as her car had disappeared through the gate. There's something good about being with someone you like. But, right now, there was something better about being a free agent. I was sick to the teeth of people trying to hold me back. Maybe now I could get on.

I opened the door and went into the squat. It was still very early and there was little sign of life. So I decided it was time to take a look at the basement which had been so carefully refurbished by Eigenschappen after the eviction of the original squat.

When I reached the bottom of the stone stairway, it took me a few seconds of feeling around in the dark before I found the light switch. When I flicked it on, the whole massive area was lit up with clear white light, quite different to the dinginess upstairs. The walls and ceiling were painted white and the floor was covered with light grey ceramic tiles. The whole basement was empty too except for a lot of flat packages stacked at the far end. I couldn't believe that such a large area would have been refurbished just to keep within the squat laws. My footsteps echoed in the sterile space as I walked over to the packages and slit the top one open. The contents looked something like a kitchen worktop, a workbench or something similar. Pel must have had plans for this area, otherwise why were these fittings here? And why would he need a basement like this if the building was being made into luxury apartments?

When I got back upstairs, it was still very quiet. It didn't take me long to find Pat's room. I hammered on his door. "Pat, are you there? I need to talk. It's Cameron."

There was a muffled groan from inside the room. "Huh? ... Oh fuck ... WhadyawantCameron?"

"Let me in Pat, I need to talk to you. I need to talk to you right now."

There was more muffled cursing and moaning and then the key rattled in the lock and Pat's sleep-creased face appeared around the half-opened door.

"Cameron, it's not nine o'clock yet, what the f–"

"I was attacked and threatened last night. I need to talk to you about it."

"Shit, you winding me up, woman?"

I gave him the death stare.

"Huh, damn, you mean it. You better come in."

He opened the door and I walked into the dim and stuffy sleep-filled room. A figure stirred under the covers and then Emma's head appeared, her eyes blinking as she tried to focus on me.

Pat tossed a T-shirt across to her. "Hey Emma, Cameron and I gotta talk. Go make us a coffee, willya?"

She scowled at me and I turned away, as much to avoid her stare as to give her some privacy whilst she dressed. She slammed the door on the way out, muttering something in Dutch that translated as an insult to English women in general, but presumably was intended for Carrie and myself in particular.

Pat smirked. "Sorry about Emma, she's a little sensitive."

I looked at him in amazement. "Well, if you turfed me out of bed so unceremoniously, I think I would be annoyed!"

He grinned. "Hey, you wanna try it?"

"Dream on, buster," I smiled back, "you have no chance. I butter my bread on the other side."

"Yeah, I guessed. Pity. A real waste."

"That depends," I countered, " on your perspective." I looked him up and down from his raggy yellow T-shirt to his bright pink boxer shorts. "You look very fetching."

He winced and pulled on a pair of jeans.

"OK, so you've been threatened. Huh, it sure doesn't seem to have improved your manners. What happened?"

I went across the room and pulled back the curtains to let some clean light into the dinginess. Then I moved a pile of clothes off the only chair and sat down.

"I don't know who they were, Pat – I didn't see any of their faces

– but there were three of them. One on a motorbike, the other two in a black Merc. The guy on the bike screwed up but the other two got me. They both had their faces covered. One of them held me, the other, the smaller one, threatened me. Said that if I didn't leave, he would kill me."

I told him the whole story – from when I left the Juno Bar to my arrival back at Hellen's from the airport. He never said a word until I had finished. Then he drew a deep breath and whistled through his teeth.

"Cam, sweetheart, it sounds like you have upset someone real bad." He shook his head in disbelief. "Holy shit – first me, then you. What the fuck is this? Hey, you want my advice, you should get out, babe – and fast – this is not safe."

I stared hard at him and spoke through my teeth. "Pat, the next person who tells me to go home is going to end up in intensive care." I paused to let the message sink in. "Let me spell it out for you as well. I am not giving up. I am staying right here. I am going to find out exactly what happened to Carrie. And no one, not thugs, not the police, nor my friends are going to make me change my mind."

He held both his arms up. "OK, OK. Jeezus ... you've made your point, babe."

"And don't call me babe!"

He shut his eyes under the force of my barrage. "Sorry ... OK, Cameron – just calm down will you? Jeezus!"

"Anyway, you were threatened and you are still here."

He stood very erect at that. "Yeah, but I'm a –" He noticed the expression on my face and stopped himself.

"So, can I squat here awhile?"

He smiled, relaxing again. "Yeah, sure you can. You can use Carrie's old room if that's OK. No one else seems to want it after what happened to her." He put his arm round my shoulder. "Huh, you know I'll help you all I can, don't you? I can't abide people who threaten my friends."

"Thanks," I said, a little guarded over his offer, but touched nonetheless. "As chauvinists go, you're OK ... Sorry I got mad."

"Hell, you should be!" He shrugged good-humouredly and then studied me more closely. "Woman, you know, you're just as pig-headed as your sister. You'll get yourself killed, man, just like she did."

"Ah-ah." I shook my head. "Not me, Pat. I'm too fucking wild."

"Yeah, you aren't kidding, Cameron. You sure aren't kidding."

I dumped my gear in Carrie's old room and stood by the window, looking out across the water. Traffic was heavy. Huge tankers passed incessantly; small boats struggled across the choppy sea, busily running errands; barges plodded past, heaving their heavy cargoes through the grey water. Occasionally, a police boat would sail officiously past on its way to check some cargo, sort out some complaint – or, perhaps, very occasionally, fish a body out of the water.

I wondered why Carrie had particularly asked for this room. Pat said he had needed to go to some trouble getting it for her, persuading someone to move out first.

Then I saw the Nordmag. Of course, how stupid of me. I could see this building from over there, so the reverse had to be true as well. I stood and watched for perhaps half an hour but, from here, I couldn't see anything strange at all.

In the end I gave up and unpacked my bag, being very careful to hide the laptop behind a beaten-up chest of drawers. I took out Carrie's scrapbook and wondered guiltily how Marriette was feeling, this morning. The scrapbook had upset her, it probably hadn't been a good idea to show it to her. I flicked sadly through the pages of press cuttings and articles. So much good work, so many good stories. She had been a courageous woman.

I was about to put it down, when I reached the page about her kidnapping in Ethiopia. This was the one that had upset Marriette. I remembered again how bitter Carrie had been over her treatment.

There was a picture of her, looking drawn and ill, and another one of her captor, Peter Karst, being led from court by the police. He was a surprisingly small man, stocky, with a pinched, mean face and a mass of dark hair.

I closed the book in disgust, thinking how unfair life could be. Sure, the fraud was stopped, and more food got to the people who needed it, but Carrie was marked for life by her ordeal. They never managed to prove that Karst was involved in her kidnap either, so all he got was ten lousy years in jail for theft. I walked back over to the window. He would be free again now, and my sister was dead.

I was still deep in thought when Pat knocked and came in looking hyper. I couldn't tell whether he was high or just simply glowing with excitement.

"Hey, Cameron, we heard on the grapevine yesterday that the police are coming to evict us in the next two days. You want to come and see what we're doing to defend ourselves?"

"Mmm, I'd like that … Hey, but aren't you scared?"

"Nah. This is what the squat movement is all about. We have to take on the system and beat it, man. We have to show that ordinary people have rights too. Word is there's going to be a big squad of riot cops, horses, water-cannon, the works. We're not going to get thrown out this time. This time, we will be ready.

"Come on – prepare to be impressed."

I followed him out of the room and along the corridor. He spoke over his shoulder to me without slowing.

"You trying to figure out what she used to watch, out of that window?"

"Yeah … Pat, did you know that the warehouse opposite here is owned by Pel's lot as well?"

"No, I didn't, but so what?" He was walking so fast that I could hardly keep up.

"So, what if something going on over there has something to do with what is going on over here?"

He looked blank and stopped. "Hey, my English is good but you've just lost me."

"Look, they got that squat evicted over two years ago on the pretext of rebuilding. All they did was refurbish the basement, just like here. When it was re-squatted, they evicted it really fast. Doesn't that ring any bells?"

"The same pattern as here, exactly."

"Except there is now another squat in the Nordmag."

"Huh, I didn't know that. It's a dump."

"Well, they call themselves a squat – but there's something odd about it. The guy I spoke to was very aggressive and unhelpful. Also, I'm pretty sure that's where the black Merc came from."

He stopped by the main door. "The car that followed you? You think the squat's a front?"

"Could be, Pat. That could be why Carrie was watching it. Like I say, maybe there is some kind of connection with this building? Maybe they are planning something like that here as well."

He turned and pushed open the door. Suddenly we were outside again, blinking in the brightness after the dim light of the corridor.

"Are you saying that your sister's death could have something to do with the Molen as well?"

"All I'm saying is that there could be a connection." I was surprised to find myself shouting over the noise.

It was after ten now and the squat had woken up. Everywhere I looked, people were working urgently: building defences, collecting materials, as if preparing for a long siege. Above me, several hammers kept banging in and out of time with each other. People were shouting, some were singing loudly as they worked, others just yelling things at the tops of their voices. Everywhere I looked, there was frenzied activity and excitement.

Information passes quickly in small communities and, already, most of the squat knew who I was and nodded at me or smiled when I passed. There were about thirty of them living there: roughly equal numbers of men and women, most of them in their twenties, with a few older people. They were a colourful if motley crowd, working in an urgent, good-humoured way.

An older man waved at Pat as we passed and came running over, asking in Dutch how wide he should make the trench across the gate. Pat discussed the logistics of JCBs and water-cannon with him and they made a decision. The man nodded, satisfied, then smiled broadly at me, exposing only half a set of teeth. He raised a finger – "Fuck the pigs!" – then returned to work with his stonecutter, marking out the trench.

Pat grinned and nodded in the man's direction. "That's Max, he's been around the squats for years – always likes a good fight."

I watched Pat as he showed me round. The squat, like many others, was run as a collective, but Emma had been right, he was undoubtedly regarded as some kind of leader.

A handful of people were collecting stones and bricks, anything that could be used as a missile, and taking them into the squat in an old wheelbarrow. A wiry woman around thirty with shoulder-length hennaed hair, wearing leggings and a faded T-shirt that proclaimed, 'Climbers do it roped together', passed by and Pat shouted out to her:

"Hey, Rosa, you got the water rigged up OK?"

"Surely," she said in a Florida drawl. "Come and see for yourselves, guys."

We went outside and she took us along to the end of the building nearest the road. There on the ground was a long length of fire hose – not the normal kind found in offices, this was the real McCoy – about three inches wide and connected to one of the building's fire hydrants. She picked up the heavy metal nozzle, weighing it in her hand and smiling ruefully.

"I've tried it, honey, and I can tell you that it's strong enough to knock a six-footer like you off his feet at ten yards ... Care for me to demonstrate?"

Pat laughed. "Nah, I'll take your word, Rosa." She smiled broadly at him as we moved on. He looked at me and made a face. "See, she likes being called babe." I didn't react. Then he asked: "Hey, you think the same people threatened both of us?"

"Hellen thinks not – what about you?"

"Mmmm, maybe, maybe not. They were not the exact same guys at any rate. Different styles. Yours sound nastier, mine hurt more. Cars were different as well. Shit! But at least I could see who was working me over."

We walked on. There were barricades appearing everywhere. Outside the building, by the gates, Max was shouting above the noise of the stonecutter at a group of women and men who were wielding sledgehammers, pickaxes and shovels. Pat nodded in their direction.

"We're aiming to make it wide and deep – it's the only way we can keep the diggers and the cannon out – or at least hold them up for a while."

Inside, in the entrance lobby, Emma was showing two of the women how to make Molotov cocktails. She briefly acknowledged me but there was scant friendliness in her smile. Pat nodded to her as he passed and she nodded back, flushed with the anticipation of the battle to come.

I don't know if he was winding her up on purpose but I winced inwardly as he made a show of putting his arm around my shoulders as he took me up the wide stone steps to the first floor. Three guys were up there, nailing boards to the window frames. One of them smiled and nodded at Pat, who gave him a thumbs-up sign.

"They're boarding up the windows so that the smoke bombs can't get in ... Little Rudolf over there is a joiner – he's trying to free some of the window casements, so that we can open them to throw rocks and bombs."

Two more women, one about ten years older than me and a younger companion, were carrying old tins of paint up the stairs, stacking them in a corner.

"Hi girls."

"Hi Pat." The older one put her load down and came across, giving my guide a big hug. "How are you doing, love?" Her younger companion went on ahead.

"Well, Martha, I wasn't so good until I saw your beautiful face," he joked.

"Pat, you are incorrigible!" The woman looked at him censoriously but I could tell she was charmed by him all the same. "Hello." She smiled in my direction, then turned back to Pat. "We got all this paint for free from a skip just off Haarlemmerweg." She grinned mischievously, and proffered her cheek. "Didn't we do well!"

Pat chortled, "You sure did sweetheart!" and gave her a kiss. "You'll have some great bombs there. Huh, colourful as well!" He waved goodbye and we started walking back.

"By this time tomorrow, Cameron, we will also have rocks, Molotovs, fireworks and smoke bombs up here so that we can repel the pigs." He took me back to the top of the stairs where another team was piling up furniture and planks. "This is our secondary line of defence. If they get in downstairs, we retreat up here." He grinned, sweeping his arm expansively across the huge floor of the warehouse, then pointing down the wide stairwell. "They'll have a hell of a job getting up those stairs and over the barricade with us throwing all we've got at them!"

We started down again, just as a young blonde-haired woman appeared, carrying a plastic sack over her shoulder and punching the air victoriously. "Hi Pat, goed nieuws!" she yelled. He looked at her enquiringly. She waved the bag at him. "Gas masks, man, forty of the fuckers" – she did a little curtsy and spoke as if reading a formal message – "from the brothers and sisters of the Spui Squat."

He laughed out loud and gave her a big hug. "Goed gedaan, Linde." He congratulated her in his deep, rich voice, sounding genuinely amazed. He turned to me, passing on the good news. "Cool, now even the gas can't get us." They whooped and smacked each other's hands. "Sound ... see you later, sweetheart."

Pat almost bounced as he ran down the stairs, me struggling to keep up again. He took me to a room off the main lobby. "This is our food and water store," he said, opening the door on to a room packed with five-litre drums of water and boxes of canned goods. "We're getting ready for a long siege. I reckon we can probably hold out for a month with this lot. Tomorrow, we disperse it around the building ready for any eventuality."

He turned to me. "Good shit, huh?"

"Yeah, impressive, man. You've got a good team." Damn, I was even talking like him now.

"Yeah and it'll get better. I've been promised a hundred more people tomorrow from other squats. This is going to be one of the greatest fights of the movement – even bigger than the Keyser in '79. After this, the city planners are gonna have to take notice for good, man."

I smiled and nodded, patting him on the back.

He stopped at the door to my new room. "Hey, you think we should attack this other place across the water? Catch them off guard?"

"Mmmm, maybe not at the moment, but thanks for the offer anyway."

"That's OK, don't mention it … babe!" he said, walking away, chuckling loudly.

I liked Pat; I wanted him to be one of the good guys.

I didn't trust anyone at the moment, not even Hellen. She was just a little too keen to get me off the case. If I was an incurable romantic, I could easily convince myself that it was because she was falling in love with me, but I knew better than that. Besides, for all the intimacy of the other night, we hardly knew each other.

On the other hand, she seemed well in with Hugo Dankmeijer.

I hadn't asked Pat about the laptop because I also didn't know whether I could trust him. There might be information in its files that implicated him; then again, he'd just had two months in which to get rid of it, but had handed it over to me instead.

I was the only person in the squat café. It was still only late afternoon, but darkness had fallen and work on the defences had stopped for the day. My shoulder ached from hauling stones up to the first floor of the building. It hadn't been very bright doing heavy work after the episode with the Merc, but I wanted to do my bit for the squat. I was dying for a good soak in the bath but the best I'd been able to manage was a luke-warm shower. Still, I had got to know a few of the women and discovered the squat's resident computer nerd, a dyke from South Yorkshire, who had promised to meet me here. She was late.

The door opened and Claar, the dark-haired woman with the generous mouth – the one who had served us coffee the other evening – came in. She saw me sitting by myself and came over smiling.

"Hi, Cameron, you OK?"

I smiled back, nodding my recognition.

"I'm sorry, Toni says she'll be here as soon as she can." She raised her eyes, looking for divine guidance. "I seem to spend half my life apologising for her being late. She's so easily side-tracked!"

"It's cool," I said, "I'm in no hurry. I'm just pleased that she might be able to help."

"Oh she'll help all right. The harder the problem, the more she likes it. You've heard of golf widows; well, let me tell you, I'm the original computer widow. I could cope if it was another woman but Jeez how the fuck do you compete against a box full of semi-conductors?"

I raised my eyebrows. "Maybe you should take up a hobby too?" I joked.

"You kiddin'? I got no time for anything other than Toni – she is a full-time job, I can tell you. Still," she relented, "she's cute with it. Hey, thanks for your help today. "

"Oh, I didn't do much, but I did enjoy the exercise. It was certainly busy around here, I was really impressed with how everyone worked so hard."

"Yeah, well that's down to Pat. We're a lazy lot really, but he knows how to bully us. I don't know how he manages it – there's no way I would normally dig a six-foot wide trench for anyone, but somehow I find myself doing it for our Patrick."

"You known him long?"

"About two years. We came here around the same time. I was just a kid and scared as hell. He helped me a lot, you know, took me under his wing, so to speak." She paused, suddenly looking reticent. "Sorry about your sister. I didn't know her well. Pat was really close to her, though. Ever since the eviction, he's been really down. I stayed with him in the Spui squat for a while and he never stopped roaming the streets looking for her."

I couldn't help showing some surprise. "But he told me they just had a casual relationship!"

"Yeah, they had. Truth is, though, that Pat really fell for your sister, but she didn't feel the same way. I think she liked him all right, they certainly seemed to hit it off in bed, but nothing else. Huh, he's a real womaniser normally, I've never seen anyone get to him the way she did. She kind of used him, I guess."

Claar coloured up. "Oh, I'm sorry, it's your sister that I'm talking about. I shouldn't have said that."

"It's OK, my sister wasn't perfect," I said, bristling inside. "What exactly do you mean by 'used him'?"

"Oh, y'know ..." She coloured up again. Now she looked like she would like to dig herself a hole and disappear into it.

"It's OK. Go on, tell me."

"Well ... for one thing, she got him to find her the best room in the squat. He even moved poor old Jonny out so she could have it. And ... oh I dunno ... she just did her own thing – though what that was, we never found out. She just didn't seem to fit in, if you know what I mean."

She groaned. "Goddess, I'm sorry, Cameron, I'm such a blabbermouth. I've said too much, I always put my foot in it. I guess we were all just a bit sore 'cos she monopolised him … Sorry."

We sat in silence for a while, a veil of awkwardness between us. I wished she hadn't told me. I didn't want to believe that my sister could be anything but popular. Not Carrie.

Claar spoke again, trying to bridge the gap which had opened up between us. "Pat's really upset, you know, but he's pretending to be all right. That's why he's so manic. He's been like this since he found out she'd been murdered. He's driving us all so damn hard."

"But he seemed OK earlier today."

"Huh, he's just good at hiding it. Look, I know Pat, and I can tell you that he's really cut up inside. He thought she had walked out on him after their row. That was bad enough. Now that he knows she's dead, he feels like he is somehow responsible."

"Well, thanks for being honest with me."

Claar looked towards the door in some relief. "Ahh, here's Toni at long last! Hi sweetie!"

Toni grinned and ambled across the room towards us. She was a slight woman with a craggy face, a shaven head and a multitude of piercings in her eyebrows, lips, nose and ears – and those were only the ones I could see. Her skin was almost white, presumably from the long hours of being closeted away from daylight with her favourite toy.

"Hiya darlin', sorry I'm late!" When she spoke, the flat vowels of her Barnsley accent seemed to fill the big room. She gave Claar a hug and sat down. Hearing her talk made me feel homesick for Yorkshire and for Tibby and Becky. I just hoped that Marriette hadn't told Becky that I was on my way home.

"Guy up corridor had a problem with his AUTOEXEC.BAT," she explained, dropping her aitches. "Wiped the whole friggin' file, can you believe? Anyhow, he's made up now. I reconstituted file for him."

"Really?" I'm easily impressed when it comes to technology.

"Bloody piece of cake, love." She grinned mischievously. "But it don't half impress some people!"

She looked across at Carrie's laptop, rubbing her hands together. "Now, blossom, what exactly can I do for you?"

I started by telling them why I had come to Amsterdam. After what Claar had said about Carrie, I didn't want them to feel that I was using them or being secretive, so I told them my suspicions about a police cover-up – and that missing women and drugs were involved. I told them about Carrie's career – more, I guess, for my own sake than heirs. I wanted to even the scales, make them see she was a good person, someone who had principles and believed in other people. Someone who sometimes, maybe, got a little too caught up in her work and forgot about the social niceties.

Toni took hold of the laptop and pulled it across the table towards her. "So you think she maybe recorded her investigation on here?" she mused.

"I'm certain of it, but I can't get in because I don't know the password."

"Oh wow!" Her eyes lit up. "I just love breaking codes. When does t ask for t'password – in Windows or in DOS?"

"In Windows." It took a supreme effort not to lapse into Barnsleyspeak as well.

"Good, good, good! This should be a piece of piss."

She switched the machine on and waited for it to start booting up. Then she pressed one of the command keys. The start-up procedure stopped and a list of options appeared on-screen. She took a floppy disk out of her jacket pocket and inserted it into the machine. "I'm bypassing start-up and going into DOS files – it's faster this way ..."

Her fingers alternated between the various keys. Banging in options and file names, hitting enter, then doing it all over again, her tongue playing with the silver ring in her lower lip as she concentrated. "Doing it the other way would take days. This way, with just a little luck ..." She stopped momentarily, thinking hard, and then began hitting the keys faster than ever, her skin no longer anaemic – the woman was positively glowing with pleasure.

"Yeahhhh, bingo! 'Sparrow653.'"

"Great!" I laughed with sheer delight. "Aren't you clever?" Carrie once had a cat called Sparrow. The numbers were the month and year of her birth.

She blushed but, just the same, I could tell that she was pleased with herself.

"Heck, it's no big deal, Cameron, you just need to know how, that's all," she laughed as she removed the floppy, holding it up significantly, "and have right software. Now let's get back into Windows and see what's in there." She pressed a few more keys then 'enter' and the Windows screen appeared with the password request. She keyed it in.

"We're in! Where to now?"

"Try Works. I think she used the WP package for her notes."

She clicked on the icon as my stomach did a series of somersaults. It did several more in quick succession when the list of recently used files appeared.

Right at the top was a file called AMSTERDAM.

We all looked at each other. "Open it up," I said.

Toni clicked on the name and a page scrolled down. But it wasn't what we expected. Carrie's notes had been replaced by a terse message:

> CAMERON, THERE ARE NO LONGER ANY FILES ON HERE OF
> INTEREST TO YOU. IF YOU HAVE GOT THIS FAR, THEN IT
> WOULD SEEM THAT YOU ARE ALL TOO SERIOUS ABOUT
> INVESTIGATING YOUR SISTER'S DEATH. STOP AT ONCE
> – OR YOU WILL BE KILLED TOO.

Toni whistled under her breath. Claar touched my arm.

I might have known this was too good to be true. "Toni, is it possible to find out when the file was deleted?"

She looked at Claar, surprised by my lack of reaction to the warning. "Yeah ... I can, as long as trail is still intact ... I'll just get back into

DOS … yeah, here we are." She tapped again, moving effortlessly through the files in the computer, then stopped, a satisfied expression on her face. "Here it is, here's babbie … It says the file was deleted at 5.18 a.m. on 11th November."

Claar looked startled. "That's the day before yesterday! The day Pat got beaten up!"

"Yeah," I replied. "So, whoever told Pat to get out is warning me off as well."

"More than that," gasped Toni. "They copied the file first. Whoever they are, they know everything that your sister knew."

Thirteen

Just after ten on a damp, cold Tuesday evening. I could think of nicer places to spend the night than crouching under the dripping timbers of the Nordmag jetty: my bed, for one, or even better, I suppose, Hellen's bed. I shifted my position to ease the cramp that was spreading through my left calf, working my foot to get the blood flowing again. Pat was roaming around between the slime-covered timbers, looking for the best (and hopefully the most comfortable) vantage point.

Earlier in the evening, he had become very subdued, his relentless drive gone. I guessed he was coming down from the excitement of the day and was left with his own thoughts and no displacement activity. I gave up trying to make conversation and went out through the big doors in the café on to the balcony overlooking the water.

The outline of the Nordmag was just visible on the far bank, perhaps a quarter of a mile away. It was very peaceful out there as the occasional brightly lit tanker slid past in the black sea. But the warehouse itself, and the area round it, looked dark and desolate.

I thought about Carrie and the window in her room. Had she been watching the Nordmag or something on the water? It seemed inconceivable that anything bad was going on – it all looked so normal, so pleasant. The movement of the water, the lights on the sea traffic, the car lights ... coming and going ... on the opposite bank ..

I suddenly realised that what I was watching didn't actually make any sense, so I went back inside to find Pat. He was rolling up a new 25 guilder note ready for his first snort of the evening. I let him finish before I went over – if he offered me some, I might be tempted.

"Pat, has anyone got a pair of binoculars?"

He breathed in deeply, pleased with himself. "Sure babe, mmm, think that Lili has a pair. No, you stay there, I'll go get them for you, my dear."

I raised my eyebrows – things really do go better with coke – and grabbed my leather jerkin which was hanging on a chair. It was cold out there on the balcony. The pattern of the lights by the Nordmag continued sporadically. After about fifteen minutes, Pat returned and handed me the glasses. "What you looking at in the dark, woman?"

I didn't reply but I put my eyes to the binoculars and focused them on the far shore, watching intently for some minutes. When I was sure, I passed the glasses back to him.

"Look over there, Pat. The piece of land next to the Nordmag. Tell me if you see anything strange. Take your time."

He looked for a while and put the glasses down, puzzled. "There's nothing to see, woman, except a car driving away."

"Yeah, and if you keep watching, you'll eventually see another car arriving. Doesn't that strike you as odd?"

"Should it?"

I snatched the glasses back. "Look, that area is derelict, Pat. There are no bars, no housing and no through roads. Yet cars keep coming and going all the time."

"Mmm, you want to take a closer look?"

"You mean, like, more powerful binoculars? Or were you thinking of a very close look?"

He grinned broadly. His eyes shone with excitement. "Go put on lots of warm clothes, Cameron, and then I'll show you Betsy."

"Betsy? Sounds like something out of a John Wayne film!"

He guffawed. "Yeah, I'll meet you back here in five."

When I returned, Pat was waiting for me with two sets of dirty grey oilskins. "Here, put these on or you'll get soaked."

I struggled into the clammy oversized trousers and jacket, turning up the trouser bottoms and the sleeves so that they didn't get in the way. If I had a beard, I could have starred in an advert for Fisherman's Friend. Pat looked equally ridiculous so we sneaked out quietly and walked across the railway line to the edge of the small dock.

"So, come on Pat, what's Betsy? A rowing boat? A motor boat? A cruiser?"

"Naah, better than all those." He located a ladder and climbed over the edge. I followed him and we descended into a small black rubber dinghy.

"Oh," I said, not making any effort to hide my disappointment, "you sure this is seaworthy?" I shone my torch over it, dubious about both the size and the condition of the craft. "It seems to have a lot of patches."

"Cameron, stop worrying, it's fine: we use it most days to go into the city. It takes ages by road but with Betsy we can be in the centre within minutes."

"OK," I said, not entirely convinced, "I'll take your word for it."

I sat on the slatted wooden floor whilst Pat set himself on the small seat next to the outboard. He turned on the fuel line and then pulled the starter cord three times until the motor stuttered lamely into life. After revving the engine for a few minutes, we picked our way through the debris floating in the abandoned dock and hit the choppy, open water, skimming, none too smoothly, across the surface of Het Ij. The waves buffeted the light craft, making the outboard scream every time it lifted clear of the water; the sea spray cascaded over our heads, stinging our faces and running off our oilskins. My stomach lurched in perfect rhythm with the boat.

Ten minutes later, he cut the motor and we rowed the last two hundred yards, coming quietly under the ageing timbers, mooring the dinghy out of sight beneath them.

So now here I was, sitting under a rotting jetty, feeling cold, sick and wet; cramp shooting up my left leg, and Pat acting like he was having real fun.

"Hey, Cameron!" he hissed, signalling to me from about ten feet away. I eased myself up, relieved to change my position, and picked my way across the timbers.

"I guess this is the best place. We can see the door into Nordmag and we also have a good view of the area."

"Great, I'm also pleased to see that there is somewhere to sit."

"Woman, you are always grumbling!"

I made a face at him as we positioned ourselves just under the edge of the jetty on a cross-member that was about two feet above the water. We were well hidden from above and far enough out along the jetty to have a clear view of the building and surrounding area.

It was a dark, cloudy evening. The car lights to our right seemed to have stopped as we arrived, but it wasn't long before we heard the crunch of feet on the cinder track above us and saw a man emerge from the door where I had tried to gain entry to the squat. He walked quickly, back on to the side streets, as if he was in a hurry to get away. After a while, we heard an engine start and saw the lights as a car drove off.

A few minutes later, more lights as another car drew up and parked. I supported myself with one hand whilst I focused the binoculars with the other. A man appeared from the street. Smartly dressed in a dark overcoat, he walked through the gates towards the warehouse, nervously glancing around. He didn't look like a squatter.

He reached the door and knocked. The panel in the top of the door slid open and, after a short exchange, he was let in. Over the next hour, there were a number of comings and goings. They were all men, all reasonably well dressed. Though some were casual, they all looked like they had money and none of them looked like the sort of people who would frequent a squat, even a squat café. They were too middle-aged, too straight, too tense.

By the end of an hour, the men who had first entered were leaving.

I looked at Pat through the gloom. "Some kind of illegal brothel, I guess," he said, anticipating my question. "The legal joints have to stick to rules. Illicit ones offer specialities."

We both turned our heads as we heard an outboard motor, and

retreated clumsily along the wet timbers into the darkness, the sea splashing below our feet.

The dinghy came almost alongside us – only feet away from our hiding place – with two men in it. The smaller one cut the engine, laughing at some comment that had been made, whilst the larger of the two tied the craft to one of the wooden pillars. Then, picking up a package from the dinghy, the first man started to climb the ladder up to the jetty.

The bigger man shouted after him: "Wacht! Ik moet pissen." He urinated over the side of the dinghy, directing the piss out in a long arc. Pat drew back in disgust when it landed only a few inches in front of him, and I stifled a laugh.

"Schiet eens op, klootzak!" The man on the ladder, unimpressed with his companion's full bladder, was shouting, "Hurry up, you asshole!"

After much banter, they climbed the steps and ambled across to the warehouse door. I climbed up after them and peered over the top. The package, which looked like a plastic container about twelve inches square and deep, seemed valuable. For all their fooling, the first man was holding it protectively to him. We waited until they were let into the building.

Pat looked at me. "Drugs? That could be their speciality."

"That's it then," I said, satisfied. "We can hand this over to the police now."

He blenched. "Are you joking, Cameron? The cops will never believe either of us."

"What?"

"Look, however sure we are that this is some kind of racket, and however sure we are that it somehow involved Carrie, we can't prove anything. We need to see more, we need to get in there if we can."

"Oh come on, Pat, it's pretty clear already what's going on. A police raid would do the rest."

He looked at me like I was simple. "Yeah, and who's going to persuade the cops to go in? Cameron McGill, the well-known trouble maker, or Patrick Breckelman, the coke-sniffing squatter? Come on, sweetheart, get real!"

"I know someone who can persuade them."

"Yeah? Who?"

"You know her. She's a cop, her name's Hellen."

He looked at me, stunned. "Hellen! That Hellen. A cop! Fuck!"

"Come on," I said firmly, "it's time-to-go time."

"Hallo" – Hellen's voice was sleepy and slightly irritated – "wie is dat?"

It was just after midnight. I knew she would be asleep but, frankly, I didn't care. After all, it was her who had been so insistent about handing this over to the police. Well, I wanted to do that now and I needed her help. The phone seemed the least hazardous way of making contact.

"It's me – Cameron."

"Cameron! Are you all right? What's happening?"

"It's OK, Hellen, I'm fine. I just need your help. We've found out something important."

"Who's we?"

"Me and Pat. We went out in the dinghy tonight and watched the Nordmag warehouse across the water from the squat. It's what Carrie was interested in, Hellen. We think it's an illegal brothel."

I told her about the evening in detail. "I'm sure that Dankmeijer won't listen to me, but do you think you could get him to raid the place?"

"I'm sorry, but he'll need grounds. All you have are suspicions. The court wouldn't grant a search warrant just because a number of men were going into a building. They could be playing cards, eating at a squat café – anything."

"Oh, come on, it's obvious. Do we have to go back there and take photographs?"

"It's not obvious, Cameron. Hugo will need hard evidence before he can do a bust. And no – don't you dare go back there yourself!" She paused. "Look, just let me think a moment, will you? I'm still half asleep."

Whilst she thought, I paced impatiently up and down my room. Pat was sitting on the chair in the corner, looking disconsolate again. He didn't like the fact that Hellen was a cop at all. He was even less enthusiastic about me ringing her and asking for help. I looked across at him and thought how moody and changeable he was. He caught me looking and turned away.

"Cameron, you'll have to leave it with me. There's just a chance that I may be able to persuade Hugo to mount a surveillance operation. But you will have to promise me that you will leave it for now. No more playing detectives, OK?"

"Yeah, OK," I replied, disheartened again. "Everyone keeps telling me to leave it with the police; then when I try, you say there's not enough evidence."

"You'll just have to trust me, OK?"

I frowned. "Yeah, OK … If you say so."

"You promise to stay out of it and let me do this my way?"

"Yes, OK Hellen, I promise. Keep in touch will you?"

"Of course. Bye Cameron."

I put the phone down, dejected.

Pat looked across at me. "What's wrong?"

"The police will need more evidence before they can raid the place, but Hellen thinks that they may be persuaded to carry out some surveillance."

"Aggh," he cried. "Surveillance? How the fuck can that help? Let's face it, Cameron, they're stalling. And that includes your attractive girlfriend. They all think that if they sit around on their arses, everything will go away." He wiped his mouth with the back of his hand and walked towards the window. "Well it won't, sweetheart, because I'm not going to sit around and let those bastards at the whorehouse get away with killing her."

He stopped suddenly and turned round. "It must be a crack-house."

"What must?"

"The Nordmag. Listen" – he was suddenly very intense – "whilst you were on the phone, I was thinking about Carrie. She didn't tell me much, but she did say something about women disappearing off the streets; women crack addicts. It fits. The Nordmag has got to be an American-style crackhouse. You know how it works?" he demanded.

"Crack for everyone – the women and the customers?"

"More than that. Crackhouse business stinks. One: crack gives a massive sexual high. Two: it's extremely addictive. Three: taken with high testosterone levels, men turn abusive. So for the crackhouse pimps, it serves a triple purpose: it procures and keeps the women under their control and it brings the customers back for more and more."

"So the women are trapped?"

"Yeah! They are really trapped. Shit, I know you think I'm sexist, but I like women and I don't like to see them being abused." His voice was loaded with anger and disgust. "More than that, I don't like to think of Carrie being abused."

"You think that's where they took her after the squat battle?"

"Yeah, it figures. You say that Pel's company owns both build-ings, so why not? They could easily have taken her there in all that confusion."

"And you think that's what she was investigating. The crack-house?"

"Cameron," he stared at me intently, "crack is bad news – six times stronger than cocaine. Anyone who takes it in excess goes downhill: weight loss, acute insomnia, nausea, lung disease and, often, paranoid psychosis." He looked mean. "It is not a nice drug, Cameron. Believe me, I know."

"How? You taken it?"

"Me? Hell no! No ... it's a long story, someone I was fond of a few years ago." He turned away, letting his feelings settle. "Your sister must have known, but those bastards got to her before she could expose them."

"We can't be absolutely sure of that, Pat."

He looked at me defiantly. "Well, I'm sure."

"OK," I reflected, "if you're right and the police watch the building, it will all become apparent."

He shook his head vigorously and shouted: "Jeezus, Cameron! They're not going to see any more than we did!"

I looked across the water to the hazy outline of Nordmag on the far shore. "OK, so what do we do?" I was trying to be patient. Patrick's anger was not constructive.

"You don't do anything, woman. You promised your friend – the cop – remember?"

I turned round, stung. "Does that mean you are planning something?"

"Me? Maybe ... maybe not." He was edgy and very angry.

"Pat, please, promise me that you won't do anything rash."

"Look, Cameron. I've been beaten up, and you've been threatened. There's a bunch of women over there being exploited, probably killed off slowly one by one and being replaced by others, picked up off the streets to fill their places. The police don't give a shit. And your sister – my friend – has been murdered because she cared enough to try and stop it."

He ran his fingers through his hair then, more calmly, continued. "I've had enough of these jokers. I can't sit back any more. Somebody has to stop them. Besides, you say Pel is involved with Nordmag as well, so it may somehow be linked to our problems here."

For once, I wanted to keep the lid on this. If it was a crackhouse, then it was not something we could handle on our own. "Pat, please give it a day or two," I appealed. "Give Hellen a chance to sort it first. Apart from actually going into Nordmag, there is nothing we can do."

He looked as grim as hell. I suddenly felt cold, pulling my jacket around my shoulders.

"Please, Pat."

"Yeah, OK, I hear you."

We sat in a sombre silence for a few minutes. God, I was tired. For the first time that evening, I let my mind go into limbo. Earlier, I had intended to confront Pat about the message on the laptop, but now, I was glad I hadn't. Now I knew that I could trust him. My mind drifted back to his description of the attack. He really must have been threatened badly that morning. His attackers knew that Carrie had been there at the Molen. They had taken Pat outside – away from his room, so they could search her things. It was them who wiped the file and replaced it with a warning to me. So, if Hellen was right, I had now been warned off by two separate factions.

I turned to Pat, suddenly very awake again. I wanted to ask him what he thought, I wanted to talk about that early morning. I wanted to know everything I could about those men and about how long he was away from his room.

"Well, I'm hitting the sack, Cameron. I'm beat and we gotta finish the defences tomorrow." He got up and hugged me. His eyes were tired and glazed again, his manner downcast. He had retreated back into his shell. My questions would have to wait.

After he had gone, the room felt very empty. He'd helped me a lot and I liked the guy. I would talk to him about the laptop in the morning.

I sat up for some time, dissatisfied and uneasy, watching the lights near the Nordmag out of Carrie's window. Like Pat, I wanted to move things forward, without depending on the police. But I wasn't so certain that Carrie's death had just been about a brothel over the water. I was still confused. Every time I found out something new, it just got added to the growing pile of information, building up like a bonfire that never ignited. Missing women addicts, police evasion, eviction notices, threats, a crackhouse. I was going round in circles and the circles were getting bigger all the time.

It was one o'clock by the time I crawled into my sleeping bag. I was tired but I couldn't get my brain to stop turning. Half an hour later I got up again, dressed and wandered along to the café to make myself a drink. It was pitch black, but I managed to find the bar lights and locate the kettle. I sat on one of the stools, propping myself up against the bar, trying to relax.

The room was warm, the wood-burning stove in the corner still pushing out heat, and our waterproofs had dried out. I took the first jacket and trousers off the backs of two chairs and folded them. But when I tried to find the second set, they were nowhere to be seen.

I felt my stomach turn and tried to tell myself that Pat must have taken them back to his room. But that didn't explain why he had left the other pair. Deep down, I knew the real reason. Pat was using them again.

He was out on the water with Betsy.

I left my drink on the bar and ran down the corridor to his room, hammering frantically on the door. There was no sound inside. I turned the handle and the door swung open. The bed had not been slept in.

I didn't know whether to wait until he came back or find a car and go after him. I wanted to make sure he was safe, but if he was at Nordmag, my unexpected presence could put him in great danger, especially if, as I suspected, he was posing as a customer. What could I do there anyway?

I went back to the bar feeling helpless. Damn the man! Why had he gone on his own? Why couldn't he just leave it for one night? I slumped forward, resting my head on my arms whilst I figured out what the hell to do. My brain felt overloaded with insoluble problems, shrouded in a muzziness that became thicker and thicker until I fell asleep.

I must have lain like that for some time, because when I awoke, the stove had burned itself out and I was shivering. What woke me was a noise ringing in my ears, an electronic alarm.

I tried to focus on the noise rather than my discomfort. I sat up, wrapping my arms around me for warmth, confused. My mind was holding all the pieces of the jigsaw, but somehow I couldn't put them together. The noise got louder and clearer as I came to and I realised, with a start, that it was the mobile in my pocket.

I pulled it out immediately and pressed the call answer button. The line crackled and I came fully awake.

I could almost feel his hot, excited breath. His voice was a hoarse uneven whisper, as if he was talking as he walked, anxious not to be overheard.

"Cam ... thank God. Listen ... being followed. We were right. It's a big, big crackhouse. But more ..."

"Pat, get out of there, get away, tell me later!"

"No, they're on to me, Cam ... gotta tell you now, sweetheart ... this is important, get the cops, the crackhouse is –"

I heard a screech of tyres in the background and then there was a clatter as his mobile hit the ground.

I yelled into the phone: "Pat!" But there was silence. Then somewhere far off, a car door slammed and there were footsteps.

Someone picked up the phone and the line went dead.

Fourteen

I stared at my mobile. The moment had the quality of a bad dream. My first instinct was to get over there and help him. But it was a fifteen-minute road journey, even at this time of night.

I needed to alert the others. My stomach sank. I feared the worst, but it wasn't fair for me to go without breaking the news.

I knocked on Claar and Toni's door first. Claar answered. I didn't know what to say, how to tell her that the man she so admired was probably dead. In the end I just said that he'd been attacked and that I didn't know if he had survived. Claar went straight to Emma's room and within minutes the four of us were driving in Toni's car through the road tunnel to the area round the Nordmag.

We didn't have any trouble finding him. We could see the flashing blue lights from streets away. A wet wind was blowing off Het Ij as we got out of the car and walked across the cobbles to the police tapes; behind us, only a few hundred yards away, the Nordmag warehouse.

An ambulance and three police cars were parked in a half-circle. One of the bigger cars had an extendable spotlight which shone bright white light on to the road as if it was a stage. Screens had been erected but I could still see into the enclosed area when people came and went. Pat's body was laid on the road face-up, one leg twisted behind, the rest of him limp and lifeless. His mouth hung open and his eyes were staring into the dark night sky. Someone was taking photographs whilst other cops were combing the road for any evidence.

We stood behind the police tapes with a small crowd of reporters and ambulance followers, watching in disbelief. I felt sick inside. I was angry with him for being so bloody stupid. I was angry with myself for getting him involved. This was my battle and I should have been fighting it alone.

On the way, I had told the others about our recce earlier in the night and how unsettled Pat had been on our return. Claar, Toni and Emma said very little, but it was clear that they resented his involvement with me and my sister. I didn't say much more to them, it was pointless.

Emma was stood next to me, white with shock and, superficially, very subdued. But I could tell from her eyes that the pressure was building up inside.

I put my hand out to her and touched her arm. "I'm sorry, Emma."

She stared at me for an instant, her face a blank. Then she ducked under the tape and ran across to Pat's body. A woman cop ran out and restrained her. She fought wildly and another cop – a guy this time – came across to help. Eventually, they got her away from the body and put her in a car whilst they talked to her.

I looked around me. I caught Claar staring at me, but she turned away quickly when I looked. Emma had lost her lover and the squat had lost its leader. I wondered if I would still be welcome at the Molen now. I was an outsider who had taken their hospitality and caused them grief.

The police had finished and an officer and an ambulance woman were preparing a body bag. I'd seen enough. I walked away, seeking solace in the dark, empty streets away from the brightly lit scene of crime.

The Nordmag was in darkness: just another derelict warehouse amongst so many others. I walked through the gates and down the steps to the waterline, no longer caring much about whether I was seen or not. Betsy was still there, under the jetty, tied in the same place as before. The missing oilskins, cold and wet, were bundled on the floor, still waiting for the return of their owner. I untied her, started the engine, and headed back to the Molen.

I got back wet and cold. We hadn't woken any of the others before we'd left, and I certainly didn't feel like doing it now, so I put the oilskins over a chair in my room and went straight to bed.

I wanted to cry but somehow the tears wouldn't come. I wanted to sleep but that was impossible too. It was a relief when daylight finally came – and with it the police.

Hellen glared at me. "Cameron, do you realise how hard it was for me to get on this detail? The very least you can do is talk to me."

At any other time, I might even have been turned on by Hellen in her dark blue, police regulation blouson and trousers, her Walther P5 in the holster on her hips, her blonde curls falling out from beneath her peaked hat.

But not this morning. This morning I was angry. And I was upset. Pat was dead and now she was giving me a hard time. I looked out of the café window at the big dirty warehouse. I didn't need this. Certainly not from her.

Her colleague had done the decent thing and disappeared for a few minutes and, in the circumstances, I expected a little kindness, but the Career Cop was showing through again and all I was getting was hassle.

I grunted contemptuously.

"Cameron, this is absolute madness. It's not a game!" Her voice had risen an octave or two. "This is real life, woman. It was irresponsible of you both to go back there last night. You promised me! You could have been killed as well!"

I couldn't take any more. "Don't you come over all righteous with me, officer. I told you what was happening and asked for your help but all I got were bland assurances!"

With some effort, I lowered my voice. "As a matter of fact, I didn't go there with him last night. I promised you, remember? In fact, I didn't know that he was going back there myself until it was too late. I would have stopped him if I could."

I could feel the tears welling up inside me, but I was damned if was going to let her see them. I glared at her and she looked back, fire in her eyes. The stand-off seemed to go on for ever.

In the end, Hellen gave in and slumped into a chair.

"I'm sorry. You must be very upset, and all I'm doing is lecturing you." She looked down awkwardly. "It's just that ... well, I am fond of you and it worries me that you are so involved in something so dangerous ..." She leant across and took hold of my hand. "Can't you see now that you are up against people who are ruthless, who don't give a shit about human life? Do you really think that Cameron McGill and her one-woman army is any match for them?"

"Please, don't start going on again." My eyes were misting up again. I steeled myself. "I do know what they are like. They have killed Carrie and now Pat ... and, in a different way, the women they entice off the street."

"You don't know that."

"I know enough. It's almost certain they are keeping women imprisoned in there, dealing in illegal prostitution, and drug-running. Any one of those is grounds for a police raid."

"Yes, well ... you'll probably get that now. After Pat's death, I don't think even Dankmeijer could resist such a move."

"Resist? Why should he want to do that?"

She sighed wearily. "I don't know, and even if I did, I couldn't tell you. I just wish this whole affair would go away." She looked at her watch. "I must go – I'm not even supposed to be here."

"Hellen! What is it? There's something you're not telling me." She looked decidedly fed up, touching my arm and speaking softly: "Just leave it, Cam, eh? Leave it, please. I don't know."

She stood up, pulling me to my feet so we were facing each other. She pulled me close and I slid my arms around her back, confused. We stayed like that for a few moments and then we kissed. She hugged me again.

"I'm sorry if I was a little aggressive. I just want you to be ... well, you know. I don't have to keep saying it."

"Hellen, believe me, I want to get to the end of this as well. If Dankmeijer raids that building and arrests the men behind it, then, as far as I am concerned, that will be the end of the matter. Then we can relax."

"Together?"

I nodded. "Yeah, sure."

She looked relieved and we kissed again, longer and deeper this time. It was just what I needed.

After a few minutes, Hellen pulled away. "I've really got to go. Anyway," she said, squeezing the tip of my nose, "snogging in uniform isn't allowed."

"OK," I said, running my hand down her back and across her bottom, suddenly wanting the comfort of her body, "no one is insisting you keep your uniform on. Let's go to my room."

She laughed. "I don't think so, somehow! Hugo will be here any minute and I don't think he'd be too pleased."

"Oh shit, no! Do I have to talk to him?"

She put her head on one side. "You think you have an option?"

I grunted. "I guess he won't be in such a good mood, huh?"

She smiled ruefully. "If I were you, Cameron, I would be very careful what you say. You might be able to get round me all right, but I don't think you'll manage it as easily with him."

Hellen bumped into Emma as she left the café. It's Sod's Law that you meet the very people that you don't want to meet at the very time that you don't want to meet them. Emma recognised Hellen's face and stopped in her tracks, her eyes running up and down the blue uniform. Hellen looked straight back at her.

"Jig bent en smears!" (You're a cop!) She gave Hellen a long, nasty look, spat at the floor and walked through the room, ignoring me.

I went over to the bar and made myself a good strong coffee. There was an air of deep shock hanging over the squat. A sort of numbness. The reality of Pat's death hadn't sunk in yet, the grieving and the sorrow was yet to begin. Right now though, it didn't seem possible that such a big man could be wiped out so suddenly or so easily. I just hoped that the police would wrap the whole thing up soon, so that I could go home and forget about it.

I knew, without looking, when Dankmeijer came through the door. The feeling of hostility was tangible; I swear that I felt the air move as it vibrated across the room towards me. I braced myself and turned round to face him.

The Inspector indicated a table in the corner, away from the few other people who were in there.

"Good morning, Miss McGill. As you would expect, there are certain formalities to conduct over the death of Mr Breckelman. I will need a full statement from you, covering everything you have done since I saw you at the police station last week."

His tone was even and official, but his eyes betrayed the anger inside. I didn't argue, I just gave him the statement he wanted about Nordmag, in detail. But I didn't tell him anything about Helga, the message on the laptop, or about Eigenschappen and Pel. I still didn't trust the man. I still didn't know why he was holding back on the death of my sister. When I finished, I waited for some comment, perhaps some acknowledgement that Carrie's death was suspicious after all. But he said nothing, simply folding up his papers, preparing to leave.

"I presume you will be staying here for a few more days, Miss McGill?"

"Yeah, I'll be here a while yet."

"Don't leave without informing us. I shall need you to come to the police station to make a formal statement and ultimately to make yourself available as a witness in the event of an arrest."

"So you are treating Pat's death as murder?"

"Yes, that is correct."

"What about my sister, do you accept now that she was murdered too – probably by the same people?"

He looked guarded. "Miss McGill, I am not going to discuss your sister's case. My advice to you is to stop getting involved in investigations that are best left to professionals. You have not only been endangering your own life, but your recklessness has now resulted in someone else's death. Please stop interfering" – he looked at me sternly – "or I may have to take some action to restrain you."

"Inspector," I said evenly, "I am very happy to assist you with your enquiries, but I haven't done anything wrong or broken any laws, so do expect to be treated with your normal standards of courtesy."

"I think it is a matter of opinion as to whether you have broken any laws, young lady," he said coldly. "I am very close to charging you with interfering in a police enquiry. If I have any more trouble, then can assure you that I will."

I waited until he had gathered up all his papers.

"Are you going to raid the Nordmag now, Inspector?"

He looked at me warily. "I can't say, Miss McGill."

I took that as a yes.

Most of the anti-eviction activities had stopped. Small groups of people sat around talking, sometimes hushed, sometimes angry. Slowly, people started to drift in from other squats around the city – Pat's promised army of supporters, now come to learn of his death. So far, only Emma had appeared hostile to me, the others seemed indifferent. But then, I had made no effort to mix that morning. I wasn't in the mood to share my feelings with anyone. It had been hard enough talking to Hellen.

Whatever Dankmeijer had said, I didn't exactly blame myself for Pat's death. But it was inescapably true that I had been the catalyst for it. If I hadn't got involved in this thing, he would still be alive. I had wanted Hellen to tell me that it wasn't my fault. But she hadn't – no one had.

The air of hopelessness around the squat was making me edgy. I needed to get out. I borrowed a large black overcoat and stuck the big hat on my head again as a makeshift disguise. Claar said it was OK if I took her bike, but she didn't want to talk.

I pedalled along the shore road towards Centraal Station, my insides churning. I had lost my sister, and now I had lost someone who had tried to be a friend, too.

Well, maybe this would be the end of it. The crackhouse at the Nordmag would be raided and the killers would be caught. More important still, Carrie's wishes would be realised and the loathsome activities of the illegal brothel would end and the perpetrators be punished. Goddess, I hoped so, I really hoped so.

By now I was cycling through the centre. I reckoned that I was safest among the crowds and, in any case, my need was for anonymity rather than solitude. I got off the bike near Dam Square and chained it at a parking spot.

I was feeling thirsty and stressed. What I wanted now was a strong coffee and a spliff. So I was making my way purposefully across the big square, towards the Kadinsky Coffee shop on Rosmarijnsteeg, when I noticed a BMW pull in to the kerb and a familiar figure get out of the passenger side. She walked around the car and talked earnestly to the driver. I walked faster to try and get a better view of him, but he drove off before I got anywhere near.

The woman left, moving across the square, weaving through the crowds of tourists and shoppers. My need for stimulation became irrelevant as I focused on my quarry. Keeping the hat well over my face, I moved nearer – close enough to follow her and find out where she was going.

She picked her way across Dam Square, avoiding the pigeons, making her way irritably around the knots of tourists with their bird food and cameras. I was sure it was her, but she looked different. A little less formal, more relaxed in her movements ... but unmistakably the woman I knew as Helga Wassenheim. The woman who had supposedly left for Hanover two days ago and, I now realised, the woman who, with a wig and dark glasses, had been watching both me and my tail at the airport.

I followed her out of the square, past the Royal Palace and along Raadhuisstraat, crossing the Herengracht and then turning left by the canal. She walked quickly with a sense of purpose. A woman who knew exactly where she was going and what she was doing. After a few hundred yards, she turned right by the side of a small branch canal. About halfway along, she paused, taking keys from her handbag and letting herself into a smart canalside townhouse. It was no business office and no client's house. She acted like she lived there.

I waited until she had gone in and then followed her to the door. My curiosity was pushing me to press the buzzer and find out why she was still in the city, at this house. My Common Sense told me to stay well clear – this woman was trouble, and I had promised Hellen that I would back off until after the raid.

I pressed the intercom. Almost immediately a sharp, rather impatient voice answered. "Yes? Who is it?"

The accent was American.

I hesitated, thrown by the change of nationality. "It's Cameron McGill, Helga. I met you at Marriette's Guest House last week – I'd like a word with you please."

There was a long pause.

"Ohh ... Yeah ... Yeah, of course. Do come up."

The door buzzed and I entered a small hallway and climbed the steep stairs. At the top was a spacious passage and three doors. I made for the open one.

Helga's lounge was large and stylish, sumptuously furnished with fine antiques, Persian rugs and original oils. The deep burgundy and navy curtains were dressed with swags and tails and the whole room was lit by a giant glass chandelier, high up in the centre of the ceiling. I whistled softly under my breath. Not my style at all, but elegant and impressive nevertheless. And very, very expensive. If this really was

Helga's house, then she was some rich bitch!

"Hi Cameron, what a nice surprise!"

I turned to see Helga entering the room behind me, smiling, putting on her sociable hostess act. Her German accent had been replaced by a mid-American drawl and there was an unmistakable edginess about her. I appeared to have caught her unawares.

"You wanna coffee or something stronger?" She opened a vintage drinks cabinet, revealing a vast array of bottles. I asked for a Campari and tonic and wasn't surprised when she produced a bottle of the deep red spirit. My favourite drink is not to most people's taste, but then Helga seemed to have something of everything in there.

I sat in one of the antique armchairs, probably a Louis the something-or-other; anyway it wasn't from Ikea, that's for sure. She sat opposite me on a fancy chaise-longue. I took my time before I said anything. She was obviously waiting for me to speak first.

There were three things I wanted to know. "I thought you lived in Hanover, Helga? I thought you were here just on business?" I smiled sarcastically. "I thought you were German?"

She smiled confidently, lapsing back into what now seemed like a stage accent. "Ach, I'm so sorry, liebchen. Sometimes, in business, one has to tell little white lies." She laughed lightly, pleased with herself, and sipped her drink.

I glared at her.

"Aw, come on, sweetheart, don't be sore, there's a simple explanation. I told you I was in business, didn't I? Well, one of my companies is publishing a new guide to hotels in the Netherlands. We have a team of researchers working on it right now but, well ... I thought it would be fun for me to check out one of the women's places myself."

She pouted. "My work is so boring sometimes. It was a little adventure, some fun. I didn't mean any harm."

It sounded convincing. "So, did Marriette pass?"

"Oh sure, of course, she'll get the highest grade in her category."

"Oh, that's good. She will be pleased," I said sarcastically. "I could just about buy that if you hadn't got Pat turned over."

She looked blank. "I beg your pardon?"

I sighed wearily. "Helga – or whatever your name is – you know very well what I'm talking about. The same morning that you got me Pat's address – the morning that you got up early because you couldn't sleep – Pat was threatened and Carrie's computer files were copied and replaced with a warning to me."

She looked like she had no idea what I was talking about.

"Then a woman speaking with an American accent rang the squat to say that someone answering my description would be arriving shortly and was a spy."

She waved her hand dismissively, laughing at the incredibility of it all. "Ah! You can't seriously think that was me, my dear! For goodness sake, I'm just an entrepreneur – why on earth would I be involved in things like that? Coincidence. It happens." She paused for an instant, then looked at me quizzically.

"Yes?"

She waved her hand dismissively. "Well it's probably ridiculous, but Marriette was keen to stop you – you sure she's not implicated? She knew about everything too."

"You're right," I said, without hesitation, "it is ridiculous!"

"Well, she must have gossiped, I guess." She shrugged and then, unfazed, her eyes lit up. "Say, why don't you come round to dinner one evening whilst you're here Cameron? It would be nice to have a chance to, er … relax a little with you." She arched her eyebrows, throwing me a mischievous look. "Maybe you like American women more than German ones."

I think I blushed.

She laughed at my self-consciousness and I decided this was becoming just too embarrassing to endure. I had satisfied my curiosity and I didn't want to push my luck. Another little tête-à-tête with Helga – German or American – was more than I could stomach at the moment.

"May I give you a ring to arrange something? Where are you staying?"

"Well, actually, I'm on my way home," I lied, "so I'm really sorry, but I won't be able to take up your kind invitation."

"Well, that's a real pity, maybe some other time."

For some reason, she looked quite pleased.

Wednesday night and the squat café was crowded. I had taken up residence at the bar early on and I was already on my fourth Campari. Tonight, more than most nights, I needed the reassurance that only alcohol could give. Now, all the chairs and tables were occupied with perhaps another thirty people sitting and lounging on the floor. I had expected the place to be closed because of Pat's murder and, in a sense, it was – because the drinkers were activists rather than ordinary people. This was no routine evening at the Molen squat.

During the afternoon, whilst I was away, the mood had changed dramatically. The numbness and shock had given way to anger. It seemed that Pat could galvanise people into action even in death. More and more of his friends from other squats had drifted in and, slowly, the hopelessness that pervaded the Molen had been replaced by a sense of outrage. Word had got around that Pat had been killed by the owners in an attempt to break the spirit of the squat. Everyone was ready to believe this – it suited the circumstances, it suited the politics, and in truth, it suited me too.

Maybe there was a stronger connection than I had first supposed – I knew that the people who had killed him did want the Molen emptied and, maybe, they had seen Pat as their greatest obstacle? If Pel was involved in drugs and prostitution, then he wouldn't worry about killing a few people to protect himself. I knew that his ownership of both the Nordmag and the Molen must be significant too. I just couldn't work out why.

People were leaning over me, ordering drinks from the bar. I looked up as an older guy dripped beer on my shoulder. He apologised but I was beginning to feel claustrophobic. It was impossible to find any privacy. I had returned to find that I was sharing my small room with three other women. It seemed to be the same all over the squat. Extra food and water was being stashed all over in preparation for a long hard siege. Work on the defences had begun again, and now there was a sense of grim expectancy. Lookouts had been posted on a twenty-four hour rota – the riot police were expected at any time. Everyone was fired up for a long hard fight.

Someone banged loudly on a table and the babble of voices trailed away. Emma stood on a chair and waited for absolute silence. She spoke in Dutch but it wasn't hard to get the gist of her message – even for a failed linguist like me.

Up to now, I had regarded Emma as a mere ideologue and a follower. But maybe circumstances do maketh the woman, because tonight she was transformed. Her language was the same, but the manner of her delivery was impassioned and intoxicating.

"Brothers, sisters, this is the hour of our destiny ... Pat Breckelman, a fellow activist, a good man who gave his life for the movement ... killed by the established order because he was a threat ... We've had enough of exploitation, of greed, corruption and rules ... The people must take control again ... reclaim our space, our homes, our city from the forces of big business and the conservative establishment ... The Molen's fight is everyone's fight ... representatives of the greater good ... of decency and honesty ... fighting for the rights of ordinary people everywhere against the forces of centralised business and government."

She seemed to know, instinctively, how to work the crowd: her voice rising and falling with passion and commitment; her eyes constantly scanning the sea of faces, looking at each of them in turn; the way she paused, using silence to underline her points; the way she enunciated every word. As she spoke, there were shouts of agreement and support, clapping and cheering.

"Brothers, sisters, we welcome you to our squat. We are proud that you wish to fight alongside us. We are proud to be part of the great squat movement. We are proud to have been chosen by circumstances to represent all the squats of Amsterdam in this historic battle." She paused, looking around the room. "You are all – all of you – part of what will be a very special victory, a victory which our children and our children's children will talk about and celebrate. A victory which will be hard fought and difficult to achieve." She paused again, building up to her passionate ending. "But, brothers and sisters, a victory which will be ours, fought for side by side with the strength and passion of true comradeship."

She sat down to tumultuous applause, whistles and shouts. Then others, Emma's lieutenants from the other squats, all men, began to speak, organising everyone into squads, apportioning jobs and weapons, setting rotas and training sessions. Preparing for war.

Maybe it's the cynic in me, or perhaps I just don't like the thought of being organised, but I really couldn't take any more. I slid quietly out of the door and went back to my room, which for now at any rate, was thankfully empty of guests.

I'd been waiting all evening for the raid on Nordmag. I knew it would be after dark and I looked out regularly across the water from the café for evidence of the bust.

Now, when I looked again, I could see blue lights flashing from the cars around the building and from the two police boats on the water. The Inspector had gone in big.

I sighed in relief; it looked like it was all over. Carrie's death would be vindicated and the record set straight. The crackhouse would be closed and the women given decent hospital treatment. I hoped that the customers would get their come-uppance too.

I should have felt a sense of great relief; I should have felt exhilarated. But, for some reason, I felt flat and strangely uneasy. I pressed my forehead against the glass, enjoying the coldness against my skin, allowing myself to be mesmerised by the strobe-like blue lights.

Even if the crackhouse was all wrapped up, there were still questions that needed answering. I still didn't know what it was that Hans had refused to tell me at the drug agency, and I still couldn't work out what the police were trying to hide. And where did the Molen fit into all this?

God knows how long I spent running all the information through my brain again, but when I looked up, the Nordmag was in darkness once more. I closed the thin sheet that acted as a curtain and laid down on the bed. Maybe if I wasn't a Virgo, detail wouldn't be so important.

I was almost asleep when the mobile rang.

"Hi Cameron." It was Hellen, sounding tired and drawn. "Just thought you should know, Nordmag was clean. All they found was a small squat in an empty warehouse. Nothing else."

Fifteen

I was sick with disappointment and Hellen didn't sound too good either. She didn't actually spell it out, but the way she spoke and the tone of her voice made reading between the lines child's play: I was doing OK before you came along – good job, promotion imminent. Now I get a steaming for compromising my professional integrity, I'm close to losing my promotion ... and, on top of all that, I have you to worry about.

I didn't try and argue. I liked Hellen and, for all her misgivings, I believed that she liked me too. But she wasn't the reason that I was here and I needed to remember that. There were enough complications in my life at the moment and I could do without this particular one; it was beginning to hurt just a little too much.

This was the second night in a row that I hadn't been able to sleep. The other women in the room were asleep on makeshift beds on the floor. I had to pick my way between them to get to the window. How could the Nordmag be clean? Had Pat been mistaken? I didn't think so.

I put the binoculars to my eyes yet again, scanning the sea and the far shore, wishing I could penetrate the walls of that building, see what was going on inside. The stream of customers had stopped – scared away, I supposed, by the raid. But, as I watched, I saw the little boat and the two roughnecks arrive again. I couldn't be certain but, from the way he walked, it looked like one of them was carrying something – just like the previous night.

Me, well I was certain that the building contained a crackhouse. The lack of visitors now was hard evidence that the punters had been scared off. Secondly, people don't usually kill without due cause. Thirdly, it seemed likely that the two men in the boat were delivering the drugs, the crack, to the Nordmag. Fourthly, Pat had been there and he'd said it was.

I was sure that he must have got into the building. That he had discovered where the brothel was located, and had tried to tell me. "Gotta tell you … this is important … the crackhouse is …" It had to be there – there was no way they could have moved everyone and everything out before the raid.

I remembered that Hellen had said something the previous morning, inferring that the police, or Dankmeijer at any rate, were reluctant to raid the building. Maybe they didn't look in the right place? Huh, maybe they hadn't wanted to find anything?

I thought back, yet again, to Carrie's last letter. "It's an issue that affects women … is being ignored (hushed up?) by the authorities." Whatever it was that Pat saw, it had been enough to make him into a threat and, just like Carrie, that meant he had to be killed.

I was sick as hell of all this. The rows with Hellen, the barracking from Dankmeijer, the threats from the thugs and the killings. More than anything, though, I was heartily sick of pussyfooting around and getting nowhere. I'd been here six days, raking over Carrie's last few weeks in this city. The whole thing was a mess and it was beginning to make me very angry. Either I had to make some bold moves and sort it out or … well, I wasn't going to stop now.

I resolved that things were going to be different from now on. And damn Hellen! If she didn't like what I was doing, then she could go to hell.

Hans Knaapen was looking out of the window when I burst into the room.

"Cameron, you made me jump!" I didn't reply.

He shifted his feet. "I hope you have had a worthwhile few days since I last saw you."

"Like hell I have!" I wanted him to know how angry I was.

"Hans, since I last saw you, I have been threatened with my life. One of Carrie's friends has been killed. The police are being evasive. And, in the Northern Docks, a crackhouse is flourishing with impunity."

The drug agency administrator swallowed hard. "I thought you were going to leave things to the police."

"No, *you said* I should leave things to the police."

I moved a pile of papers and sat on the edge of the table. "I'm up to my eyes in this, Hans – just like my sister was. I can't – I won't – back off now. I have to find out what is going on and stop it. It's the least I can do." I waved my hand in a dismissive gesture and dropped my voice, "And, if I get killed, like Carrie did, then that is too bad."

He looked crestfallen, I thought for a moment that he was going to cry. He'd shaved since I last saw him, but he still looked tired in his denim shirt and old blue jeans. "You held something back before, Hans. Something you told Carrie, but not me. I need to know everything. It could make all the difference to my chances."

He closed his eyes.

"Ohhh, Cameron … Cameron!" He sighed and pulled out a chair, sitting down opposite me. "OK … Whatever I say, it looks like you've made your mind up to see this through."

I waited impatiently.

"I think I was telling you that there was evidence that some young women – users – were disappearing from the streets. What I told your sister – but not you – was that their disappearance is, I think, involving a very addictive new drug. So far, only users are getting access to it and, even then, never on a take-away basis. We have not managed to get hold of any – nor, I think, have the police."

"When did this start?"

He slumped into a nearby chair and rubbed the back of his neck. "Not long ago. I think the first indication was in the spring when one of my field workers was starting to report stories of some women being enticed away. But the stories were from third parties;

we have never managed to talk to anyone who is taking it. It is strange, almost as if someone is conducting field trials.

"I do not know much more, except that there are some powerful people involved and that a similar thing is happening in other cities of Europe. Naturally all the agencies are worried about the potential mayhem that a very addictive new drug could create, but, so far, the police, and Interpol, have been very uncommunicative. They seem to be playing their cards very close to their chests, but I am sure they are worrying too. I would guess that they don't know where the new drug is coming from either."

"You said 'powerful people', Hans. Just what do you mean by that?"

He rested his face on his arm and looked up at me, sighing with resignation. "Look, I only hear what I hear, OK? But the word from the field is that organised crime is involved. That is why it is so dangerous, Cameron. That is why I was telling you to stay out of it."

"Yeah, I understand, Hans. But do you think they, whoever 'they' are, could have killed my sister with this new drug?"

"Sure, why not? She was investigating the stories and from what you said about the police report, there seems to be some indication that she was given an exotic drug of some kind."

"Yeah, well they are certainly being evasive as to what it was."

"I'm not surprised. Everyone – the city council, the police, the agencies – are playing this one down for all they're worth. If it gets out – if the media gets hold of it – then there will be red faces everywhere. Questions will be asked and the authorities won't have a single answer."

"So, neither the people who are peddling the new drug, nor the authorities, would have wanted a journalist like Carrie to complete her investigation."

"You kidding? She must have been scaring them all stupid!"

***

Back at the Molen, everyone's energy was focused on the imminent battle. Most of the defence work completed, the emphasis had shifted to the political – the struggle to be seen and heard by the world outside the squat.

I carried Claar's bike across the narrow, springy plank that bridged the defensive trench at the gate, picking my way around the various barricades. It was a clear sunny day and the place was packed. Around two hundred people were sitting and standing in small groups: some chatting, others debating heatedly; some playing cards; others just laid back, smoking weed and enjoying the late autumn sunshine.

Colourful hand-painted banners were everywhere: hung from the railings, festooned across the walls and draped on the barricades proclaiming: 'Vrijheid' (Freedom), 'Wij zijn vrij' (We are free), 'Gekraakt!' (We've squatted!). Flags were draped high up on walls and from makeshift poles. Big and white, painted with the squatters' symbol – an extended hand holding a crowbar and a hammer, a powerful image with its mixed undertones of both communist revolution and anarchy. Bright red and blue bunting was stretched across the roadway between the small dock and the buildings.

The whole place seethed with the heady atmosphere of revolution. But until someone from outside the squat turned nasty, it was going to stay a determinedly good-natured, if angry, protest.

More signs and banners were leaning against the building, ready to be taken up and waved for the assembled media whenever there was an opportunity. A black squatter with dreadlocks sat near the door with a double turntable and a transmitter, broadcasting news and music on 'Radio Vrij Molen'. Over by the dockside, Emma and others were holding a press conference with a small group of reporters, and following me into the squat was a film crew.

I spotted Claar and Toni. "Thanks for the loan of your bike," I said, handing Claar the key. She nodded and took it. I smiled back tentatively, still worried about my reception.

Toni, the one from Barnsley, was more forthcoming. She gave me a big friendly smile and hugged me. "You all right, blossom? I hope you're being careful – these people you're messin' with aren't playing games, love."

For a moment I was overwhelmed by Toni's kindness.

Claar noticed and touched my arm. "I'm sorry if I was not very nice with you earlier, Cameron." She put her head on one side and reassured me. "It's OK, you know. Nobody blames you."

"Thanks," I replied, "but if I hadn't been here, Pat wouldn't have gone out last night."

"Hey, come on, Cameron." Toni pitched in. "You might have started it off, but we all know what an 'othead Pat was. Uh, once he got an idea in his head, there was no shifting it. Anyhow, it's happened, and no amount of soul-searching by any of us will bring him back." Toni's flat vowels had a comforting quality. "Everyone's been talking about it this morning and we all reckon t'best way of remembering Pat is to carry on wi't fight. It's sort of like a big wake here now. We're doing this for him."

"He would have liked that," I said sadly. "How's Emma taking it?"

Claar grunted. "Huh, she's got the skin of an elephant. I thought she was really shaken up when we saw his body, but she seems to have got over it. Call me a cynic, but I think she always wanted to be in charge, that's why she stuck so close to Pat. I hate it! I hate the thought of her stepping into his shoes. Still, there are other activists here too, people who know what they are doing. They've all turned out to support us because they know what an important symbol this squat is."

"And they've come here 'cos of Pat," Toni looked proud. "Most of these lot met him some time or another and they want to pay their respects to his memory by showing solidarity."

I nodded. I wasn't surprised by the reaction, he'd been a nice guy. "Anyway, are you both ready for the fight?"

"Oh, yeah, everything's cool," Toni responded. "This is what you call t'lull before storm. We're making as much noise as we can – the more we get noticed, the harder it is for them to get us out. The public's with us, Cameron." She raised a clenched fist.

Claar started pointing to different people. "See him, the guy with the grey hair in a ponytail, and those two women, over there, they've been fighting in squats for nearly twenty years. They were among the very first activists, right in the early 70s ... Those guys over there" – she pointed to a small group of more mature men and women – "They took part in the legendary Coronation Day Squats in 1980. Can you believe it, I never thought I'd ever –" Her voice trailed off as she looked over my shoulder. "Huh, huh. Watch out Cameron, here comes Emma!"

Emma hadn't changed too much – she still didn't worry about social niceties.

"Cameron, I need to have a word with you about your duties. If you stay here, you must fight with the rest of us."

I took her arm, steering her away from the two women. "Emma, I need to talk to you. I wanted to say how sorry I am about Pat. It wasn't my fault, you know, he went without telling me."

She stared at me coldly. "Huh, first your sister and then you. If you had both stayed away from him, he would still be alive."

"Yes, I know. All I can say is sorry. He chose to get involved, I didn't ask him to."

"And to make matters even worse, you brought a pig into the squat."

That made me furious. "Emma, Hellen is a friend – and the only reason she came here in the first place is because you locked me up. If she'd really been acting like a 'pig' she'd have charged you with kidnapping."

She drew breath, stung by my remarks.

"Look Emma, I know you are upset, and that's understandable, but I liked Pat too and I feel really bad about all this. Can't we be friends, please?"

"You should report to Jan Smithers as soon as you can, you will be working on his detail."

I resigned myself to her hostility. "Yes, of course, I'll do all I can to help. I owe Pat that ... but, in the meantime, I need to ask you a favour. I need to borrow the dinghy tonight. Is that OK?"

I steeled myself for a refusal, but instead she looked at me warily. "I suppose so. Why exactly do you want it?"

"Oh, just a little trip over to the other side," I said, as off-hand-edly as I could. "There are things I need to check out."

"To do with the brothel?" She raised her eyebrows. "You don't give up easily, do you, Cameron?" I saw her eyebrows raise a fraction and she shifted her feet. "Well, just take care, that's all. We don't want anything to happen to you as well."

Recovering her composure, she gave me a detailed rundown of the defence plans and my own small part in them. I was to be positioned on the first floor with the stoning and bombing crews in the secondary line of defence. Her manner was precise, impersonal. A commander approaching a crucial battle. A woman covering up her feelings, just like her lover, Pat, had done with Carrie. There was a certain irony about it all. Not for the first time, I wondered how many leaders were driven by heartache in one form or another.

"You miss him badly, don't you, Emma?"

She looked at me for a moment too long. "We expect the attack at any moment, day or night, so please be ready to go to your post at any time."

I watched her as she walked away. I didn't feel any warmth towards the woman, but I admired her guts – and she wasn't as cold as she pretended.

As she disappeared into the crowd, I looked around for the woman with the hennaed hair, the one with Pat's fire hose. I eventually located her over by the gate.

"Hey, Rosa!" I shouted across a sea of heads. She smiled, broke off her conversation and started pushing through the crush to meet me.

"Hi, how you doin' girl? Nasty business. You OK? You taking care?" She looked concerned.

"Yeah, I'm OK. And you?" We talked a while about Pat. Like everyone else, she was putting on a brave face. Rising to the occasion, as she put it. Thing is, it would have been a damn sight easier with the man still around.

Eventually the time seemed right to ask. "Rosa, you were wearing a T-shirt the other day that said something about climbing." I looked again at her strong limbs and wiry body. "Do I take it that you're a climber?"

She shook her head, regretfully. "Was. 'Bout five years ago, before I came to Amsterdam – not many mountains round here, honey. Ohh, I use the climbing wall near Centraal, but apart from that, I only use my skills when the movement needs them."

I looked at her quizzically.

"Breaking and entering," she whispered. "I specialise in breaking into new squats."

I was pleased. "Yeah, that's what I heard."

"No, no, Cameron! Look just hold it there, honey. Start again. The object is to get the grappling iron to move in ever-increasing circles. That's right. Hold the rope nearest the iron with your right hand and move your arm like you were on the end of a skipping rope, so the iron describes a small circle. Great! Now feed more rope through and slowly increase the iron's circle. OK, that's it. You got it. Now remember. You let go just as the iron is coming to the top of its circle. Yeah! That's it, hon! You got it!"

It hadn't taken me long to persuade Rosa to teach me about breaking and entering, though she had big reservations about my intentions.

"Look, Rosa," I pleaded, "I need to get into Nordmag and I need to do it without being seen."

She whistled through her teeth. "Shit, Cameron, you crazy or what?"

"Maybe." I looked intently at her. "But Pat was murdered because of what he found there. The police have drawn a blank so it's going to stay that way unless someone else does something. Anyway," I lowered my eyes, "he went in there because of me. I need to know what he died for."

She deliberated a moment. "You want I should help?"

I shook my head. "Thanks, but this is personal and, after Pat, I don't want to put anyone else in danger. I just need you to show me how to do it. Right?"

She frowned. "OK, but look, if you're gonna do this then you sure as hell can't afford any mistakes. When do you plan to go?"

"Tonight."

"Tonight!" She shrieked. "You're joking, woman!"

I shook my head. "No, Rosa, it has to be tonight. Business has been hit by the raid, and, for once, it is quiet at the Nordmag. I won't get such a good chance again."

"OK!" She smiled wryly. "Then, we better get to it, sweetheart!"

Now we were by the side of the Molen. Her with her instructor's hat on, me with a lightweight grappling iron in my hand. We were aiming for the gantry, way above us. A feature of all Dutch buildings, this beam or small girder sticks out from the top floor so that furniture and other goods can be pulleyed up and pushed through a window into the relevant room. The gantries on the Molen and the Nordmag were industrial size and situated above the line of loading doors which ran vertically, one above the other, right up the building.

It took me about ten attempts before I hit it for the first time, and, to begin with, the bruises on my shoulder made my action a little stiff. But, within a half-hour, the blood had worked its way through the muscle and I was remarkably supple. What's more, I was getting the grappling hook on to the gantry nearly every time.

"Great!" Rosa was impressed. "OK, you can do it. Just remember, keep your rope loose and follow through. And when you get in, find out what you must, then get the hell out – OK?" She gave me a hug. "Good luck, huh?"

I nodded and smiled at her.

As I walked away she shouted after me. "Oh, and Cameron …"

"Yeah?"

"Bring the fuckin' iron back, will ya?"

By the time Rosa and I had finished, it was well past dark. I wished that I had more time. It wasn't just getting into the building that bothered me. I didn't have a floorplan, I didn't know the layout, or the exact location of the 'squat' in the building. I was going in completely blind. On the plus side, I knew it would be quiet. I also knew from my observations of car lights from Carrie's window that business didn't really start until around ten o'clock. If I was careful and just a little lucky, I would have plenty of time to get the rope over the gantry and shin up to one of the loading doors. Once inside … well, I would just have to be very careful, that's all.

I went to my, now communal, room and ate a makeshift meal of tinned pasta and bread: I needed the carbohydrates for the work ahead. I put on a thermal vest and several layers of warm clothing, making sure that my outer layer was dark coloured – not difficult for someone who habitually dresses in black. Then I picked up the bundle of oilskins that Emma had left on my bed and made my way out into the night.

Betsy was still moored in the small dock area on the landward side of the squat. I climbed down the ladder into her and sat down on the wooden floor to unpack the oilskins – I certainly couldn't afford a soaking tonight, it was too cold. I unfolded the jacket and slipped into it. Then, as I attempted to get into the trousers, a package, hard and metallic, fell out of them. When I undid the string and tore open the plastic bag, there was a small handgun and, even more surprisingly, a note from Emma.

"You may need this – it is loaded, remember to remove the safety catch. Take great care, sister."

I don't much like guns but, right now, it was reassuring to have it with me. I said a silent thank you to the strange woman and stuck it in my jerkin pocket, zipping it closed. Then, as soon as I had got into the trousers, I pulled the boat's starter cord good and hard. To my surprise, the outboard sprang to life immediately, belching out a cloud of petrol fumes as the engine caught. I edged the craft forward along the side of the railway embankment until I reached the dock mouth and accelerated, pushing out into the cold wind and the choppy sea of Het Ij.

I could see the street lights to one side of the Nordmag, so it was easy to see where I was going, but I knew that I needed to keep my eyes open for the big cargo boats, the barges and the tankers that navigated this channel day and night. I wound my way across in fits and starts, speeding up to cross in front of a tanker and then slowing, almost stopping to let a container ship pass in front of me in the other direction, staying as clear of their wakes as I could. All the time, my fragile craft was being buffeted by the wind and bounced around by the sea, the outboard howling as it left the water at the edge of each successive wave, my stomach churning from both the movement and my own fear.

About two-thirds of the way across, I noticed movement by the Nordmag jetty. It was quite dark but through my binoculars I could just make out two figures getting into a small boat. I cut back my motor, maintaining just enough power to keep the bow facing forward, and watched as it sped across the sea to my left, towards the opposite shore, somewhere about a half-mile to the north-west of the Molen.

The wind was blowing away from Nordmag, so I didn't need to cut the engine until I was close to the shore. I rowed the last few yards, slowly and with difficulty, fighting against the wind, until I reached the lea of the building, where the water was calmer. I slid under Nordmag's jetty and tied the dinghy out of sight. So far, so good.

I took off my ungainly waterproofs and stashed them in the bottom of the boat. My shoulder had stiffened up a little from the practice earlier, so I spent a few minutes exercising it until the muscle had warmed up again. Then I lifted the grappling iron and gathered up the 25-metre length of lightweight rope. Looping this over my shoulder, I made my way under the jetty to the ladder and climbed until I had a clear view of the building and its environs.

Clear, not a soul in sight. I pulled myself up on to the jetty and ran along the side of the Nordmag until I was at the opposite end to the well-used 'squat' entrance. The loading doors were above me now: three of them, one on each floor with the big wooden gantry coming out of the building at the top, some seventy feet above. I stood back some way along the wall so as to get a good trajectory.

The other night I had watched this building for a long time and I had only seen light coming out of the doors on the ground floor. It seemed reasonable to suppose that the other floors, like the Molen, were empty. But, to be on the safe side, I was going for the top floor first – the one least likely to be occupied.

Around me, everything was thankfully quiet and, just like the other night, very dark. I listened for a moment for the sound of a car. Nothing. Just the wind eddying gently around the building. I laid the carefully coiled rope on the ground, holding some of it loosely in my left hand, transferred the grappling iron to my right hand, and began to swing it in a circle, anti-clockwise.

I tried to concentrate, but my stomach was churning and my heart beating so loud that it was making my head ache. I had to get this right first time. I had to focus properly. I stopped the swing and let my hands drop to my sides. I breathed deeply, like an athlete, concentrating on relaxing, focusing on the task ahead, closing my mind to everything else. Visualising what I was going to achieve.

I began to swing the iron again, letting the rope extend until the circle was about a five-foot diameter, turning it faster and faster all the time, concentrating my eyes on the gantry above me, willing the iron to seek its target. When I let go, the metal soared into the air above me and across the gantry, stopping suddenly as I held on to the end of the rope, and then resting, dangling from the beam.

I sighed with relief and carefully pulled back on the rope. The grappling hook rose nearer and nearer to the beam. As it got closer, I pulled more slowly – it was critical that the sharp hooks made contact firmly so that the rope would hold my weight. Inch by inch, the hooks approached the beam. I closed my eyes. If the rope came loose now, then the iron would come tumbling down. It didn't. The line became taut and, as I pulled, I could feel that the hooks were securely fixed under the gantry.

I was about to start climbing when I heard a car. It was dark but I couldn't take any chances, so I left the rope dangling and hid around the side of the building. A man knocked on the door at the far end and I heard voices as the panel opened in the top of the door. A few seconds later, he went in and I returned to my rope.

Before this afternoon, I hadn't climbed a rope since school. It's easy, provided you have strong arms and legs … and it's … well … pleasurable too – but maybe not in these particular circumstances.

I got hold of the rope above my head and wrapped my legs around the lower part, pulling myself up with my arms and then gripping the rope tightly with my thighs and legs, pushing myself further up the rope. It was starting to rain and sharp drops of water began to sting my face as I climbed. I smiled to myself as I recalled the school rule which said that only boys were allowed to climb the ropes. I had discovered why when I was about thirteen and finally sneaked a go myself – why should boys have all the fun?

When I got to the first floor, I rested on the narrow ledge of the loading doors for a while, listening for any sign of occupation. There was none. If my calculations were right, all the activity would be on the ground floor at the other end of the building. When I climbed up to the next – and top – storey, it appeared just as deserted, but the doors were still quite solid. I didn't know if I could force them, but I had to try – it was the only practical way to get in and out without being seen.

I tied the rope securely around my waist so that I could hang there and work, my feet supported on the ledge. There was one gap in the door at the top, where some rot had set in. I took the small jemmy off my belt and jammed it through the hole, levering as hard as I could to ease some of the planking from its frame. The dry wood came away bit by bit.

Once the hole was big enough, I pushed my arm through until I found the cross-member. Good! The doors here were secured, just like at the Molen, with a piece of timber held across both doors and resting in metal holders at each side. This should be easy.

It wasn't. I pulled upwards, but the wood was tight and I couldn't move it. I removed my arm, rubbing the aching muscles and feeling back in my belt for the jemmy. I needed more purchase. Longer arms would have been useful but since that wasn't possible, the jemmy would have to act as an extension. I put my arm back through the hole and hooked the curled end of the jemmy under the wood. Now I could lever it backwards and forwards, gradually prising it off the holders. When it was almost free, I stopped, put the jemmy back in my belt and lifted the bar with my hand to stop it falling. Then I quietly pushed the doors open.

Once inside, I found myself in a large open area with ornate iron columns every fifteen feet. It was, as I expected, quite empty. I pulled the rope up behind me and closed the doors again, before making my way carefully through the pitch black, using my torch intermittently to find my way, until I located the stairs. They were wide stone steps in the middle of the building on the landward side. I stopped at the top and listened. I could hear nothing, but I was loathe to just walk down when I didn't have a clue what I was walking into.

I turned off the torch completely and waited a few moments whilst my eyes adjusted to the darkness. When I looked around, I could make out the loading doors to my right at the far end of the building. At the other end, a small, weak patch of light was shining on the rafters at the seaward corner. I crept towards it.

In fact, the light was leaking upwards from a structure just above floor level – some kind of sack chute between floors, the wood worn smooth with use. I put my ear to it and listed. I could hear voices, but only just. They were far away, maybe on the ground floor, certainly not on the floor below. OK, so I could risk going down to the next level.

I went back to the stairs and felt my way down without risking the torch. The air in the stairwell was stale and musty and there was a thick layer of dust on every step, another good sign. Halfway down, the stairs turned back on themselves and I followed the wall around before descending again to the emptiness of the first floor.

This was pretty much the same as the floor above except that the light from the sack chute was stronger, but lighting up the landward corner this time. And, even by the stairs, I could hear the murmur of men's voices. I crept across, careful not to make a sound, and knelt down by the chute, praying that my knees wouldn't crack.

The chute was old and dusty and led down to the ground floor and, presumably, what had once been a sales area – a very different sales area to the one it was now. I peered down. The chute was boxed in for the first part of its descent, opening out halfway down I could only see the door and the area around it. But I could hear all right.

There were two voices. They weren't talking much, but when they did it was casual banter in Dutch and very relaxed. It didn' much sound like anything illegal was going on. I waited for nearly ten minutes. The men were playing a game of some kind. There was a gentle rivalry between them, some laughs, some moans, a lot of obscenities. I had to see more. I put my hand down on the chute and pushed. Gently at first and then with more force, until I was quite sure that it would hold my weight.

I took off my boots and socks, reasoning that I would be less likely to slip on the smooth surface in my bare feet, and climbed on to the smooth wood, crouching, the sweat on my feet giving me enough friction to prevent slipping. Inch by inch, I worked my way down, my guts churning wildly, scared of making the slightest noise.

I was nearly at the end of the boxed-in section when the chute moved beneath me, creaking a little. I froze, my heart beating so loudly that I was sure they would hear that as well.

"What was that?" One of the men was on his guard.

"It's nothing, klootzak." (Asshole.) "You're just nervous, Pel's got to you. It's just the building. It's old and it's windy outside. It's been creaking all night."

I waited a few minutes and I was just about to move a little further down when there was a loud hammering on the door. The 'klootzak' shouted out in surprise. His companion laughed cruelly, amused by his discomfort, then ambled over to the door.

I sat there rigid as he came into my line of vision and opened the panel on the door. A tall man, perhaps six-foot-two, with black matted hair, he wore boots and faded denim jeans with a heavy black jacket and scarf. He peered through the shutter and asked for a password. When he was satisfied, he let in a prosperous-looking middle-aged man, then turned round to walk back.

If he looked up now, he would see me crouching in the chute only a few feet above his head. He didn't. But I saw enough of him to recognise the tattoo on his face. He was the man who had turned me away a few days ago.

Whilst they were distracted with their customer, I crept the last two feet to the end of the boxed-in section and peered carefully around the edge of the boards.

Below me was a small open area, perhaps twelve feet wide. Beyond that, panelled walls had been erected along both sides of the building: like the ones in the Molen, but better, more robust, making up what must be the living accommodation of the fake 'squat'. The two men had been sat playing cards at a table below me – a lone fan-heater blowing warm air around where their legs had been. The whole area was lit by a single lightbulb, hanging just above the table.

The card players took the man and blindfolded him in what looked like a well-practised routine. Then Tattoo-face led him round in a circle, presumably to disorientate him, whilst his colleague opened the door to the first room of the squat. From my position, I couldn't see the whole room, but I could make out that it was only sparsely furnished and that the floor was covered with a large, thick, grubby-looking rug. Klootzak lifted the rug back and then raised a new metal trapdoor – the sort you see outside pubs. Except that this was no pub and there were stairs rather than a barrel ramp.

I thought about Pat's phone call: "gotta tell you … the crackhouse is …"

… Is in the basement – of course.

The man was brought to the stairs and helped down. Klootzak put his arm around the customer as he guided him. "You have your choice of women tonight, my friend, we are very quiet."

"Oh, thank you. You have some of the new stuff too? You know, not crack, the other. Wow, it is so good, I have been dying for some more since the last time!"

The trap closed slowly and the two men sat down again.

The basement. The perfect cover. A fake squat above, and a long-forgotten basement below, accessed by a simple, hidden trapdoor. My mind went back to the basement at the Molen. Pat had described it as 'beautiful'. In a way it was – clean, spacious and well lit. Even the fittings were there. Benches or worktops. It maybe hadn't been refurbished to use as a brothel, but my guess was that it had been Pel's intention to use it for something illegal.

Then Pat and his friends had returned. Returned before Pel had managed to install his fake squat – the cover for whatever he intended doing in the basement ...

The men were playing cards again.

"Slow tonight ... Pel will not be happy."

"Oh, fuck him, he only cares about money. Anyway, I'm out of this soon." Tattoo-face was not a happy man.

"Oh, so you are going to retire, are you?" Klootzak softly mocked his fellow guard. "You think Pel will give you a pension. I think not! We are stuck with him, my friend. No one retires from The Foundation except in a wooden box!"

Tattoo-face spat on the floor. "Yeah, The Foundation, I've been here since the beginning, my friend, and I've had enough. I want to go somewhere warm, a place where the sun shines. I want to get out of this freezing hell-hole for good. Pel will understand, you'll see."

The light above the card table flickered on and off twice and the two got up, lifted the trapdoor and another man, blindfolded, came up the stairs, was walked round whilst the trap closed and then released into the night.

OK. So I could see the connection between the Molen and the Nordmag. I could see what had happened to the missing women and I was beginning to see the power of the new 'designer drug'. I gathered that 'The Foundation' was a Dutch mafia of some kind. But I still couldn't work out what had happened to Carrie and why.

I thought back to my conversation with Pat on that first night in the Molen. I was missing something, something important. Pat had said she was uncommunicative with the rest of the squat; he had tried to get close to her, tried to help ... No, there was something else, something to do with the court case.

The two men talked on sporadically, complaining mostly. I was getting cramp. I shifted my feet carefully so the chute didn't make a noise. The court case. Why was Carrie so interested in Pel during the court case? Why, when she had just recently arrived in the city, was she staring at the face of a property developer? And why, if he was such a big shot, was he worried about it?

I couldn't crouch like this for very much longer, my legs were seizing up. In any case, I had seen all I needed to see.

I was just about to call it a day when there was an impatient hammering on the door. I retreated a little way up the boxed-in part of the chute, so that I was in the shadows, and waited. This didn't sound like a customer.

It wasn't.

"Meneer Pel!"

The man standing at the open door was not in a good mood. "Zo het is rustig!" (So, it is quiet!) he snarled, in his rough, gravelly voice.

Tattoo-face let him in and whined an apology: "It's the fucking cops' fault, boss."

The man stood for a moment, just inside the door, scowling. I was looking directly at him. He was only small, five-foot-five maybe, stocky, and in his late forties/early fifties but still showing a generous head of black hair. He was dressed smartly – and expensively – in a mohair suit and black overcoat, but his face was pinched, mean-looking with deep-set eyes and a long scar down his left cheek. He exuded both an authority and an unpleasantness that you could almost cut with a knife.

This wasn't the first time I had met him. It wasn't the first time I had heard his voice. But it was the first time I had seen his face up close. He was the man in the black Merc who had threatened me; he was the man with Helga in Dam Square – and he was the man who Carrie couldn't take her eyes off in court that day. Now I knew why.

Images of Carrie flew around my head. Poor Carrie: trapped

dehydrated in her African prison; struggling for her life in a basic hospital in Addis. Poor Carrie, who years later still carried the scars of the ordeal in her head and the clippings of the story in her scrapbook. Brave, courageous, reckless Carrie, who couldn't let sleeping dogs lie.

The man standing a few feet below me was Stefan Pel all right. But he was also Peter Karst.

Sixteen

"Thank God you're still safe." Hellen's face was ashen, her manner grim as she answered the door.

"I'm OK," I said, pleased with myself and still buzzing with adrenaline.

She gave me a cursory hug. "No you are not, Cameron. You are in deep trouble."

We went up the stairs in silence and I sat down on the settee apprehensive by now: I didn't want another confrontation. If she was going to start preaching, then I was out of there. But I needed her help; I had to know who I was up against and she was the only person who could tell me.

I had rung her as soon as I got back to the Molen. I wanted to tell her what I had seen but, more than that, I wanted to ask what she knew about The Foundation and Peter Karst. She went all quiet on me when I mentioned the F-name and told me to come over at once. It had sounded like an order.

She made us both a strong coffee. "Drink this," she said, "you're going to need it."

Then she sat on the chair opposite. I couldn't believe the change in her since I was here last. Any warmth between us appeared more and more fragile. OK, I knew that we could both be arrogant and pigheaded; I knew that she was worried about her job prospects; I supposed she was even worried about my safety – but, somehow, all these only seemed to add up to a part of the problem. It was like there was something else – something I was missing.

Whatever that was, the woman I had made love to only forty-eight hours ago was sitting across from me like she was on duty.

"Why do you want to know about The Foundation?"

"Just something I overheard tonight, Hellen – I thought that maybe they were involved in Pat's death."

"Go on."

"I'll tell you after you've told me." Suddenly, I wasn't feeling very co-operative.

"OK." She composed herself, reluctant, perhaps, to give me the advantage. Her voice became cold and factual as if she was briefing a junior officer.

"I don't have to do any research on The Foundation, Cameron. It's standard briefing material – and it's confidential. I'm only telling you because I think this has gone far enough. Right?"

I nodded disconsolately. I felt like a child being reprimanded.

"The Foundation is Dutch organised crime. We know some of the people involved, but we can't prove anything. It only started two years ago: very small at first, but growing big and powerful at an alarming rate. Initially they targeted local criminals, starting with the smaller ones, extracting protection money in return for the freedom to operate on 'their' territory. Those who objected were, apparently, wiped out – quite a lot of Amsterdam's criminal element seems to have met with fatal accidents around this time.

"They moved on to general extortion, prostitution and drug dealing with amazing speed. But we still don't know who runs The Foundation. There is a strange solidarity amongst the criminal element, borne mostly out of fear – they know from experience that anyone who shops a member of the organisation will be killed within days – no matter where they are held. These people have a network of contacts and spies everywhere. All equally scared."

"But there must be some chink in their armour," I said. "No one, however powerful, however frightening, can buy total silence."

"You're right. There were two informers last year – Henk Smoulders and Henrik Wittigen – both arrested for petty misdemeanours. The police were tipped off anonymously – probably retribution for not paying their protection money. They were extremely pissed off with The Foundation because they thought that it was betraying some kind of criminal ethic. Anyway, they wanted revenge so we did a deal with them and they both made statements giving information and naming names. Not the big shots, admittedly, but it was an important start – and both were ready to testify."

"So, what went wrong?"

"For their own safety, they were held in tight security at the remand centre. We virtually cut them off from all the other prisoners, giving them the sort of protection that is routine for paedophiles and the like. We needed to ensure that they reached court: they were our first real hope of nailing the thugs behind the organisation. We actually pulled a number of people on the basis of their statements ... then all hell broke loose.

"Smoulders and Wittigen withdrew their evidence, claiming that their statements had been given under duress. Then, only days later, they were both found dead. One hung himself, the other overdosed on pure heroin. Since then, information on The Foundation has been nearly impossible to obtain."

Hellen sighed. "So, it is not a record that the police are proud of. We have caught and convicted some of the smaller players, but so far we haven't been able to touch the main people."

"What about Karst?" I asked.

"I checked with Central Records before you came. According to them he was a Belgian criminal who was involved in a number of scams in the 80s. He was jailed in the spring of 86 after being found guilty of fraud involving famine relief in Ethiopia. He was acquitted for the attempted murder of a journalist. He's not been heard of since he was released, just over two years ago." She looked mystified. "Why do you ask about him, Cameron?"

"Because, Hellen, the journalist that Peter Karst tried to kill in 1986 was Carrie."

"Carrie! ... My God!"

"And he is also on the board of the company that owns both

the Nordmag and the Molen."

She looked surprised. "We know that the same company owns both buildings – I checked – but you're wrong about Karst, he's not a board member."

"He is. But, now, he uses the name of Stefan Pel."

Hellen gasped.

"So that explains why your sister acted so strangely at the Molen court hearing. But why did she expose herself like that? He was bound to go after her."

"I think she was leading him on, Hellen." I sighed, sadly. You've got to realise, she wasn't rational about Karst."

"You think she came to Amsterdam to get him?"

"No, she wrote to me telling me there was a story she wanted to investigate in Amsterdam. When she got here, I think she started digging around and came across Pel first, then realised that Pel was Karst. She wanted him to know that he was going to be exposed."

"Cameron … how did you find out that Pel is Karst?"

"I didn't connect the two at first. It was when I saw Karst tonight that I remembered his photo from an old press cutting in Carrie's scrapbook –"

Hellen held up her hand to stop me. "Wait a minute … you saw Karst tonight?"

"Yeah. He's older now, of course, but there's no doubt that it was him or that he now calls himself Stefan Pel. The real surprise came when I also recognised him as the man who had threatened me and the man I had seen with Helga. Then, I began to see the connection between him, the crackhouse, the squat and Carrie's death."

She looked at me, not quite comprehending.

"I've been inside the Nordmag building tonight, Hellen."

She started. "Inside!"

"Yeah, inside! And whatever your friend Hugo may think, it most certainly isn't 'clean'. What's more, I not only saw Karst there tonight, it was also clear that he was high up in the Foundation hierarchy – at any rate, his men were scared of him." I paused again, adding quietly, "And I saw the entrance to the brothel that your people missed."

She looked shaken.

"Pat was right, Hellen. I knew he was. The crackhouse is there, and it's still functioning. It's under the building. It should have been obvious to even the greenest cop." Then I added more quietly, "But then maybe they didn't want to find it. You all seem to have been working very hard to stop me uncovering anything!"

A mixture of emotions swept across her face: embarrassment, confusion, surprise – and anger. I'd wounded her. "There is no need to talk to me like that, Cameron. Hugo may have given you a hard time but I've been trying to support you."

"OK," I said contemptuously, "I appreciate it, I'm very grateful. But you've almost given me as much hassle as bloody Dankmeijer."

"What!" She reacted at once, glaring at me, hurt in her eyes. "All the fucking things I've done for you. You ungrateful bitch!"

"Really?" I said, my anger spilling over. "You could have fooled me. You didn't tell me anything about the Foundation. All you were interested in – you and Dankmeijer – was getting me to give up."

"What do you mean?" Now we were both boiling.

"I mean that you have never approved of what I am trying to do. You're so tied up in your fucking career. You've done your damnedest to get me to quit. That's all that you've seemed concerned about. Christ, it's been every time we've met, every time we've talked on the phone. Even the information you have given me is couched in terms of a warning. What is it with you?" I couldn't hide the sarcasm in my voice. "It's almost like your friend Hugo has told you to warn me off!"

The room went deathly quiet. I saw her eyes flicker first, then I saw an uneasy look cross her face and the truth dawned on me.

"You've been assigned to me, haven't you?" I couldn't believe it, but I knew from her expression that I was right.

She looked at me, a mixture of sorrow and embarrassment showing through her attempt to cover up her feelings.

"How long? When did they tell you to work on me?"

"I'm sorry, Cameron, it's not the way it looks, honestly."

"Huh!"

"Cameron," she spoke urgently, "please listen to me! After you had that row with Dankmeijer and we bumped into each other, I felt very angry. The whole station went on about it for days, I was ribbed mercilessly. It was twice as bad because they could see that you were a dyke as well. Anyway, I mentioned to my boss that I had seen you in the Juno Bar that night and that I had a go at you. For your own safety, he asked me to try and persuade you to give up your reckless project."

"So you thought it would be a laugh, I suppose, to mix business with pleasure and have a good shag whilst you were at it?"

"Cameron, will you listen to me! Please? I didn't know you at the time and it seemed reasonable to try and get you to back off. Then when I had to rescue you from the squat, I was convinced that you really were endangering yourself."

"So the police have known what I have been doing all the time. Huh, what did they think of our night together?"

She replied softly, patiently, "Cameron, it's been an informal thing. I haven't told them about everything. I haven't mentioned Carrie's laptop or your visit to Freebase or your chats with the users at the methadone bus. I could have, of course, but I didn't ever intend to spy on you. All I was asked to do – all I ever agreed to do – was make you aware of the real danger that you were, that you are, putting yourself in."

She leant forward, holding out her hands to me. "And whether you believe it or not, the better I got to know you, the more I cared about your safety."

"Great!" I felt hurt and disappointed. "And I thought there was something between us!"

She touched my arm. "Cameron, there is something between us. Do you think that I could have faked the other night? Do you really think that I'm that sort of person? Sweetheart, it's only been a few days, but the more I have got to know you, the more I have wanted to protect you. When I worry about your safety now, it's got nothing at all to do with the police."

She sounded like she meant it. Jesus Christ, however angry I was, I wanted to believe her.

"Cameron, I like you. I like you a lot. I want to spend time with you. The last thing I want to do is go to your funeral." A tear ran down her face.

Part of me wanted her to be upset, to suffer for the deceit; but then, when the chips had been down, she had really helped me. And, shit, I wanted to believe the best of her. She was the one thing that had brightened me up in months and I didn't want to lose that. For once I didn't want to destroy something that was good for me, so I ignored my simmering feelings and pulled her across on to the settee beside me. When I put my arm around her, she moved in close and buried her head on my shoulder.

We sat in silence. Hellen nuzzled into me persuasively. I resisted.

"What's going on with the police, Hellen?"

"I honestly don't know, lieveling." She looked up at me. "Honestly, I don't. They are worried about something big. I suppose it's to do with The Foundation, maybe even Karst, but I really haven't been told. Whatever it is, it is obviously highly classified and I am not a party to it. I have told you all I know."

She kissed me on the cheek and ran her hand down my arm. "Can we be friends again ... please?"

I capitulated. "Yeah, I guess ... but no more trying to stop me. Promise?"

I promise."

"OK, you want to know about the crackhouse?"

I told her the whole story: the dinghy, the grappling iron, the sack chute, the secret entrance to the basement, Karst's appearance and my eventual escape. She shook her head and groaned.

"Oh, I despair of you, woman. Have you no regard for your own safety?"

I shrugged and smiled back shyly.

She squeezed my arm. "It's all right: you must do what you feel is right. I still think you are very brave though. I thought that when I first met you."

"Thanks." Now I was embarrassed. "I'm just doing what I need to do."

She gathered up the coffee cups and took them to the kitchen. Then she poked her head out of the kitchen door. "Where's Helga fit into all this then?"

I screwed up my face. "I've been thinking a lot about that. I told you I've seen her with Karst so, superficially at least, it looks like she's working for him."

"But?"

"But, it doesn't quite fit does it? Remember we thought there might be two factions. The men who threatened me – Peter Karst and his gang – and the men who threatened Pat – Helga's lot.

"So? They could be working together."

"Maybe … I don't know."

Hellen disappeared back into the kitchen, shouting through the open door, "So what now?"

"Well, somehow, I'm going to have to tell Dankmeijer about my visit to the Nordmag." In case she hadn't heard, I shouted louder. "You want to tell him?"

She came back into the room. "Uh-uh, not me, sweetheart!"

"OK, I don't mind, doing it," I said big-heartedly, "I love helping the police. You got a pen and paper?"

"Why don't you ask to see him in person? It's after midnight, they would have to wake him up – you'd like that."

I shook my head. "Tempting but no, I have other plans."

She handed me a pad and pen, smiling enigmatically.

I drew a detailed plan of the ground floor area, marking the room where the trapdoor could be found. I gave a detailed description of Tattoo-face and his friend 'Klootzak', and of Peter Karst aka Stefan Pel Then I wrote a brief statement of everything that I had seen and heard there. At first I signed just my name at the bottom, then I thought about Dankmeijer reading it and took it back out of the envelope adding 'with love' and two kisses for good measure.

I sealed the envelope, then wrote in big letters, underlined in red ink: "INSPECTEUR DANKMEIJER – PERSONAL – EXTREMELY URGENT – TO BE READ AT ONCE."

Hellen reappeared just as I finished. "You want me to give you a lift to the police station?" she asked.

"Please. It will be quicker than by bicycle," adding, as off-hand edly as I could, "then I need to go to the Westpoort and watch the shipping."

"What? ... Now?" she shrieked.

"Yes. Now!" I had to laugh at the expression on her face. I took hold of her hand and pulled her down next to me, feeling relaxed for the first time in days. "I'm glad we're friends again. I just have one more thing to check out and then I'm through." She fixed me with that concerned look again. I held up my hands. "I know what you're thinking, but I'm not sure exactly what I'm looking for, so I can't tell the police just yet."

She studied me carefully.

"You have no intention of letting the police interview you tonight either, have you?"

I shook my head.

"And you're going to go and get involved in yet another reckless adventure?"

I nodded, smiling awkwardly.

"I can't talk you out of it, can I?"

I shook my head.

"Well, in that case –" she disappeared for a few seconds and returned with her coat "– I'm coming with you."

I looked at her, gobsmacked. "It could be dangerous, Hellen."

She put her hands on her hips and gave me the sort of look that said, 'Wise up woman, I'm no girlie.'

"Well ... what about your job prospects?" I said, genuinely concerned.

She kissed me on the lips, looked deeply into my eyes and then, very quietly, whispered, "Fuck my job prospects."

We sat in Hellen's car on Danzigerkade, taking it in turns to look through the binoculars, scanning the jetty in front of Nordmag, the water and the area around us. We were parked close to where I believed the speedboat from the Nordmag had moored. The clouds had dispersed and now it was colder and clearer. We had a good view of all the comings and goings on the channel.

We waited for over an hour, huddled in layers of warm clothes. Over the water, there was some movement by the Nordmag: a few cars parking nearby, business progressing slowly again. But no speedboat yet and, thankfully, no police.

I had dropped off the envelope at the duty desk just after midnight, smiling pleasantly to the desk officer, like I was just dropping off a birthday card. Then I got out real quick and back into Hellen's waiting car. As soon as he read it, he would want to talk to me – and there was no way I was going to get tied up in a long round of statement-making just at the moment.

I hoped that my note by itself would be enough to justify another search of the warehouse but I was sure it would take the police a few hours to organise another warrant and I needed that time to check out the movements of the speedboat.

Hellen shivered. "Come closer," I said, "let me explain McGill's Theory of Bodily Warmth to you." I put my arms around her, snuggling up to her back.

"OK," she said, indulgently, "just don't distract me."

"Not many people know this," I said, bored by the long, cold wait, "but the warmth from two bodies is greater than the sum of each. That's why you should always take a double survival bag on mountain expeditions: two people cuddling up together are far less likely to suffer from exposure, especially – and this is a known fact – if they are both dykes." She laughed. "No, it's true. Research has proven that it's something in the genes: homosexuals apparently give off more warmth. Besides," I said, nuzzling up to her neck, "it's much more fun."

She put the glasses down a second and turned her head, giving me a long, lingering kiss. "I don't believe you. You're just sex mad ... and, you are distracting me."

We both laughed and kissed again then, ever the professional, she put the glasses back up to her eyes.

"Cameron, I've got a boat." Her voice was taut with excitement. "It's just cast off from this side, somewhere to our right. No lights, so you probably won't see it without the glasses." I waited whilst she watched. "It isn't going across to Nordmag ... it's going more to the left ... in mid-channel now and stopping." She paused, watching intently. "They're doing something in the boat, I can't see what ... wait, there's a small flag, a pennant, on a pole ... there's something on it ... I can't make out what ... Now they're putting it in the water." Then, sounding puzzled, "It looks like they're fishermen laying a crab pot."

She handed me the glasses and I focused on the boat, just as it turned around on its return journey. The marker was bobbing in the water almost in mid-channel, a small green light winking on the top of the pole. The whole thing was so small that if we hadn't seen it deposited, we would have missed it.

"Come on, let's see where the boat moors."

We ran along the coast road, then along a dirt path at the water's edge, stopping about twenty yards from where it moored, hiding behind a stack of old pallets. Two men got out. They tied the boat to a barge and then walked along the shore and up a long metal ramp to get on board.

The barge was one of the big ones: a converted sea-going boat that looked as if it was living or working accommodation now. Moored so that its bow was facing us, it was around seventy feet long by twenty feet wide and painted in a dark colour. It was in almost total darkness: one porthole was lit on the seaward side and a small deck light at the top of the ramp.

Meanwhile, Hellen was still watching the water, or more specifically the marker buoy. She tugged at my arm.

"Look," she whispered, "There's a tanker coming, heading right for the marker."

She passed me the glasses and I focused on the marker, leaving her to follow the progress of the boat with her eyes. "There's a man on deck now ... with something in his hand ... a pole. Can you see him? ... He's standing at water level ... There must be a low deck around the boat. I can't see what he's doing."

I could. As the boat came into my magnified area of vision, I saw that the pole had a large net on the end, and the man was scooping up the package from the sea.

"Very neat!" breathed Hellen. "Drugs."

"So, if they are drugs, the barge could be The Foundation's store or even, perhaps, a manufacturing base," I said.

"Yeah, and the shipping will be their distribution network – all over Europe, perhaps even beyond." She touched my shoulder. "Cameron, I need to get back to the station with this."

"Yeah. I guessed you might," I said irritably, turning away from her.

Hellen shook her head in a show of mild disbelief. "OK, what's your plan?"

"I want to see what's in that package. I want to finish this."

"Cameron, no!"

"It's OK, you go. There's no need for you to be involved. Just drive me to the Molen, so I can pick up the dinghy."

She sighed. "I just don't believe this!"

I took her in my arms. "Hellen, I've been through hell to get this far. I'm not stopping now. You didn't really expect me to, did you?"

She kissed me on the cheek. "I should have known better."

"Go on. Drop me off by the dinghy and then go and see Hugo. I'll be fine."

She shook her head vigorously and then looked into my eyes. "I'm not leaving you now, sweetheart. If you're going, then so am I."

It only took us a few minutes to drive to the Molen and find Betsy, moored in her usual place. We left the car parked on a side road nearby and within half an hour we were sitting in the dinghy watching The Foundation's barge from a few hundred yards downwind. It was just gone 2 a.m.

We waited, shivering in our exposed position for another hour. The barge was in a quiet backwater – we hadn't seen a car or a person all night – and the area was run down. Just onshore was a wide strip of empty waste ground littered with scrap cars, rubbish and weedy scrub. In the water, most of the boats looked like they were seldom used, some were having trouble staying afloat, one had given up trying. It felt like a giant marine scrapyard.

We huddled together, a blanket around our shoulders, keeping as warm as we could against the biting cold breeze. We were beginning to think there weren't going to be any more pick-ups, when, just after 3 a.m., our resolution was rewarded. We heard muted voices, then we saw the two men get into the speedboat and push off from the side of the barge, starting the engine once they were in clear water.

Another tanker. Another pick-up. More of the new drug, destined for somewhere in Europe? I remembered Hans telling me that it had been reported in every major city.

We watched them move out into the channel. Last time there had been less than five minutes between the setting of the home-made buoy and the pick up, so we knew that we would have to act fast. Once the speedboat was in mid-channel we pushed off and started our outboard – I was glad we had thought to stay downwind of the barge as the noise seemed excessive in the still of night. We moved out into the water, making a broad arc to our left – away from the speedboat's return route. If we had timed it right, we would reach the buoy just after the speedboat had moored and the men had disembarked.

Hellen steered whilst I watched. We were both dressed in black, in a small black dinghy with no lights. There was little chance of us being seen, but even so, we delayed our rendezvous a little to give the two men time to get back on the barge. We heard their motor as they passed upwind, to our right, on their way back to shore. Through the glasses I could just make out the marker in the murky blackness. It took us another two minutes to reach it, by which time I could see the lights of the tanker bearing down on us fast, only a few hundred yards away.

Hellen accelerated up to the marker and I leant over the side near the front, catching the pole as we passed, pulling its contents on board. As soon as I had it, Hellen slewed the stern round hard 180 degrees and gunned the motor, propelling our light craft away from the area, back to the relative safety of the shore. Looking back, I saw the man with his net, searching the darkness for the flashing marker light.

We tied the dinghy up close to where we had been before, hidden between two boats, and shone a torch on the package. It was a black polystyrene box, a two-foot cube, held tightly together with four thick black bands of polypropylene. I took out my knife and cut through the bands. Then, between us, we worked the top half away from the bottom to reveal the contents.

Hellen whistled softly under her breath.

Inside the package were row upon row, layer upon layer of small glass phials, hundreds of them: each containing a white, cloudy liquid.

She took one out and examined it, turning it over in her fingers, looking for all the world like she had discovered the holy grail.

She turned off the torch and looked at me. "It's drugs all right," she gasped, "but fuck knows what!"

"Whatever it is, it's big business." I whispered back. "There must be millions of dollars worth. I reckon we should bail out now, don't you? Let's get this to your boss."

"Yes please."

As I picked up the lid to put it back on the base, I noticed a small device taped underneath. "Shit! Hellen! Some kind of signalling device. It must be there so the guy on the ship can locate it."

As I threw it in the water, she pulled hard on the starter cord. "Let's get the hell out of here!" she exclaimed. The motor coughed into life, then died on us. She pulled again, and the same thing happened.

"It could be the cold or just a blocked fuel pipe."

"Or no fuel at all," I said, after checking the gauge with the torch. "Let's go!"

In a flat spin, we clambered aboard the barge next to us – me hauling the awkward package under one arm – and pulled ourselves around the edge until we reached the narrow stretch of quay, ready to make off across the wasteland to the road just three hundred yards away.

I thought it was going to be all right. I thought we were going to make it. Then we heard his sickening, mocking voice.

"You going somewhere, ladies?"

Seventeen

He was a massive, thick-set brute: around eighteen stone of solid meat, with a shaved head and a mean, moon-shaped face. Somehow I didn't think he was enquiring about our social life when he asked us where we were going.

We both froze only a few feet away from him. I don't know about Hellen, but just looking at him scared the hell out of me and there was no way I wanted to engage him in conversation – or anything else for that matter. I looked back, thinking that maybe we could swim for it. But my eyes met those of a second man, sitting on the back of the barge, blocking our way out. He was only a fraction smaller and I wasn't encouraged by the psychotic smile that radiated from his ugly pock-marked face.

I was wondering what the hell to do next when, without any warning, Hellen launched herself bodily at Moonface, shouting, "Run Cam!"

I could have run. The idea did have its appeal. I could have taken the handgun out of my pocket and waved it at them but I guessed that neither of these two was going to be persuaded by a bluff. The obvious defence was to aim and shoot. But I had never used a gun before and there was every chance that I would hit Hellen instead of her attacker. So, instead, I grabbed Moonface from behind, my arm round his neck, trying to choke him, trying to pull him back, away from Hellen. She grappled from the other side, using her self-defence techniques with little effect.

He grunted with contempt, as if we were crazy to even try and resist him. And he was right: our combined efforts were no match for his inordinate strength and weight. As I swung from his neck, he ripped Hellen with his left hand and elbowed me hard in the ribs with his free arm. I heard the sharp crack as one of my ribs gave way, and a searing pain shot across my chest as I brought my foot up underneath his groin.

He winced and swore with real feeling: "You fucking bitch!" He yelled and twisted around, trying to grab me.

It was clear we were fighting a lost cause and, meanwhile, the Psychotic was moving ever nearer, working his way along the edge of the barge, his big round eyes fixed on me. Like it was Christmas, and I was the present he was going to take apart.

"Go! For fuck's sake, run!" Hellen was screaming at me.

"No, you go."

"You stay here, both you," growled Moonface.

Hellen screamed furiously at me: "I can't! Get the hell outta here!"

I froze, my Common Sense telling me to go, escape, get help; but my heart asking how I would cope if I escaped and Hellen died. I had already lost a sister and a friend to these hoods, now I was terrified for her. It was happening all over again and I felt sick and raw inside. I wanted to stay and fight – however futile that might be. I got her into this and if she was going to die, then so should I.

But the conflict in my mind evaporated as soon as the Psychotic lunged at me: his big hairy hands going for my neck. I had to get away, find help. It was Hellen's only chance. I ducked and made a run for it, taking off across the derelict land towards the road, holding my ribs and wincing with pain every time my foot hit the hard ground.

I heard him curse in Dutch behind me and pushed myself even harder when I heard the thud of his feet close by. He might be bigger and more powerful than me, but I was fitter. I knew that I could outrun him over a distance, if only I could keep ahead for the first hundred yards.

The pain in my ribs exploded through my body as I careered on, my Docs skidding off the rubble, broken glass and other shit that littered my way. Psycho was only a few feet behind – if I stumbled just once, then he would get me. I swerved this way and that, straining in the dark to see the old crates and dumped furniture. I daren't look behind. I might trip.

Teasels stuck to my clothes as I brushed past the scrub. The smell of burnt-out cars and rotting garbage filled my mouth and nose. My lungs were burning, my clothes were sticking to my body and the desperate animal fear deep inside me was driving me on, giving me more strength than I owned.

I was almost halfway across. I could see the lights from the traffic, less than two hundred yards away. If I could get to the road, I could flag down a car and escape. The thudding of feet behind me became fainter. I glanced quickly over my shoulder, relieved to see that I was leaving him. A few minutes later, he had stopped, his legs apart, hands on his hips, gasping for breath.

I slowed down to a jog, holding my ribcage, trying not to think of Hellen. I concentrated on relaxing, looking ahead and focusing on the road. Breathing deeply, getting the oxygen to my aching muscles. Cooling down. Recovering.

Then I heard a distant roar and the night lit up from behind, casting my shadow forward: a long thin spectre propelled crazily ahead of me, as if it too was trying to escape. I looked back over my left shoulder to see a single headlight coming at me fast. It flashed erratically to and fro as the big motorbike bumped over the rough terrain; the deep, heavy growl of the engine warning me that I was the prey again and that this time, I couldn't outrun my pursuer.

I staggered on, my heart in my mouth, glancing over my shoulder and waiting until the machine was so close that I could feel the breeze from it in my hair. Then I veered hard to the right, stumbling, almost falling, with the inertia. He missed, but he was close enough for me to feel the wind from his machine and taste his exhaust as he passed.

Fear forced me on again: faster, harder. I pumped my arms for extra power, stretched my legs, increased my stride, swerved, zigzagged. I made for every obstacle I could find: anything to impede him. As I cleared the wreck of an old van, he came for me again, his light illuminating the area all around me, casting long ghostly fingers across the litter-strewn ground. I threw myself violently on one side to avoid him, hitting the rocky ground at speed, grazing my hands and face, crying out with the intensity of the pain.

I almost passed out. My legs, arms and ribs ached so much that it was getting difficult to co-ordinate. The pain was beginning to take over. I wasn't sure I could avoid him for much longer. I managed to scramble up before he could get to me again and staggered on, slower, much slower now, sucking great lungfuls of air into my body. Only willpower and fear were keeping me going.

The road was only a hundred yards away now but there was little traffic, and once on good ground I would be at his mercy. I looked around. Fifty yards to my left was a high wire fence, bordering some kind of warehouse building. If I could get over that fence, then I might survive. But my chances didn't look good.

He was coming at me again. I stood still and waited, as if ready to give up, using the time to recover my breath. He slowed down and, for one moment, I thought I'd misread him. Then, when he was less than twenty feet away, he opened up the throttle and shot towards me again, blinding me with the halogen headlight. I put my hand over my eyes, peering beyond the light, trying to see him. But I could see nothing but the brightness, bearing down on me again, like some vengeful demon.

I managed to step out of his way, but this time, he lashed out with his hand as he passed, catching me on the face and sending me staggering backwards to the ground. I screamed in pain as I fell over a boulder, banging my ankle and landing hard on my damaged ribs.

For a moment I couldn't move. I just lay there, sweating with pain, my lungs heaving. He braked hard, slewing his bike around in a cloud of dust. I could almost see the evil grin on his face as he prepared to come at me for the kill.

I knew I couldn't get out of his way again; that I wouldn't be able to get to the fence before him. He had all the power and I was exhausted. My body hurt like hell and my will to fight was going.

In those few seconds, I thought how arrogant I had been to believe that I could take on these thugs and win. My sister was cleverer than me and they had got her. Pat was one of the toughest men I have known, and he hadn't stood a chance. The entire Amsterdam police force hadn't been able to pin them down. Yet there was me, pig-headed Cameron McGill, who thought she could beat them single-handedly.

Then I thought of Hellen. For all I knew, she could be dead as well.

My eyes began to burn with tears of anger. As I heard him rev his engine, I knew that this could be my turn to die. I guessed that the thug on the bike had a personal score to settle from our previous encounter. He wasn't about to let me off the hook.

But I had a score to settle as well. Two, maybe three, of my friends were dead and if I was going to join them, it wouldn't be without a fight.

I rolled over and into a crouching position, and took the safety catch off Emma's handgun, holding it with both hands like they do in the movies, arms extended, my finger on the trigger. I knew that I would only have one chance. That if I missed, it would be the end. I waited until he was accelerating towards me again, then I aimed at the headlight, squeezing the trigger and bracing myself for the kick-back. He was only feet away when the gun went off.

The bright light exploded and the gun kicked upwards as I fired, throwing me backwards on to the ground as the bike shot past me into the blackness. I rolled over, the gun still in my hands, pointing after my attacker. I heard him cursing as he turned his bike round, an orange glow replacing his halogen headlight.

I got up, stuffing the gun into my jerkin, and limped stiffly towards the fence, my body screaming with every step. I could hear him coming at me again, but now he was slower, driving with difficulty across the rock-strewn land in the darkness. I tried to zigzag, stumbling badly, my own vision blurred from staring into the light.

With one last supreme effort, I filled my burning lungs with air and ran as hard as I could, using every fibre in my body, focusing on the wire of the fence. Closer ... closer. I could hear the roar of the engine coming up behind me. I stretched my hands into the air and threw myself forward, catching the fence as high up as I could, feeling the wire cutting into my fingers with the force of the impact, pulling my legs from under me and using my velocity to propel my body upwards and over.

I felt the fence shake as I went over the top. And when I landed on the opposite side, I turned to see both man and machine enfolded in the mesh.

I stumbled off into the depths of a big timber yard. Ahead of me were stacks of huge tree trunks piled neatly together. Beyond them was a Dutch barn with huge stocks of cut timber stacked on three floor levels along its length. I limped painfully through the piles of weathering timber, making for the cover of the building.

Once under the curved, corrugated roof, I stopped, leaning against a pile of tongue-and-groove, catching my breath and giving myself a chance to think. The guy on the bike wouldn't be the last of my attackers. There would be others following. I picked my way through the darkness of the yard towards the main road on the other side. I had to get help for Hellen – if it wasn't too late.

I flipped open the mobile phone and punched in the emergency code. It took a few seconds to connect, time that I couldn't spare. I gave the location of the barge and told them that Officer Hellen Van Zalinge was either a prisoner there or had been killed nearby. It was chilling to put it into words and I felt light-headed and sick.

I didn't have time to say any more. I heard the first man shout angrily as he reached the fence, his voice echoing off the metal roof above me. "De teef is hier!" The bitch is here.

I had to cut off the call, just as the police asked for my name and location.

"Woman, give up. You cannot get away."

"Be sensible ... We will not hurt you."

Oh sure, and I'm a Dutchman.

I looked around at the stacks of timber around and above me: if I had to make a stand, then this seemed as good a place as any.

I found the nearest ladder and climbed up to the first level, taking as much strain as I could with my arms and protecting my ribs. I felt like a wounded animal going to ground as I picked my way quietly amongst the neat stacks of cut timber that lined the open edge of the floor. The smell of pine resin filled the air around me, scouring my lungs and clearing out my nose, helping me to breathe more easily – and more quietly.

I stopped behind a stack of four-by-four wood, each piece around twelve feet in length, the whole pile about four feet high, sitting on pallets and running parallel to the edge of the floor. I peered over at the yard immediately below: an empty, open area. Beyond was the perimeter fence and the road. Around my feet were strips of rusty metal banding, once used to hold bundles of the timber during shipment. As quietly as I could, I took out one of the pieces of wood and pushed one end beneath one of the pallets under the woodpile, so that the free end was somewhere just above my head height.

I could see them coming towards me now: three of them, some twenty feet below. Moonface was there, holding a sub-machine gun at his hip. I wondered what he'd done with Hellen. The other two had a handgun each. Perhaps it would be best to avoid a gunfight.

I grabbed one of the metal bands and tossed it over the edge. It fell to the ground, rattling lightly, making just enough noise. It was a corny trick but it worked. One of the thugs below stalked cautiously forward, his gun extended in front of him, towards the source of the noise. I waited until he was right below me and then reached up and hung on the free end of my lever, pulling it down hard and tipping the woodpile ... The timber rolled forward and fell, rumbling menac-ingly, over the edge. Then I heard the man scream as the wood hit him, pinning him to the ground.

There was a moment's shocked silence, then the shooting started. First, a single shot from the ground on my left, a white and orange explosion that ripped the timber around me and showered me with shards of wood. I dropped to the floor and was crawling for cover by the time the others came. I got behind another stack of wood and then stood up, moving quickly along the wooden gantry away from the shooting.

I moved just in time. Moonface opened up with the automatic. He was on my level now, spraying the area that I had just left. The scream of the bullets and the rich, dark smell of the cordite primed my body again, producing enough extra adrenaline to ease my pain as I dodged around stacks of wood and along the walkways. I found another ladder and climbed up to the next level, where I stopped and listened.

I heard a car passing by on the road but now, in the woodyard, there wasn't a sound. Somewhere in the darkness, the two men were waiting for me to make a mistake. I crept along the upper level, ducking underneath the iron roof spars that criss-crossed the walk-way at chest level, feeling my way carefully through the darkness. When I was halfway along, I stopped, crouching, waiting for them to come to me.

I saw the flashes from their torches first. The first almost imme-diately below me, the other on the same level, some distance away. I fingered the gun in my jacket. It would give away my position and, besides, there was no guarantee that I could hit either of them. My only chance was to get away. I climbed a pile of timber and eased myself on to one of the metal roof spars, absent-mindedly rubbing at my left shoulder and registering some stickiness on my hand.

The roof spar was narrow but I managed to pull myself along it until I was on the overhang, well clear of the storage floors and above the yard – above various large, wide pallets of board, some stacked four high. The top pallet was still around twelve feet below me, but I reckoned I didn't have much choice.

I hung by my arms from the spar for only a moment but already the pain was excruciating. As I dropped down on to the pallets beneath me, I braced myself for the landing.

I rolled as my feet touched the wood and the pain exploded. Up through my body, tearing at my nerve ends and hammering against my skull. My vision started to blur, and I could feel consciousness slipping away from me as I swung myself over the edge again, dropping down to another pallet below me, then dropping finally to the ground.

I slumped against a pallet, exhausted. My body was screaming in agony, my head awash with multicoloured fireworks. My breathing was shallow, my body starved of oxygen. I gasped painfully, trying to force enough air into my tortured lungs to fuel my body's desperate need.

I could see the light from their torches flashing above me. I looked out towards the road. I would have to cross fifty feet of open yard to reach the fence. There was no way I was going to make it. There was no point in moving at all now: my only chance was to stay here and to shoot them, before they shot me. Reluctantly, I took Emma's gun out of my jacket again and pulled myself, still sitting, to one side so that I was looking straight down the gangway between the pallets and into the open yard beyond. It was a good defensive position, provided I saw them first and didn't miss. If I did ... well, then it was a lousy place to be.

The sensation in my left shoulder grew stronger and I noticed that my hand was sticky and wet. Blood was leaking from a wound on the top of my shoulder. Once I noticed, it started to throb like hell.

I pressed my shirt against the wound, cursing, waiting for them to come and finish me; feeling the Grim Reaper breathing down the back of my neck. I said a silent 'sorry' to my sister for letting her down and heard Pat's voice again coming to me on the mobile just seconds before his death. I thought about Hellen … and what could have been.

I thought about life and how I had never really valued it.

I was bracing myself for the end when there was a shout to my left and then a sound of hurried movement. Gingerly, I crawled to the edge of the pallets, just in time to see Moonface and his friend disappearing over the fence on my right and into the darkness.

To my left, I saw three welcome flashes of blue as two police cars and a motorcycle approached fast but silently along the road. I broke cover, staggering to the fence and hauling myself painfully over, just as the cars shot past … on their way to the barge.

By the time the thugs would have realised that the police weren't stopping, I was on the main road, following the cars. The tarmac wound around the edge of the scrubland and, though my progress was slow, it wasn't long before I could make out the lights by the shore-line. With effort, I quickened my pace, wincing at the pain in my chest and the dull throbbing in my shoulder. But at least the road was even. After what seemed ages, I finally made it round the last bend, just thirty yards from the shore.

To my right I had a clear view of the activity. I could hear the hissing and spluttering of the police radios as the cops communicated with their control. I could see the blue lights still flashing on their cars. I could see the officers themselves as they combed the shoreline, searching the boats along its length.

But what struck me most of all was what I couldn't see. What really frightened me was the big black hole at the water's edge. The police had arrived too late. Both the barge and Hellen were gone.

There was only one person who could help me now.

Eighteen

The lights were on in the house, even though it wasn't yet 5 a.m. A few people were passing by on the street, making their way to early morning jobs. I kept away from them. I must have looked like something out of a Hammer Horror film: blood-smeared face, filthy clothes, torn jacket – all topped with lashings of congealed blood.

I rang the bell and waited. The security phone crackled to life. "Yes?"

"It's Cameron, Helga, let me in."

There was a moment's silence. "I'll come down."

She answered the door dressed in a stylish cream jacket and skirt, her hair and make-up immaculate.

She recoiled when she saw me. "Jeezus!" Then, urgently, very quietly, "Cameron, I can't explain, but will you please leave?"

I may be reckless sometimes. But, this time, I knew exactly what she was trying to tell me. I had to find Hellen, and this was my only chance.

So I shook my head, pressing the gun against her. "No, not until I've talked to you."

She shook her head in disbelief, whispering through her teeth, "Jeez! You silly cow!"

"Shut up!" I motioned with the gun and, reluctantly, she led the way upstairs and into the lounge.

She sat down on the chaise-longue and lit a cigarette. If my theory was right, it was no surprise that she was angry – and perhaps a little scared. I sat across the room, on the arm of one of the antique chairs, pointing the muzzle of Emma's gun straight at her. Her two packed suitcases were already standing near the door.

"It's taken me a while to figure everything out, Helga, but I'm almost there."

I could see the apprehension beneath her cool facade, but she needn't have worried – I knew exactly what I was doing. I was even prepared to bend the truth to protect her.

"Hans at the drug agency must have contacted you straight after I first saw him to tell you Carrie's sister was in Amsterdam, asking questions. He can't work for you full-time, but I guess he must be one of your paid informants. The guy has access to some valuable street intelligence after all."

I watched her eyes. This woman was good. There wasn't a flicker. "Anyway, he told you where I was staying. Then you talked to Marriette, found out about my search for Pat and realised that, if you made a show of helping me, you could find out his whereabouts and get to him first."

She was belligerent: "And why, exactly, would I want to do that?"

I smiled grimly. "Because you needed to make contact with Stefan Pel. Your drug agency contacts couldn't help and you certainly couldn't ask the police for his address. But Hans had told you that Pel had murdered Carrie, so you figured that if you could find her notes, you would be home and dry."

She was relaxing now, feeling safer with the abridged version of the story.

"You also wanted to stop me finding out any more – I was going to get in your way. So when you told Marriette that you had got up early to go for a walk, you were actually at the Molen; and, whilst your friends kept Pat occupied, you found Carrie's laptop, copied the files and then left the message warning me off."

I could tell from her face that I was hitting the mark.

"Then, for good measure, your friends threatened Pat and you fingered me as a spy – hoping, I suppose, to scare both of us off, so that we didn't get in your way. But you misjudged us, Helga: people like Pat and I don't run, we just become more determined to stand and fight, and your interference made us into allies."

She shifted awkwardly in her seat.

"And Carrie's notes did lead you to Pel very quickly, didn't they? I would guess that you are in close contact with him by now, no doubt arranging supplies for your American friends."

The last bit was pure guesswork, but she nodded in resignation.

"I guess I underestimated you, Cameron. You're a very bright woman. But you won't pull that trigger." Her eyes glanced almost imperceptibly over my shoulder and I had to stop myself from following them.

I levelled the gun at her. "Oh, I will if I need to, Helga. But I would rather not. All I want at the moment is to get Hellen away from Pel and his thugs, and you are the only one who can take me to her."

She glowered at me in her careful, controlled way. I could tell she was trying to figure out what the fuck I was up to: she'd warned me and I had ignored her.

She shook her head slightly. "I can't take you to her, I don't know where she is."

She stood up, and I raised the gun threateningly, motioning for her to stay seated. She ignored me. "Aw, honey, I just want a drink." She walked across the room to the cabinet, pouring herself a large Bourbon, then turning to me. "You wanna drink?"

I shook my head. I did, but I knew that, in my present state, even a little alcohol would finish me off.

She leant casually against the cabinet and sipped her drink. "Don't worry, your friend is still safe for the moment."

I caught my breath, dizzy from the news.

"Like I said, I can't take you to her – but maybe I know a man who can." She raised her eyebrows quizzically. Then, as I waited for her to continue, she looked beyond me again. I braced myself and turned my head …

Just in time to see Stefan Pel bring his gun down on my skull.

***

J Arthur Rank was pounding my head with his big hammer as I came to.

It was pitch black and, instinctively, I tried to touch my aching head with my hands, but I couldn't: my arms were tied securely behind the chair that I was sitting on. For a few moments my brain was a dark, muzzy sponge sitting on top of a body that was empty, disoriented and nauseous.

Somewhere above me a generator hummed, but otherwise, there was no indication of where I was. I had to make a big effort to focus my thoughts.

Slowly, the events of the early morning started coming back to me, starting with Helga's face, ending with the freeze-frame sight of the gun coming down towards my head, me sitting there, watching in slow motion and waiting for the impact. Then blackness, interrupted by a feeling that I was a bundle being despatched through some strange postal system.

"Oh, shit!" I groaned out loud.

Another voice spoke quietly, somewhere nearby.

"Cameron, you're conscious!"

I wasn't sure if it was my imagination.

"Cameron! Can you hear me?"

"Hellen? ... Is that you?" Fuck, it even hurt to talk.

"Yes, sweetheart. Thank God! How are you? I thought you were dead!"

Jesus, it was so good to hear her voice.

"You OK?" It was hard putting the words together and my voice sounded distant and woolly, like it belonged to someone else.

"I'm fine ... You looked like shit when they brought you in."

Thanks Hellen, I really needed to know that. "Actually, I feel like shit as well." I coughed and my head felt like it was going to fall apart. "Where the fuck are we?"

"On the barge, I don't know where. They moved it when you ran off."

"I know ... I called the police. They know you're a prisoner." I suddenly felt dizzy and had to stop and breathe deeply.

"You OK?"

"Yeah, fine." I felt like I was going to throw up.

I gave it a few minutes and then managed to tell her about my visit to Helga's. "It was the only way I could find you."

"Great plan, Cameron – except that now we're both going to die."

I remember closing my eyes, just for a rest. But I must have passed out, because when I opened them again, the lights were on.

The pain in my head started up again as the light penetrated my eyeballs and cut into the raw tissue beneath my skull. I blinked and looked around. It was a massive room, almost the entire cargo hold, converted into a gleaming white workshop with workbenches arranged in rows across the width – laminated white workbenches. Like others I'd seen, somewhere else.

Hellen was on my left almost within touching distance – if we had been able to touch. She looked pale and frightened. We were in the middle of the hold with three long worksurfaces behind and another three in front. On another, wider bench, right at the end of the room was a large, complicated framework of tubes, flasks and car-boys held together with giant retorts – it reminded me of the physics lab at school. On other benches, packaging equipment, boxes of empty phials and large bottles were arranged neatly.

Moonface, Psycho and a couple of others I hadn't seen before came into the room and began dismantling and packing the equip-ment. Stefan Pel aka Peter Karst walked slowly and deliberately around the benches until he was facing us. He leant against the bench behind him, gently nodding his head, studying us, a nasty smile on his face.

Then he leant forward and ran his thin scaly fingers down my cheek. I winced as he brushed the wound on my shoulder. His voice was cold and sarcastic. "Tut, tut. All that effort!" He wagged his fin-ger at us. "You should have known that in the end you could not win." He came closer, peering into our faces, trying to intimidate us.

His halitosis hadn't improved.

"I told you, young lady, that if you didn't leave, I would kill you." He leant back again, looking at me pityingly. "I have a business to run and I can't afford distractions like you and your friend."

I just stared back. It wasn't worth the effort of a reply.

He turned to Hellen, lifting her chin so she had to look into his face. I wanted to hit the bastard. "As for you, officer, you really should know better than to mess with The Foundation."

"Why don't you go screw yourself!"

He sat back on the bench, amused and smug, looking at me again.

"I knew that you would have to come looking for your queer little friend, McGill. So when I heard that you had escaped, I went to Helga's first. I thought it might save me the trouble of looking for you and, anyway, it was quite convenient; we had a deal to finalise." He affected a sick, sentimental expression. "It would have been such a pity if you two had lost the chance to die together."

I glowered back. My mind was clearing now.

Hellen reacted before I did. "You are sick and very, very sad!"

He snarled and brought his hand down, hard across her face, making her cry out in pain.

"Oh, very brave, Karst," I mocked. "Do you ever fight fairly?"

He stood back and sneered. "It's Stefan Pel now, McGill – and you haven't seen what I can do yet."

"No, but I've heard – and none of it sounds very glorious to me … Karst."

He turned on me, controlled, but plainly furious, his smugness gone. "I don't like you, McGill. I don't like reporters or dykes or fucking cops. You've all caused me a lot of work with your meddling. You've badly injured two of my best men, shut down my operation at Nordmag, screwed up my chance of using the Molen for a base and now I am having to move out of Amsterdam. Still, you won't bother me for much longer – very soon, I am going to kill you. Just like I killed your nosy sister."

I lashed out at him with my foot, catching him hard on the shin.

"You fucking asshole!" He shouted out in pain and raised his hand to hit me, but he stopped himself and, instead, signalled to Moonface and Psycho.

One of them held my head whilst the other taped strong vinyl across my mouth. I felt panicky, totally helpless. Now, even breathing was a major effort. They did the same with Hellen. She looked scared to death. Karst sat back and watched. "There, that's much better. Now you won't annoy me with those rude interruptions."

He was smiling benignly now. "None of what you have done will harm me in the end. The loss of Nordmag is a nuisance, nothing more. What makes me very angry is the loss of the Molen. You must be very pleased with yourself, McGill." He walked over to a small box and took out one of the glass phials we had seen earlier, holding it up and studying it theatrically.

He turned with a flourish. "This, ladies, is BX3, the drug for the new millennium, and you are going to be lucky enough to try it very soon." He smiled vainly. "I am an entrepreneur. Protection schemes and sexual services have made me very rich, but they are a relatively slow way of making money. Now this –" he held the phial up, looking at it adoringly "– is a major scientific breakthrough which we ... er ... acquired earlier this year from an associate."

He turned as the door opened.

"Ah, Helga, my dear, do come in. I am just telling our guests how my new drug is going to have a major impact on the world's recreational activities."

Helga walked across, a superior smile on her face. Karst put his arm out to welcome her, kissing her on the cheek. She didn't even wince.

He looked pleased with himself. "As you have already gathered, McGill, Helga represents some of our most important potential customers, a number of powerful syndicates in the States who are very keen to buy a licence to manufacture over there. We have been negotiating. Haven't we, my dear? Now she is taking samples back for appraisal. Soon, all of us will be partners in the biggest drugs business the world has ever seen."

Helga looked very at home with Karst and, when she spoke, sounded almost as fanatical as he did. "You are so right, Stefan, this is a wonderful product. For the first time ever, we all can manufacture something that really will become the opium of the people. Let me tell you two: this is dynamite. If you thought that crack was powerful, well, guys, this is, like, mind-blowing. It's the first truly synthetic narcotic to ever hit the world drugs market with such impact." She looked at him adoringly. "And it's a real money-spinner: cheap to produce, more addictive than crack, more powerful than heroin and cocaine together." She turned back to him. "Jeezus, my people are so excited, Stefan!"

Karst was listening like a pussy cat, inebriated by her enthusiasm, and, I guessed, her body. She was enjoying the attention and looked at Karst coyly, priming him.

"So, I gather you knew this woman's sister, Stefan?"

"Yeah. She was able to harm me some years ago. But since I came to the Netherlands two years ago, I have put together one of the finest criminal organisations in Europe." Karst was becoming taller every second, mainlining on the morphine of his vanity. Helga listened, seemingly impressed.

"In just a short time, I have gained total control over the Amsterdam underworld. No one moves here without paying their dues to The Foundation. Businesses pay us generously to protect them from crime. Criminals pay us to protect them from the police. We have some of the more interesting and exciting brothels in Europe and a lucrative drug distribution network. But more than all of that, we have our wonderful new drug."

Then he looked back at me, his lip curling, his voice contemptuous. "We were poised to start full manufacturing at the Molen when your sister reappeared, interfering yet again. I knew someone had been poking around; then when I saw the bitch in court, I realised who was causing the trouble. Your sister found out about our new product, long before anyone else. Clever woman, McGill – too clever for her own good. She realised that we were going to base our new manufacturing unit at the Molen, in the basement. Unfortunately for her, she let her personal feelings take over. She had to keep everything to herself until she was sure that she had enough to put me back in jail for good."

He shook his head. "And this time, I wasn't going to let her spoil things for me." He smirked. "I was rather pleased – it gave me the perfect opportunity to get my revenge."

I fought to get free, straining at the ropes that held my body, trying to force the tape away from my mouth, but making no impact at all.

He laughed at me. "Oh there is more yet, McGill. If you are upset now, then wait until I tell you how I paid her back for the humiliation she caused me.

"I had suffered at your sister's hands, but even so, I wanted her to have a useful death. There has never been a drug like BX3, so we had no idea what constituted a safe dose." He affected mock responsibility. "We don't want our customers dying on us, do we? That would not be good business. They are, after all, our investment in the future. So we injected her with BX3 every hour. She did very well," he made a show of sounding impressed, "she lasted nearly all day. Oh, she had a wonderful end, I can assure you."

He turned to Moonface. "Is everything ready for our final little scene? The car, the syringes?"

Moonface nodded.

"I would like to extend the same hospitality to you as I gave to your sister." He sighed with regret. "But I am sorry, I simply don't have the time. However, I can promise a spectacular send-off for both for you and," he smiled ironically, "for those who find you.

"And you too will have a useful death. I hope you don't mind, but I have promised Helga a demonstration of the effectiveness of the drug." He smiled at her and she ... fucking hell ... she smiled back. I felt sick. This wasn't what I had expected.

He walked over to one of the workbenches. Whilst his back was turned, I gave Helga a long questioning stare. She looked back impassively and then turned away.

Karst returned with two large syringes and a box of phials, which he cracked open one by one, sucking the liquid from ten phials into each syringe. Moonface came across with a knife and ripped open the sleeves on our left arms.

I don't know about Hellen, but I was desperately trying to think of a delaying tactic. Difficult when you can't speak or move. I had just about given up hope when Helga came up trumps at last.

"Stefan –" she looked really troubled "– I know you wanna get this done, but something has just occurred to me ..."

He stopped, syringe in hand. "What?"

"Well, if the police are searching for the cop, we could get stopped on the way out. These two would be better insurance if they were still alive. You think?"

He wavered. There was a long silence.

"Yeah, OK, I'll go with that." He pointed at us both threateningly. "You got a short reprieve." He signalled to Moonface. "Take the tape off, let them tell each other how scared they are."

Moonface ripped the tape off with all the enthusiasm of a sadistic beautician. Hellen screamed out with the sudden pain. We were both left with our faces smarting and sticky.

He left, unsmiling, with his men behind him and Helga at the rear. As she reached the door, she turned briefly and smiled wickedly. I hoped that the woman was nothing worse than a tease – Goddess, I more than hoped, I was gambling my life on it.

"Cam, do you think the police will find us?"

I shrugged. "You're the cop, you have more idea than me. I just hope we don't have to rely on that – there must be thousands of barges in Amsterdam."

"What other chance is there?"

"Helga," I replied. "She's our only real hope and, right now, I'm beginning to doubt my judgement ..."

It must have been a half-hour before the key rattled in the lock again. This could be Helga – or it could be Karst. I held my breath and prayed.

Nineteen

"Hi guys!" Helga breezed in, smiling brightly, on a high, in circumstances where most people would be paralysed with fear. "Boy, oh boy, were you two shitting your pants back there!"

I breathed an enormous sigh of relief.

"That isn't funny, Helga. You had us really worried."

She took out a fold-up knife and started to cut through my bindings. "Huh, maybe, hon, but my ass is on the line. I have to be fucking good if I'm ever gonna see the sun set over Arizona again.

"OK. Listen up! I'm gonna get you outta here. But you do exactly as I say, right. You've nearly fucked up my cover once and I don't want you doing it again. Shit, Cameron, do you realise how close you came to giving me away at the house? Damn you! Karst was listening to your every word."

I rubbed my wrists and stretched my legs to get the circulation going again as she started to cut Hellen free.

"Give me some credit, Helga, it was obvious he would be waiting there for me – huh, that's why I was there. That's why I said it was Hans who told you about me and my sister. I knew all along that you must be working with Dankmeijer – that's why he's been so evasive, that's why he got Hellen to work on me – but if I'd said that, you would have been finished and we wouldn't have got to Hellen."

She grunted – a sign, I think, of some kind of grudging respect.

Hellen jumped to the wrong conclusion. "Dankmeijer?"

"Don't worry, he's not implicated. Helga, for all the signs to the contrary, is one of the good guys. My guess is that she is working with Interpol on behalf of the US Government. Who is it, Helga – CIA?"

"Christ, you gotta be kidding! That bunch of fucking … But yeah … you got it, honeybun." She held out her hand and shook ours.

"Maisie Jones, US Narcotics Agency. We heard about BX3 through Interpol. There's a joint Europe-wide operation in progress – US and European agents working in every major city to identify the source of the drug." She shook her head. "Jeez, there's panic in high places over this, I can tell you and, like I said, my ass is right on the line.

"Those silly bastards in the Pentagon fucked up with crack in the 80s when they came over all pally with General Noriega. Now the current administration is shit scared of a BX3 epidemic that could make crack look like sugar candy." She paused and added with a cynical look, "Having sex with the home help is one thing, but the Democrats would never forgive Clinton if he fucked up that big on law and order. The Republicans would walk all over them. 'Course," she smiled wryly, "I'm politically neutral, have to be."

She looked us over. "Enough talking – we gotta move. You OK now?"

"Yeah, thanks ... Maisie."

"Shit, don't thank me, sweetheart." She laughed a little self-consciously as she led the way to the door. "I'm looking after number one. See, I've just radioed: the cops are gonna raid this tub in exactly eighteen minutes. If you're still here, you'll be held hostage. That will make things very messy for them – and for me. So I want us off this boat pronto. Then the cops can kick ass without worrying about bad PR. OK? "

We both nodded, relieved to be on our way.

She stopped at the door. "I've got a boat waiting near the sharp end, so we make our way quietly, up on deck, me leading. Right? Karst and his buddies are plotting their course up in the wheelhouse. So, on deck, we stay low out of their line of vision and work our way round to the left, by the cabins. Guys, one more thing: if we meet anyone, I handle it. Understand? I can take care of things better without your help. You keep very quiet, huh?" She looked hard at us until she was satisfied that we had got the message.

"OK then, let's get the fuck outta here."

Maisie led us through the door and along a short passage. She started to climb the steep metal steps first, with us close behind. When she moved out on to the deck ahead of us, she crouched by the door, then signalled for us to follow. We were copying her every move, like some absurd game of Simon Says, dropping to our knees and crawling on all fours, across the deck; following her, bent double, around the superstructure to the side of the boat. When we got to the edge of the cargo hold, she signalled for us to go over the side, down a rope ladder and into the boat below.

She was about to follow when a voice called out: "Hey, where you go?" It sounded like Moonface.

If she was nothing else, Maisie was a good actor and her reactions were quick. "Thank God!" she shouted to him. "Come here quickly, come and look ..."

She sounded in real distress, so real that it was disconcerting. The thump of size fourteens thundered above us as the thug lumbered over the deck towards her.

"Look!" we heard her say, in a voice high on distress. "Look, down there!"

I felt Hellen tense up as well when we saw the moon-face appear over the side. His eyes lit up with surprise, quickly followed by panic as he realised that we were escaping. Then, there was a moment when time froze. He stood above us, transfixed for several seconds before the surprise turned to astonishment. Then his eyes seemed to grow to twice their normal size; his mouth fell open and his face betrayed a grim realisation. For some moments he was set in this lifeless pose, like a grotesque version of the statues on the Damrak. Then the early morning silence was shattered by his howl of pain. Hellen pressed the electric starter, as Maisie almost fell into the boat.

"GO, GO, GO!" she yelled, rather unnecessarily since Hellen had opened the throttle just as soon as her feet touched the deck. Within seconds, we were flying over the swell in the small speedboat.

Maisie took a tissue out of her pocket and wiped the blood off her ong-bladed knife before folding it up neatly and securing it back in he holder on her thigh.

"You used that on him?" I asked incredulously.

"Yeah," she said, defensively, "they confiscated my damn Smith and Wesson when I came on board."

I was going to ask her if she'd killed him when a bullet hit the bow of our boat, throwing up splinters of wood. Maisie grabbed the wheel, much to Hellen's indignation, and gunned the motor as more shots rang out, first from the deck of the barge and then from another boat which was moving out into the sea behind, picking up speed as it pursued us.

I looked around. It was still dark. Time had long ceased to mean anything, but I guessed from the sparse traffic that it must still be quite early in the morning. I could just make out the faint silhouettes of big cranes nearby. I pointed them out to Hellen. "Where are we?"

She looked around. "Somewhere in the Northern Docks." She strained her eyes, peering through the dirty grey mist at the lights on he far shore, suddenly pointing: "Look, there's the Molen."

Maisie was watching us as she crouched, her head down, behind he wheel.

"You got a rendezvous planned anywhere?" I asked.

"Shit no, woman, you been reading too many spy stories. My only plan was to get the fuck off that boat, period!"

"OK then," I said, feeling high on relief, "let's make for the Molen. Hellen's car is there."

She swung the boat round and set off, zigzagging across Het Ij, as we heard the whine of more bullets around us. The darkness was helping. But their boat was bigger, more powerful than ours, and I was worried that if they got close enough they would use their automatics.

The Molen got nearer and nearer, its ugly silhouette never looking more attractive. As we hit mid-channel, the swell increased, throwing our boat from side to side as it surged through the choppy water, stuttering and coughing. The speedboat behind seemed to be skimming the waves with ease, closing in by the minute. By the time we reached the small jetty on the seaward side of the squat, they were less than fifty yards behind us. I could see them quite clearly: Karst, Psycho and three others.

We didn't bother tying up; we leapt straight from the boat on to the ladder and up on to the narrow wharf, heading for the passageway between the squat and the 50s factory. Hellen's car lay somewhere beyond. If we could get to that we would be safe.

"We're going to make it, Cam!" Hellen grabbed my hand and squeezed it as we ran through towards safety. I led the way, feeling quite euphoric that our ordeal was nearly over.

But they were waiting for us as we rounded the corner of the building. Four of them, men in black, barring our way. I nearly ran into one of them, but I stopped just in time and ran back into the shadows of the passageway, pushing Hellen and Maisie with me.

We headed back towards the wharf. But as we got halfway, the outlines of Psycho and the others filled the narrow gap. I reached out for Hellen and held her. Maisie pulled out her knife again. But Karst moved into the passageway, his gun extended and pointing at Maisie's head. He gestured for her to drop the knife, then he kicked it away with his foot. The men in black came up behind us, pulling Hellen and me apart, gripping our arms so that we could hardly move, covering our mouths so that we couldn't shout out.

One of the other men grabbed Maisie and pushed her roughly towards us. Karst followed, wielding a torch. He shone it in Maisie's face.

"Hold her!"

Two of the men held her tightly. Karst took a step back, raising his hand high in the air and bringing it down hard across her face. She shut her eyes with the pain, but she made no sound. He moved closer until his face was nearly touching hers.

"You fucking bitch. You enjoy making me look stupid, huh? You think you are clever, huh?" He hit her again, harder than ever this time.

I thought she was going to pass out, but she raised her head and looked back at him defiantly, speaking calmly. "You dirty little shit. You're finished. You and your goddam glorious Foundation."

He smiled his nasty smile. "I think not."

Psycho appeared again by his side with the case of syringes.

"I promised you a demonstration, my dear, and that is what you will get. A little more ad hoc than I had planned, but a demonstration nevertheless." He paused, his sick smile fading. "Then, I think I will blow your brains out." He turned away from Maisie with a look of distaste and shone the light in my face.

"Now, you, McGill. You stupid, interfering little dyke. You are no better than your sister." He snapped his fingers at Psycho who placed a syringe on the outstretched palm of Karst's hand.

Even in the dark, I could see the crazy glint in his eye. "There is enough BX3 in each of these to kill you and your queer friend twice over. However, I promise that you will enjoy dying." He held the torn sleeve away from my arm whilst one of the others tied a rag tightly around my arm, exposing a vein into which Karst inserted the needle point.

"I also have an interesting little scenario arranged," he snarled. "You will be glad to hear that you will both die together – rather romantically overdosing in each other's arms, naked of course, indulging in passionate, perverted sex in the back of a stolen car." He laughed, drunk on his own power and arrogance. I couldn't see the joke myself.

But I could feel the cold liquid entering my body.

"Of course, we will arrange for the media to attend … This is, after all, the official and very public launch of our new product. The press release to Reuters is already prepared. Your British tabloids will love it, McGill: sex and drugs – and two very queer, very dead women, one of them a police officer."

He brought his face close up to mine, breathing his foul breath all over me. "Thanks to you two, the whole world will know all about

BX3 by this time tomorrow – and our lovely new drug will be in mas
sive demand." He drew away again, satisfied that he had made hi
point. "We will be unstoppable."

My body began to feel warmer as the liquid passed into my blood
stream. The pain in my ribs and around my shoulder began to ease.
was getting a weird feeling of euphoria as the drug erased both my
tiredness and the nausea in my gut. But, at the same time, I realised
that bit by bit I was moving towards the fatal dose.

Maisie looked like hell, the anger of defeat hanging over her head
like a black cloud. That's true professionalism – being more pissed off
with failing at your job than with dying. Me, I was just sorry that
hadn't managed to nail the bastard. I turned my head towards Hellen
and smiled. Sweet Hellen, I felt bad about her. When she saw me look
ing, she mimed a goodbye kiss.

That brought me back to my senses. I must fight the feeling o
euphoria that was already creeping up on me. I had to hang on to my
anger for as long as I could. I thought about Carrie, about her body
lying on the cold mortuary slab; I held on to the miserable memorie
of my parents and my home; I thought about the pain in my gu
when I first came to Amsterdam; I thought of Pat and the ridiculous
waste of his life. I thought about what would happen to Hellen.

I looked down at the syringe. Karst had emptied a quarter of the
contents into my arm. The effects were already building and it was
becoming harder to focus, harder to think.

In spite of all my efforts, I could feel myself beginning to slide
into submission, beginning to surrender to the feeling of calm happi
ness, when I heard the muffled sound of many people moving around
us. In my drugged state, I was sure I was hallucinating. Everywhere
looked, there were people – an army of people, hundreds of them –
pushing, shoving, grabbing, fighting. At first they were silent, but the
more there were, the louder they got. The thugs around us were drawn
into the crowd, absorbed and neutralised. I felt my captors hold me
tighter and I saw the look of confusion on Karst's face.

Then I heard Emma's voice, clear and loud, nothing like a hallucination. "It's Pel ... over there ... get the bastard!"

A mass of angry squatters surged around us as Karst stepped back in blind panic. All at once, the grip on my arms was released. I still couldn't make out if this was for real, but when I wrenched my arm away the needle snapped in half and tore my skin. The dark red blood that dripped from the wound was no illusion.

Karst fired his gun into the air. The noise reverberated all around the high walls of the passageway. The crowd moved back, circling him as he edged towards the wharf. I saw Maisie, now freed, following him, and I followed her, staggering a little. I think I heard Hellen calling somewhere behind me but all my senses were focused on the two figures. I felt so good. A little drunk but full of energy. Like speed with overdrive, like coke with a magic ingredient, like purest LSD, like all three of them mixed together. Now I felt better than I had felt for days, years. I felt capable of anything.

Karst, though, looked like a trapped animal, turning on the crowd in desperation, waving his gun and backing off along the small wharf-side, trying and failing to reach the boat.

Maisie followed, waiting for her moment. I knew that the wharf came to a dead end further on. Karst would only have three choices. To give himself up, to jump into the water, or to try and escape through the loading doors into the old factory.

As he approached the doors, he fired his gun into the air again and, as the crowd stepped back, he disappeared inside the building with Maisie close behind.

I waited a few seconds, then followed her through the door. Some of the others followed me and I motioned to them that they should stay back. The inside of the mill was large and open at ground level but a miscellany of pipes and tanks, rollers and crushers were rusting quietly away up above as part of a vast aerial production line. I could smell the sourness of the decayed grain, rotting in the tanks and in the big silo above me, but all I could see in the dirty blackness were faint outlines of the phantom plant.

There was no noise, but I sensed a small movement on a metal stairway to my left. I followed, pausing at the first step.

"Give up, Karst, you can't get away," Maisie's voice echoed off the metal tanks above me.

Karst answered her with two shots, one of them whining loudly as it hit the metal staircase, ricocheting off into the depths of the mill. There was little point in just following Maisie. If I was going to be useful, I needed to find another way up. So I skirted around the back wall until I found what I was looking for: an identical stairway on the opposite side.

I stopped and sat down to remove my DMs. My heart was racing but not through fear. I closed my eyes, telling myself to think. I needed some awareness, I needed to take care, most of all I needed to be calm; yet every fibre of my body wanted to run and shout. So I braced myself, pushing back the euphoria and concentrating on climbing the stairs carefully, one at a time, holding on to the metal handrail, listening for the slightest sound. I reached a small platform. The stair continued up but there was a narrow metal gangway to my right, no more than two feet wide, open except for a thin, waist-high handrail on each side. I hesitated, unsure of which way to go. Then I heard a slight noise above me, some way to my right, a loose footplate clanking as one of them stood on it.

I squeezed my eyes tight shut. Concentrate, Cameron, concentrate. I turned along the gangway and stopped halfway to look down at a row of large industrial vats beneath me. They seemed vaguely amusing and I began to think about going back down to look at them from a different angle. I shook myself, moving on, restraining an impulse to laugh out loud.

Then, carefully, painstakingly, I trod up another flight of steps holding on to my sanity by a thread. By the time I got to the next platform, I could see him. Crouching twenty feet to my right and slightly above me, taking aim at Maisie as she crept up the stairs towards him.

"Maisie! Look out!" I yelled, and she fell to the floor as Karst turned and fired off two shots in my direction. That did make me laugh.

"Cameron, are you all right?"

"Yeah," I shouted back, a big smile on my face. "Cool, sweetheart."

The sound of another bullet hitting the metal stanchion to my left brought me to my senses again and I got down, out of the line of fire, but still unruffled – and still amused.

The stairs on my side now began to climb around the side of a huge, circular silo, cutting me off from Karst's line of sight. I staggered upwards, finding it harder to be careful, almost impossible to be quiet any more. The stairs ended suddenly at a vertical metal ladder, running up the side of the silo for the last fifteen feet to the top. I climbed on to it and started hauling myself up, pausing occasionally to hang there by one hand and one foot, surveying the tangled mass of pipes and crushers below me. Beautiful, it was beautiful. Vibrant greys and rich colourful blacks, soft textures and great abysses of molten nothing.

By the time I got to the top of the silo, I was almost crying over the elegance of it all. My Inner Voice, fighting to make itself heard over the tumult of all the other sensations, was telling me to remember Carrie, remember Pat. Somehow, I focused on the morgue again and gritted my teeth.

I hauled myself up on to the narrow walkway that ran around the top edge of the big grain silo and lay there for a few seconds, trying to stay in touch with the real world.

"Give up, Karst. You have nowhere to go. You can't escape." I heard Maisie's voice coming to me from the other side of the huge container and saw him, now only a few feet above me, standing on a platform which extended over the top of the silo. His back was to the loading-bay doors and his gun was pointing down the stairs.

"Be careful, Maisie, he's got a gun!" I don't know why I said it –

even my mouth was starting to have a mind of its own. Karst turned at the sound of my voice, pointing his gun first at me, then at Maisie, who was now almost at the top of the stairs. I staggered along the curving walkway, bouncing precariously off the rails at either side as I made my way towards Karst, unconcerned about any danger but determined to get nearer.

"Get down, woman, for fuck's sake, get down!"

"S'all right Helga ... I mean Maisie ... s'quite safe."

Karst laughed, pointing his gun at Maisie's head. "She can't help you, bitch." He motioned with his hand. "Yeah, come closer, let me see your eyes when I kill you."

Maisie moved forward very slowly, very carefully, until she too stood on the platform only feet away from him.

"Kill me if you want, Karst, but it won't change a thing. You're finished!"

"Maybe, but you're not going to take me, bitch!"

I reached the edge of the platform, holding on to the rails with one hand to steady myself, feeling into my jacket pocket with the other and concentrating for all I was worth.

Karst stretched out his arms, taking aim, and slowly squeezed the trigger.

With one last supreme effort, I steadied myself and concentrated with every fibre of my body. "Fuck you, Peter Karst," I yelled at the top of my voice, "this one's for Carrie!"

His eyes lit up with sudden fear and he swung round to shoot me instead. But he was too late and far too slow.

The sudden brightness was blinding. But it was the heat and the smell of burning flesh that I remember most vividly. That and the look on Karst's face as the marine flare hit him in the stomach, searing a huge hole in his flesh and burning on and on, spitting and spluttering like a giant Roman candle. Time stood still for a few moments and the noise seemed to stop. All I could hear was the slow fizz of the phosphorous as it burnt its way into his intestines. All I could see was

Karst's bizarre mime as he stumbled around: his open, slavering mouth, his big, fish eyes, his hands, burning as he tried vainly to dislodge the fire in his gut. Then, when the pain hit him, he screamed so loud, so plaintively, that I swear they would have heard it in Dam Square.

I saw Maisie open the loading doors. I still don't know whether it was an act of humanity or the simple expedient of removing something so unpleasant that even she was retching. Karst stumbled over to the opening and propelled himself over the edge, lighting up the sky around him as he fell down towards the balm of the sea below.

I climbed over on to the platform, coughing in the dense, acrid smoke, trying not to breathe the stench of burning human flesh. Maisie looked at me as if I was some kind of alien. I tried to smile at her with relief, but the effort was too much. Instead, I held up the flare pistol that I had found in the boat and tossed it casually over my shoulder into the depths of the silo.

"Christ almighty, Cameron, you're totally off your fuckin' head!"

I remember nodding in agreement just before I fell in a heap at her feet.

Epilogue

Not many people would choose to cross the North Sea on a wet and windy December night. The ferry was only about a quarter full. Half of the passengers were truck drivers on their regular runs. The other half were tourists – Dutch and English – lured on board by the prospect of a cheap holiday.

Then there was me.

I wasn't sure how I felt as I leant against the all-night bar, Campari in hand. My Harley-Davidson was fully restored now and safely stowed below decks. Tomorrow morning, I would be back in York, back to a sane world with my friends and my cat, back to a life again. I kept telling myself how wonderful it would be to get home. But I wasn't so sure: the last three weeks had been very special ...

The police had arrived soon after I fired the flare. It didn't take them long to pull Karst out of the water, but he was well dead. I'm sure that Emma and her gang would have realised the irony of the situation when they captured the other thugs – the very people who had been trying to evict them – and handed them over to the police who, only a few hours later, had been due to support Karst in the eviction. The barge was impounded and all the supplies of BX3 were destroyed. A massive Interpol operation nailed dealers in seven other countries, thanks to the information put together by Maisie.

And 67 women were freed from enforced prostitution, some close to death, all of them in need of hospital treatment. They had been transferred to a special addiction unit where they would be given treatment and counselling. It would take a long time for them to recover and maybe some never would. But at least they had a chance. Me? Well, I was safely tucked up in the Free University Hospital and didn't come round for two days.

Hellen was there when I came to for the first time; Marriette the second time. I was so disorientated that it took me nearly an extra day to be able to think straight. By the third day, I was free of the BX3, off the painkillers and feeling almost human again.

Maisie returned to the States shortly afterwards, but not before she had called to see me in my hospital bed.

"Just where I always wanted to get you, Cameron!"

I think she was joking. Anyway, I laughed. "You're not a dyke, Maisie, so what was with that big seduction scene at Marriette's?"

"Oh ya know, sometimes the hormones rise, sometimes they don't. Truth is, you were kinda cute and I was kinda stressed. Hell, there sure aren't many perks in this fuckin' job and even government agents need some fun now and then ... Say, how come you guessed what I was up to?"

"Oh, just brilliant observation, Maisie," I said, grinning with mock modesty.

"Yeah, I guess I thought all you Limey women were quiet little flowers. Jeez, I'm usually more perceptive." She shook her head. "But how could you be sure I was one of the good guys?"

I laughed. "It was the laptop. If you'd intended working with Karst, you would have just wiped the information, or better still, just taken the laptop. But you didn't, you copied the file to disk first. Then you took the trouble to leave an anonymous warning. Not at all Karst's style."

"So OK, you knew I was one of the good guys. How come you spotted the federal angle?"

"Easy. Pat remembered that, when he was beaten up, all your guys had matching regulation handguns." I shook my head and grinned. "I don't think real criminals do that."

She laughed and blew me a kiss. I must say, I preferred Maisie to Helga. Maybe if I'd met the real woman first ...

Marriette gave me a hard time, of course.

"Cameron, how could you deceive me like that?"

"Oh, come on Etts, if I'd been honest, you'd have gone to pieces wouldn't you?"

"That's not the point, darling. All that time you were in danger and I thought you were safe with some friends in Leeds."

"That is just the point, Etts." I hugged her hard. "Anyway, it's all over now."

"Yes, Cameron, I'm so glad."

As for the eviction notice on the squat, in the end they didn't have to fight their battle. In the circumstances the court granted a stay of execution and the eviction was put on hold. Since the building was owned by organised crime, it would probably be confiscated by the state once the gang was convicted, so Emma and her squat would be likely to have at least another year of secure accommodation. A victory of sorts.

And Becky? Well ... she was relieved that I was safe, of course, but she was also delighted that I felt better about myself and about life in general. She says Tibby has missed me but I'm not sure, I bet she spoils him rotten.

My sister's death certificate was amended and I am writing her final article for her, using information taken directly from the file that Maisie copied. Her memory will always be dear to me and, of course, I'm still working through my grief. But it's different now; I feel both a sense of release and a personal involvement with her final days that was missing before. I know what she went through and why.

Dankmeijer, contrary to his name, never did thank me.

And Hellen ... She got an official caution for becoming personally involved in the private pursuit of criminals but, on the other hand, she also got a commendation for her work in discovering the source of the BX3. Even the Dutch police need their bureaucracy and double standards.

She came out of the episode with only a few cuts and bruises but three weeks' convalescence leave. The police doctor advised her to have some therapy. Together we had loads of it.

Which brings me back to the last three weeks again. I stayed at Hellen's. We spent our evenings out on the town, our nights and mornings in bed and our afternoons sightseeing. There is nothing like a shared threat to bring two people close together. We had both nearly died, so the joy of life in those weeks had been particularly sweet. But, now ... Now it was over and I was heading for home.

I drained my glass. I was looking forward to being back in York but, Goddess, I was going to miss her. I don't know whether it was what we went through, or the result of sharing those last three weeks with her, but I had begun to feel a closeness and a contentment that I had never experienced in my life before. I knew we would keep in touch, but time would pass, she would get on with her career, other people would come into our lives. And the excitement and thrill of the last few weeks would start to fade. Like it always had before.

But this time it was different for me. This time I didn't want it to die. This time, I would miss her. I laid my head down on the bar and sighed.

The barman put another glass of Campari and tonic in front of me. I looked up, startled. "Sorry ... I didn't order this."

He motioned behind me, but before I could turn round, I felt her hands around my waist and the warmth of her face against my cheek. Then I heard Hellen's voice. "Hi buddy, mind if I tag along?"

More new fiction from DIVA Books:

The Comedienne *VG Lee*

"There was nothing and no one left for me in Birmingham."

"I couldn't believe it at first – that Susan could switch from padded Valentines, eighteen inches high with 'Be mine forever', to not even stopping her car for me to cross on a zebra. If she hadn't recognised me with the added weight, she must have known it was my shopping trolley."

It's time for Joan to try her luck on the London comedy circuit. After all, everybody always said she was a funny woman...

"A touching evocation of loneliness and the complex relationship between an ageing mother and daughter. A light touch, a wonderful laconic style and spot-on humour made it a joy to read." Andrea Levy

Published late May 2000   £8.95   ISBN 1-873741-43-X

Emerald Budgies   *Lee Maxwell*

"Great flocks of emerald budgies are flying through your brain..."

Ruth is in a state. The kind of state where you might put a hedgehog under the wheel before reversing, or pull on rubber underwear before running drugs to a colleague.

Things aren't going to get any better till the memory she's been avoiding floods back into her mind – and after that, they'll get a lot worse.

Lee Maxwell's first novel is a darkly comic tale of disintegration, betrayal and revenge.

"Great energy – so much chaos – and I laughed out loud a lot too. This is a strange way to describe it but *Emerald Budgies* is really charming." Emily Perkins

Published late June 2000   £8.95   ISBN 1-873741-44-8

DIVA Books are available from all good bookshops; or by mail order on 020 8340 8644 (international : +44 20 8340 8644) quoting the following codes: *Needle Point* DVB421, *The Comedienne* DVB43X, *Emerald Budgies* DVB448.